Negligee Behavior

Shelli Stevens

Shells Bells Publishing

Chapter One

The Hunk-A-Hunk-A Burning Love Chapel smelled like stale beer and B.O..

Brandy Summers shuddered and wiped damp hands down the front of her wedding dress, trying to keep the god-awful stench out of her nose as she sucked air into her lungs.

The only light source came from the afternoon sun streaming through the stained-glass shrine to Elvis. It wasn't artful, rather it reminded her of a Shrinky Dink she'd made as a child.

She dropped her gaze to the floor. The carpet, shaggy and orange, had probably been purchased from some clearance room back in the seventies.

The fan in the room barely circulated the stagnant air but did cause the inflatable arch over the altar to lean to the right.

Be happy, this is your wedding day for goodness sake.

And it wasn't so bad. It could've been worse, right?

The fluorescent neon guitar behind the altar made crackling noises and then flickered out.

Her stomach dropped. Okay, it was officially worse.

"Brandy? Is everything all right?" Gordon whispered as the Elvis minister, who'd stopped mid-vows, flipped through his notes and muttered to himself.

Was everything all right? Talk about a loaded question.

She'd barely had time to even think since Gordon had walked into their hotel room five hours ago after his seminar. He'd dropped to his knees in front of her, clutching a wedding dress as he declared they should be spontaneous and get married.

What just might be stranger was the fact she'd decided it was a good idea.

"Everything's fine." The two words took a heck of a lot of energy to get out.

Which was a little bizarre, seeing as this should've been the happiest day of her life.

"Wonderful." For a moment she thought she saw the flash of irritation in Gordon's eyes, but then his grin widened.

She narrowed her eyes. Was it wrong to compare his glaringly white teeth to the minister's white polyester jumpsuit?

She glanced away.

Lord, her parents were going to have a conniption when they discovered she'd gotten married in some rat-infested Elvis chapel in Vegas.

No matter how often they told her to let loose and enjoy life, the wedding of the only Summers' heir should've come with a six-figure price tag.

Sweat beaded on the back of her neck. Heavens, her career choice alone had already drawn severe disapproval.

Wait. What was that? Her eyes narrowed on the small snapping sound of something in the corner. Oh, dear god. A rat trap.

She groaned, the sound barely audible behind her compressed lips.

Why? The question finally erupted in her head. Okay. She understood the wanting to be spontaneous part, but why did he choose this place?

This was the Las Vegas strip, the place was loaded with places to get hitched. This chapel—and only a mental case would even consider it one—was beyond gross.

"You know how much I love you, right, love muffin?"

She winced at Gordon's endearment. *Love muffin.*

Why on God's green earth did he insist on calling her that? She hated it and had told him as much on more than one occasion. It made her feel like an amorous Twinkie. How was that remotely sexy?

She bit back a sigh. Not that she'd ever been mistaken as sexy.

You should be concentrating on the fact that he said he loves you, not his tacky pet name for you.

Gordon was a good man. He was. Nice in appearance, charming, kind, and even volunteered with a handful of charities. Any woman would be thrilled to marry him. So what was wrong with her?

Doubt prickled in her gut, and not for the first time since she'd put on the wedding dress an hour ago. But then, the dress itself had been enough to make her hesitate.

Apparently, Gordon had picked it up at a thrift shop off the Strip. It was a huge white creation that screamed '1980' and had more ruffles than a bag of chips.

So why was she doing this again?

Because I'm in love. Right? Maybe?

Or maybe it had a lot to do with the fact that she was turning thirty next week. Thirty. Sure maybe *Cosmo* could make it look trendy to be single in your thirties, but she wasn't a *Cosmo* kind of woman.

She was a *Good Housekeeping* kind of woman and had been since she'd started pilfering her aunt's subscription in the sixth grade.

She'd been with Gordon for a year. Not too long, but it wasn't like they were rushing into this. And at least she knew he wasn't after her money. The man was a dentist for a reality TV show. He had an impressive bank account.

"Look, we can do a formal ceremony for everyone when we return to L.A.," Gordon said urgently, his tone taking on an edge as if he might've sensed her hesitation.

She gave a wan nod. That still wouldn't appease her parents. And then when the media got wind of this....

"Oh, okay, I see where we are. Sorry about that, young lovers." The Elvis impersonator looked up from his notes and grinned. "Do you Candy take Gordon—"

"Her name is actually Brandy," Gordon corrected tersely with a frown, which just made him look all that much more anal.

This just wasn't right. Any of it. She shook her head and took a small step backward.

"Right. Brandy. Thank you. Thank you very much." The minister did the Elvis lip thing. "Do you Brandy take this man to be your lawfully wedded husband?"

The nauseating smell inside the chapel seemed to double, the walls closing in on her.

Oh, god. I have to get out of here.

She took another step backward and stumbled over her wedding dress.

"Brandy?" Gordon's tone turned impatient and he took a step toward her.

Something hard flickered in his eyes as he reached out and manacled her wrist with long fingers.

Ouch. That kind of hurt.

She blinked in surprise and tugged at her wrist, but he didn't seem to want to let her go.

"Now's the part where you say I do, love muffin." His words held a steely threat that she knew she wasn't imagining this time.

Say I do?

It should've been easy enough, but her head twisted from side to side in denial.

No. No. No.

"I'm sorry," Brandy whispered and forcefully jerked her hand free from his grip. She grabbed the bottom of her dress and the acres of tulle that surrounded it. "But I don't think I can."

She spun around, drew in a ragged breath, and then ran out on her wedding.

"Brandy!" Gordon cried. His tone reminiscent of Marlon Brando's *Stella!*

Then came the sound of his footsteps pounding down the aisle.

Great. As if her fleeing her wedding wasn't bad enough, he was actually going to chase after her?

Brandy pulled her skirts higher and increased her pace, knees pumping with the extra effort.

"We don't do refunds!" the Elvis yelled and she knew luck was on her side, because Gordon was such a tightwad he would surely stop to argue.

She burst out of the chapel, momentarily disorientated by the brightness of the sun, and the noise of the Las Vegas Strip.

She needed to get away from here. Maybe she could catch a cab?

Her gaze drifted down the boulevard, crowded with rush hour traffic.

Shoot.

Not a cab in sight. Her attention caught on the big, wide black and silver Harley idling beside her at the light.

A very nice bike indeed. And the man on it...?

She took in the muscled forearm with a dragon tattoo. The man gave off a sexy, maybe even dangerous, vibe. Not that she could actually tell his sexiness level with his helmet covering his face, but his forearms spoke volumes.

"Love muffin!" Gordon burst out the chapel doors. "You don't want to do this!"

Brandy yelped and cursed herself for being distracted by the motorcyclist's potential hotness. She jerked her attention away from the hot biker and scanned the boulevard again for a cab.

Still none in sight.

She looked back at the biker, her pulse lurching. She held her breath as the idea took hold.

Was she bold enough?

Desperate times called for desperate measures....

Besides, it gave her an excuse to finally ride a Harley.

Marco Vargas tried to block out the mind-numbing traffic and cursed his stupidity again. He should have known better than to get on the Strip this time of day.

But he'd been so busy thinking how to drum up more business for the bar on weeknights, that he'd turned right onto Las Vegas Boulevard instead of taking the back roads to his home in Henderson.

And now he was suffering for it. Not just with the traffic, but also with the crazy ass summer heat. At least the Boulevard had eye candy of all varieties, from the ladies rolling into the town for bachelorette parties to the half-naked showgirls on the billboards.

Speaking of which...he glanced at one such billboard, taking in the display of barely covered tits and ass.

Seriously?

He shook his head, realizing where his mind had gone. Damn, he really needed to get laid if he was getting turned on by a god damn billboard.

Looking away, he waited for the light to turn green, the vibrations of his bike causing him to zone out.

There was a sudden flash of white out of the corner of his eye. He turned to investigate, just as a blur of fluff launched itself onto the back of his bike.

"What the—"

"Go! The light's green," the fluff—which sounded suspiciously like a woman—yelled.

Marco turned around to get a look. What was this? Some weird attempt at a motorcyclejacking?

But all he saw were wide blue eyes staring out at him from behind a stained veil.

"Great," he muttered. "Just what I need. A runaway bride."

Their gazes locked for a few seconds and then she blinked, still looking desperate.

"Please!" she cried, grabbing the sides of his t-shirt and jerking. As if that were the magic way to make the motorcycle move. "Go!"

Don't get involved. Tell her to get off your bike and drive away.

Her panic increased visibly—she must have realized he was about to throw her off his bike.

"Please," she begged. "I've got money. Lots of it. I'll pay you."

He'd been there, done that with women and money. It did little to sway him. In fact, it was more of a deterrent.

"And I'll buy you a beer."

Oh yes, because beer was the magic word. The cars behind him were laying on their horns, swerving around to pass him in the other lanes.

He glanced backward and spied one of those cheesy wedding chapels. A man in a tux burst through the doors, making his way toward them.

"Love muffin!"

Love muffin? Marco's lip curled in disgust.

Her fiancé called her love muffin? His pity level increased a notch.

Damn, he was not a pity guy, what the hell was he doing?

Marco cursed, even as he reached behind the woman to grab a spare helmet. He thrust it towards her. "Pull your dress up so it doesn't get caught in the bike."

He waited for her to roll the acres of fabric up over her legs and out of danger from the chain and exhaust pipes.

Fortunately, the ditched groom was still wading through a throng of tourists.

After she had on the helmet and her arms wrapped around his waist, he rolled back the throttle and sped them through the light.

She tightened her grip, and he could've sworn he heard her sob in relief. Or maybe it was fear. Who the fuck knew.

She damn well better make good on that beer. He sure as hell would need one after this.

He weaved in and out of lanes, leaning the bike more than once while he did so. His scowl tipped into a smile when the woman's arms tightened around his waist and she started screaming something at him.

Fortunately, he couldn't really hear what she said with the helmet on.

Where did she want him to take her anyway? She hadn't given him any instructions, but he assumed she was probably staying at a hotel on the Strip.

He pulled into the parking lot at one of the big hotels and found a spot to park. The woman couldn't climb off his bike fast enough.

She removed the helmet, which didn't even appear to be on right, and then threw it at him.

He caught it before it could slam into his chest, and met her fierce glare.

"Who on earth gave you a license? That was the—the worst driving I've ever—" she paused taking in a shaky breath. "We could have been killed!"

Wait a minute, he'd just saved her ass and now she was going to go ape shit on him? *Hmm.* The whole *I have money* part ran through his head.

Pampered and sheltered. He'd wager his next paycheck on it.

"Let me guess, princess. It's your first time on a motorcycle?" he asked, giving her a tight smile as he climbed off the bike.

"Yes. Not like that has anything to do with it." She folded her arms across her chest and her glare screamed disapproval.

They weren't quite eye to eye, but she was only a couple of inches short of being so.

She looked kind of cute in an angry, fluffy marshmallow kind of way.

He took a deep breath in, and the sudden smell of apples tickled his nose. Apples? Who the hell smelled like apples? He shook his head.

"It has everything to do with it. Besides, you're the one who jumped on my bike," he pointed out.

He slid a glance down her body, not like he could see much.

God *damn* that was an ugly dress. And couldn't she at least take off the veil?

He had no idea of what her face looked like, just those big blue eyes.

Well, if she wouldn't do it.

He reached forward and tugged the veil off of her head.

The woman gasped and reached to grab it, but he already had the veil firm in his grip.

Frizzy brown hair fell down her back as the bun came loose, while her pale blue eyes shot looks of indignation at him.

Well, at least she was nowhere near his type. Except...those lips weren't bad. So full, and pulled tight in a cute little frown.

She grabbed his helmet before he could stop her, and pried it off his head.

"What the hell are you doing?"

"I showed you mine," she said pointedly and let her gaze rove over his face, her expression was grim. "Hmm, just as I suspected. You're attractive."

"What?" He tried to decide how that was relevant, even as a spike of pleasure ran through him at her words.

"Never mind, forget I said anything."

"Okay. What's your name?"

"Brandy."

Marco lifted an eyebrow. Now that was a stripper name if he'd ever heard one. Not for one minute did he actually believe she worked as one, but it would be kind of fun to poke the bear.

"Is that your stage name?"

"My stage name? Why would I have a..." She took a loud,

outraged breath and her breasts rose impressively under the dress. "You think I'm a showgirl?"

"Stripper, actually. I mean, with tits like that, I get it. Not to mention you said you had money." He grinned. "I know a stripper can really bring in the dough tip-wise."

Her eyes bugged out, shining bluer against the red flush on her face.

"I bet you give a great lap dance, Brandy."

"Lap dance? Oh my god. I am *not* a stripper." She tossed her curls over her shoulder—which just made her hair grow frizzier—and offered up another fierce glare.

"Oh, Jesus," he breathed under his breath.

"I am not a stripper," she repeated, slow and precise. "I am a high school *choir teacher*."

His brows drew together. A choir teacher? Hell, when was the last time he'd met a choir teacher? But in an odd sense, it fit.

He folded his arms across his chest. "All right, Miss Choir teacher, why did you run from your wedding?"

She blinked, and then looked away. "What makes you think I'm running from my wedding?"

"Are you shitting me right now?" His eyebrows shot up. "The fact that you're in a wedding dress is a pretty good clue. So either you A: married the guy and decided to take off without him. Or B: left him hanging at the altar."

She stayed silent for a moment before she gave a short nod. "B."

"Ah." He shifted. Definitely the more complicated answer. "Do you...want to borrow my cell and give him a call? Or have a phone buried in your dress somewhere? Or leave him a message at the hotel or something?"

"Why would I contact him?" She reared back, alarm in those pretty blue eyes now.

"Well, what's your plan from here?"

"Plan? Yeah, like I really had a plan when I bailed on my wedding." She drew her lip between her teeth and frowned. "I just...need time to figure things out."

His gaze dropped to her mouth. How did she make that look so seductive? The biting-the-lip thing.

"Do you want me to drop you off at your hotel?" His voice came out a little gruffer than intended.

"No." She gave a quick shake of her head. "That's the first place Gordon will look for me."

"*Gordon?* No wonder you ran."

"Nice." She wrinkled her nose at him and then sighed. "I...I, oh god, I don't know what to do."

She looked so lost, so uncertain, that the pity returned in full force.

He thrust a hand through his hair and took a deep breath, not sure how to deal with a runaway bride.

Pity wasn't exactly a familiar emotion to him. He was a born and bred hard ass. But the idea of just ditching her....

So much for heading home and watching the game.

"Well, you do owe me that beer, princess."

Those full lips came together in a perfect 'O' shape. His attention lingered there a little too long.

She may not be his type, but her mouth sure was. Oh, the things she could do with a mouth like that.

His teeth snapped together.

Stop with the perverted thoughts.

She seemed a bit surprised by the offer, but also relieved. The visible tension in her body eased and she fidgeted with the front of her dress.

"Okay. Where did you want to go?"

"There's a bar in the hotel. You up for it?"

"I'm...yeah." She nodded. "I'm up for it."

He hooked their helmets over the back of his bike.

"You haven't told me your name yet." She pointed out as they walked to the elevators that led down to the casino.

"Marco."

"Marco what?"

"Vargas. Did you want to do a background check on me?" he drawled.

"Vargas from Vegas? Cute."

"Oh wow, that's funny. I've never heard that one before."

"Really?"

He shot her a hard look and she swallowed visibly.

"Okay. I guess if we go have a beer, I'll have to assume you're not dangerous."

"Dangerous? Would you really have jumped my bike if you thought I was dangerous, Brandy?"

Interesting that she'd used that word. He raised an eyebrow as the elevator doors slid shut, sealing them in together.

Brandy's pulse jumped and her mouth went dry. She stepped backward until she hit the opposite wall of the elevator.

Yikes.

Was this a good idea? She was alone in an elevator with a virtual stranger—one who seemed to fill the elevator with his presence alone.

What did he say his name was again? Vargas from Vegas, she remembered the last name.

Mark? No, Marco. Like Marco Polo.

Why was she so physically aware of him?

She caught the image of herself in the mirrored elevator and winced. Clearly, she was not at her finest.

But Marco? He was like a decadent chocolate truffle. Something sinful, but oh so worth it.

She'd never looked at Gordon that way. Then again

Gordon wasn't really the type to inspire such sinful thoughts. He was more like the granola bar you ate to help you stay regular.

"Brandy?"

Goosebumps broke out on her body as his deep, rough voice stroked over her name again.

Maybe he wasn't conventionally dangerous, but dangerously attractive for sure.

With his name, the black hair just brushing his shoulders, nearly black eyes, and olive skin, she'd guess he was Latino. And way too attractive.

From the second she'd taken off his helmet, she knew she was in trouble. Dark, mysterious, a little dangerous—he was everything she wasn't supposed to want.

Only her body hadn't seemed to get the memo.

"Do you think I'm dangerous, Brandy?" he asked again.

"Well, I would hesitate to call you safe." How did her voice manage to sound so breathy? That was so not like her. "I mean, the way you drove that motorcycle..."

She couldn't flirt to save her life. And it wasn't like she hadn't tried. There was a stack of self-help books on dating, flirting, and being a sexual goddess under her bed at home.

All covered in at least an inch of dust by now.

Marco took a step closer to her. "You're right. I'm not safe."

Before she could reply, the elevator dinged and signaled their arrival. Brandy stepped away and rushed out first, a little disappointed and not quite sure why.

She glanced over her shoulder to make sure Marco still followed and hadn't yet blown her off. Her eyes widened.

"Stop staring at my butt!"

"Sorry, it's a habit." Marco lifted his eyes from her ass and gave a roguish shrug.

Her cheeks warmed.

Easy, Brandy.

Besides, it wasn't like he could even see anything beneath the dress.

She forced herself to look away and drew in an unsteady breath. Oh, he was trouble with a capital *T*.

She shook her head as they made their way through the casino. The fluorescent lights and ringing slot machines added to the chaos that already ran rampant in Brandy's head.

Spotting the bar near the back, she weaved through the mass of people and entered the small section which was somewhat secluded from the main room.

Sitting down at the table, she watched Marco pull out a seat across from her. But he didn't sit in it like a normal person, instead, he turned the chair around and swung his legs over it. Resting his palms on the metal frame.

"What can I get you both to drink?" A waitress passing their table called out.

"I'll have a piña cola—" Marco broke off. "A Guinness."

Brandy's mouth twitched. "Do you like getting caught in the rain, too?"

The waitress let out a sharp laugh and then cleared her throat. "And for you?"

"I'll have a white zinfandel, please. One of your nicer labels."

"Well, these are on me, guys. Congratulations to you both." The waitress smiled and walked off, her bottom nearly showing under the tiny skirt.

"Congratulations?" Brandy turned a skeptical glance to Marco, who stared off into the casino looking uncomfortable.

"She thinks we just got married. Hell, it's free drinks so I'm not going to complain."

"But—but it's not true. Wave her down, get her back here! We need to explain that we're not actually married."

He looked away from the casino floor and raised an eyebrow.

"So you want to explain your situation to the waitress when you haven't even told me what's going on? Be my guest, princess."

Well, when he put it that way. She scowled and folded her arms across her chest. How could she explain why she ran from her impromptu wedding when she wasn't even sure herself?

The image of Gordon running after her sent an uneasy shudder through her.

"I just don't really want to talk about it now," she hedged. "But I'm sure I'll be feeling much chattier after a drink or two."

"I never discourage a woman from drinking," he told her with a grin as their drinks were set down in front of them.

"Somehow, that doesn't surprise me." Brandy picked up her wine and took a long swallow, savoring the warmth that slid down her throat.

She wasn't a lightweight, it would take at least a couple more glasses before she was even buzzed. She didn't drink a lot, but, thanks to overindulgence at a staff Christmas party two years ago, she knew her limits.

"Why don't you tell me a little about yourself?" she asked after taking another sip.

His eyes darkened and became unreadable. "What do you want to know?"

"Umm, what do you do for a living?"

"I co-own a bar with a friend." He wiped his mouth with the back of his hand after downing half his beer in one swallow.

Brandy stared at a drop he'd missed and had the outrageous urge to lean forward and lick it off his upper lip.

Oh, she was so out of line. She needed to stop this. She certainly wasn't on the lookout for a man, especially after she'd just run out on the one she had.

Besides, he was the complete opposite of her type. She dated doctors and lawyers...and dentists for reality television shows.

This guy was just not exactly the type of guy you brought home to meet your mother.

"So a bar?" She still watched his mouth. "Is it a biker bar?"

"We get bikers, but don't cater exclusively to them if that's what you mean." He shrugged and she noticed the way his T-shirt tightened over his broad shoulders. "We get all walks of life."

"I see." She fiddled with the necklace around her neck.

Marco's gaze dropped to her neck and then lower, seeming to hover on her chest before he looked away.

The memory of him commenting on her 'tits' flashed through her head, and her pulse kicked up a notch.

She lowered her gaze. The warmth spreading through her body now had to be from the wine. Surely he hadn't been looking at her breasts because he was interested in them. Men like that didn't look at women like her.

She bit her lip. Although it was a bit harder to dismiss the way the tips of her breasts had tingled under his brief glance.

Just what kind of lover would Mr. Marco Polo be?

She opened her eyes again and looked at him. Probably ten times better a lover than Gordon. When they'd first started dating she'd been so overwhelmed with how into her Gordon had been.

He'd charmed her, and flirted outrageously, but when they'd ended up in bed the sex had been a little... tepid. Anticlimatic.

But then Gordon seemed to breeze by the erogenous zones on a woman's body and make love like he was trying to beat the clock.

She slid her gaze over Marco's broad shoulders and another shiver of awareness ran through her.

Marco was probably a man who liked to take his time. A man who probably called it the F word, not making love. But, oh, he'd know his way around a woman's body.

The thought brought a slight smile to her mouth and her gaze grew hooded.

"I'd love to know what you were just thinking about just now," Marco said. "To have put such a look on your face."

"And what kind of look is that?" Brandy shook her head to clear it and reached for her wine glass and took another long drink.

"The look of a woman who's thinking about getting laid."

Brandy choked on her wine and set the glass down again. "You think I had the look of...."

"Yeah." He lifted his beer and took another drink. "It was definitely the kind of look that said—"

"That's quite enough, Mr. Vargas." Flustered, she reverted to her best teacher tone. Since the moment she'd jumped on the back of his bike and wrapped her arms around his six-pack abs, rational thoughts had been dangerously absent in her head.

"Mr. Vargas?" Marco laughed and gave a slow smile. "It's kind of sexy when you pull out that teacher's voice."

"What? I'm not—"

"Besides. Come on, *Brandy*, don't you think we're a little past the formal stuff? After all, you did hijack my bike."

"It was an emergency!"

"You ready to tell me about it?"

Not at all.

Brandy downed the rest of her wine. "How about another one of these first?"

"Sure." Marco finished his beer and stood up, then gave her

a considering look. "You know, you look a little familiar. Are you from around here?"

"No, I'm not." She quickly looked away, her breath locking in her lungs.

Oh god.

Did he recognize her? Most people didn't. The paparazzi had bigger fish to chase. Most of the time.

Though things had begun to change when she'd started dating Gordon.

Movement out of the corner of her eye had her turning her head just in time to see Marco get up and walk to the bar.

He was probably going to get more drinks instead of waiting for the waitress to return.

Her glance slid over his backside.

Hmm.

Impressive there, too. Gordon's butt was so flat it was almost inverted, not to mention so white it nearly glowed.

Was Marco's skin that beautiful shade of brown all over? Or was it just kissed by the Nevada sun? If she ever got him naked, she'd find out.

Wait a minute. Get Marco naked? Hello, hold up there!

She put up a mental stop sign in her head. No more of those thoughts. Jeez. It had to be the wine. She couldn't possibly be thinking about....

Besides, he might already have a girlfriend.

Or, yikes, a wife?

She hadn't even glanced at his ring finger yet. Good lord, could he hurry back with the wine already?

When he did, she locked her vision on his left hand and found it empty. She relaxed a little bit more. Until she noticed that he held not a glass of wine, but an entire bottle in his hand.

Her eyes widened and she quickly lifted her head to look at him again.

"I figure it'll save us time in the long run."

"Oh." She almost asked why he didn't get a pitcher of beer for himself, and then realized he was probably thinking about driving home.

Where was home for her tonight? If she returned to L.A., Gordon would find her immediately.

And she really, really didn't want to be found until she could figure out what she wanted.

She slid her empty glass towards Marco and decided not to think about it right now.

He obliged her silent request and filled her glass before she pulled it back from him and took a big swallow.

She immediately glanced at the bottle and sucked in a sharp breath. The label on the bottle was not unfamiliar, and this was no cheap bottle of wine he'd bought her.

"What do you think?" he asked, noticing her reaction.

"It's wonderful." She took another, slower sip. Somewhat hesitant to disrespect such a great bottle of wine by using it to get trashed. "I'll pay you back of course..." she trailed off and her eyes widened with horror.

"What's wrong?"

"I don't have my purse."

"It's on me, don't worry about it."

"No, that's not it. I mean, thank you, but I have no money. No identification. It's all locked up in our room." She started to panic. "What am I going to do? Oh god, I need my purse!"

"Easy, Brandy." He took her hand in his, his gaze gentle, and stroked his thumb across her knuckles. "We'll get it back. Which hotel are you staying at?"

Her heart, already speeding, kicked up another notch at his touch. "The MGM."

"Perfect, we're right across from it. All right, here's the

plan," he said, making eye contact with her. "We call the hotel and find out if Gordon is in your room. If so—"

"We?" she breathed. "You mean you'll help me?"

"Do you want to do this on your own? If so, you tell me when to go away and I'll do it."

"No. I don't want to be alone," she said hurriedly, surprised to realize she meant it.

Something flickered in his eyes and then disappeared.

"Then all right. We do this together."

"Okay." Brandy shivered as his thumb started doing feather-light circles on the back of her hand.

"So, we call your hotel and ask to be transferred to your room. If Gordon isn't there we sneak in, grab your stuff and get out. Do you have your key?"

"Yes. Gordon couldn't find his earlier and asked me to bring mine."

"Great. We'll go when you're ready."

Brandy hesitated. "What should we do with the wine? I hate to just let it go to waste."

Marco laughed, his mouth curving into a smile. "Never let a good bottle of wine go to waste. Bring it with you."

"Bring it...I can do that? Bring it with me?"

"You're really not from around here, are you? You're in Vegas, baby. You can walk down the street with an open container and it's perfectly legal."

"Wow. I knew I liked this city." Brandy wrapped her hand around the slim neck of the bottle and stood up. "Let's go."

They walked through the lobby, the expensive bottle of wine swinging in her grasp. Every few minutes she'd lift it to her mouth and take a sip.

If her parents could see her now...hmm. They'd probably tell her to get a second bottle of wine and go have fun.

She glanced over at Marco. He was on his cell phone calling the MGM.

"What's Gordon's last name?"

"Perry."

A second later, he was asking to be transferred to Gordon's room. He closed his cell phone shortly after.

"He's not there?" Brandy asked with a hopeful glance as they stepped outside the hotel into the heat.

"He's not answering, so it doesn't look like it."

Brandy tilted the bottle for another drink as they waited to cross the street at a crosswalk. By the time they were in the elevator up to the room, her nerves were strung taut again and the bottle shook in her hand.

Not to mention the guilt was starting to creep in.

Gordon loved her. *Loved her.* And what had she done? Run out on their wedding and was in the process of getting drunk with a sexy stranger.

She at least owed Gordon an explanation, didn't she?

Perhaps she could arrange to have a drink with him down in the bar. Maybe attempt to explain her reasons.

She bit back a giggle. Right. When she didn't even know what the reasons were herself? That was a definite no.

Maybe a phone call? Then they could discuss it without having to be face to face.

No. Even talking to him on the phone made her antsy.

I'll leave him a note.

The elevator opened and Brandy headed down the hall toward her and Gordon's room.

"Hold on a minute." Marco put his hand out, stalling her from walking any further. He rapped on the door and waited. No one answered. "Okay, where's your key?"

Her cheeks flamed. "Can you look away for a minute?"

"Why?"

"Because it's in a location I'd rather you not be privileged to know."

He lifted an eyebrow and his gaze took on an intimate look of curiosity that sent tingles through every square inch of her body.

She sighed. "Please?"

His eyes snapped shut, but the smile remained on his face.

Working fast, she lifted her dress and snatched the key from the lacy top of her stocking.

"Okay." She let the dress fall back into place. "You can open your eyes."

His eyes were already open when he reached out and plucked the key from her fingers.

"Nice and warm. Where did you say this was, princess?"

"You totally watched." Brandy gave him a light whack across his shoulders and folded her arms across her chest. "Will you just open the door?"

He laughed a low, deep sound that sent a shiver through her and made her breasts feel heavier.

She watched his large, capable hands scan the card, and a moment later there was a clicking sound.

"On your mark, get set..." He swung it open.

She moved past him and ignored the surprising tingles that ran through her body when her hip brushed his thigh.

Just go and find your purse, Brandy.

Marco laughed as he followed her inside, shutting the door behind him.

Damn, she was a puzzle. He watched as she scurried around the room, muttering to herself as she tried to locate her purse. For the most part, she seemed so prim and proper, blushing at the drop of a hat. But....

He watched her lean over one of the beds. And there was nothing prim and proper about those stockings of hers by any stretch of the imagination.

They'd probably come straight out of some dirty lingerie catalog.

And there was that peek she'd given him while she retrieved the key. Like she'd really expected him to look away.

He'd kept his eyes closed for about two seconds before opening them in time to catch a flash of pale thighs and white lace.

He'd been more than a little surprised to see such a sexy getup on the prudent little choir teacher.

For a second, the fact that she wasn't his type meant shit to him. He could almost ignore the starchy, conservative attitude and focus on those legs.

Legs that had him imagining what they'd feel like wrapped around his waist.

Her exasperated groan ripped through his sexy thoughts.

"Where on earth did I put it?"

He shifted his focus back to the present and glanced around the room. Two beds? That was odd. Maybe the hotel had been short on rooms.

"Got it." Brandy straightened from behind one of the beds holding a mammoth-sized tote bag with smiley faces on it.

His eyes widened and his lips twitched in amusement. That was her purse?

"Okay, let's get the hell out of here."

"Could you not curse every five minutes? And hold on, I'd like to change before we leave. This wedding dress is driving me nuts." She hurried to a suitcase and pulled out a wad of clothing. "I'll be right out."

He watched her disappear into the bathroom and shut the

door. Well, at least she was taking off the hideous dress. Not to mention it would make her a little more inconspicuous.

If her fiancé was looking for her she was an easy find in a wedding dress.

Marco heard the lock click as she reemerged a moment later.

Oh god. Put the wedding dress back on.

He had to bite his tongue from screaming the words.

The denim skirt she wore reached her ankles and the purple top had a puffy cat sewn on the front.

She was a couple of inches shorter now since she'd taken off the heels she'd been wearing earlier. On her feet instead were sturdy purple sandals.

"I feel so much better," she said with a big smile. "I wanted that dress off me so bad that I just tossed it in the bathtub. I can't believe—"

The doorknob jangled and she broke off, her eyes widening in horror. Brandy grabbed his hand and dove into the closet, dragging him with her. She slid the closet door shut, leaving them in darkness. A second later someone entered the room.

Chapter Two

Marco gritted his teeth and shook his head. How did he let it get to this point? How the hell did he end up hiding in a hotel room closet with a choir teacher?

She took a hurried step back when someone passed by their hiding spot. His hands automatically reached out to steady her and landed on a pair of soft curvy hips.

Well, look at that. Maybe the choir teacher was hiding something under the drab clothing.

His blood pounded a little faster and he took a deep breath in. The smell of apples assailed him again, and this time it didn't seem quite as weird.

Without thinking, he moved his hands down those lush hips and was rewarded with a stinging slap across his knuckles.

She tensed, as if worried the swat had been too loud. But after a moment came the sounds of two people speaking quietly in the room.

Hmm.

Gordon obviously wasn't alone. Had Brandy figured it out yet?

"I'm just going to shower," a man's voice said.

"Don't forget, darlin'. I charge by the hour."

He heard Brandy's nearly silent gasp as she shifted forward, trying to peek through the edge of the closet door.

Ah shit, this can't be good.

The bathroom door closed, followed by the sound of the shower running.

Marco leaned forward and whispered into her ear, "Do you have your purse?"

He felt her nod. The curls on her head tickled his chin.

"Do you want to stay and talk with Gordon?"

"What do you think?" Her tone turned waspish.

"Okay, we're going to have to make a run for it. Listen carefully." He kept his voice encouraging. "I want you to open the closet and head straight out of the room. Got it? Don't look back and don't stop to talk to whoever else is out there."

Again she nodded.

"Okay." He took a deep breath, his blood pumping faster through his veins. "Now!"

She pulled open the door and leapt out. There was a surprised gasp from the person sitting in the room.

Brandy stood stock still in front of the closet, staring in disbelief at the woman on the bed, obviously ignoring his advice to just run and not look.

He spared a quick glance at the naked woman on the bed—fried blonde hair and perky boobs—eyeing Brandy with open curiosity.

Damn it. He needed to get Brandy out before the shit really hit the fan.

"Nobody said anything about doing a group thing." The woman on the bed transferred her attention to Marco, her slow smile showing off some screwed-up teeth. "But I'm not complaining."

"A group thing?" Brandy sputtered glaring at the nearly naked woman on the bed. "You—you jezebel!"

Marco swore and grabbed her hand, jerking her towards the door. She followed, but her eyes never left the other woman.

The bathroom door swung open just as Marco closed the hotel room door after them.

He was nearly dragging her by the time he pushed the button for the elevator. The doors opened and he pushed her in, just as footsteps sounded running down the hall.

"Love muffin!" a man yelled. "It's not what it looks like."

Marco hurried into the elevator before he could get a glance at the now-infamous Gordon. The doors slid shut and a second later they could hear him pounding on the elevator and screaming her name. Well, not her name, but his choice of endearment, *love muffin*.

Brandy leaned back against the wall in the elevator, her eyes closed.

"Are you all right?" Marco watched her, his body buzzing like he'd had too much caffeine.

But it wasn't caffeine that had him on edge. It was the anticipation of her reaction. He didn't see her as a woman right now, but as a time bomb that could go off at any moment.

God, please don't let her have a breakdown. He was really, really bad at comforting weepy women.

"She had bad teeth," Brandy mumbled in dismay "I don't get it. He's a dentist. How can he be attracted to someone with bad teeth?"

The tension in his body dissipated some and he gave her a slight smile. It probably wouldn't be wise to point out that Gordon probably hadn't been looking at the woman's teeth.

Brandy gasped. "Oh! I forgot the wine. That wonderful, expensive bottle of—"

"The wine is replaceable. But we probably should've grabbed your luggage."

Brandy glanced at him and her lips parted in a silent *oh*. And then, suddenly, she did look like she was going to cry.

Fuck.

He'd just had to remind her of the luggage.

"My luggage," she said with a tiny sniff, and she blinked rapidly a few times. "I'll be fine. We—I'll figure out something."

"We'll figure something out." Had he just made a commitment to her?

But he couldn't leave her like this. Not yet. Even though he'd rather break any single bone in his body than deal with a weepy woman, he wouldn't be able to look at himself in the mirror if he left her now.

He'd get through the evening—somehow—and then send her on her way. Whereever that was. The bottom line was, she wasn't his responsibility and he would be stupid to make her so.

Brandy's blue eyes connected with his, and he could see the faint sheen of tears across them. Damn. His hardened resolve melted a bit at the sight of her quivering lips.

Who was she? Besides some uptight teacher.

Her phone began to ring in her purse and she pulled it out and then turned it off with jerky movements.

The doors to the elevator opened and they stepped out, making their way through the casino. The sound of slot machines was deafening and the floor appeared packed.

Marco, in a hurry to get them out of the hotel, grabbed her hand and weaved them through the Friday night crowd.

Soon they were back out on the Strip. The sun had set, but the lights were so bright that darkness never really fell in Vegas.

"Where do you want to go?" Marco asked as they stood at the crosswalk.

"I don't know." She glanced up at him, a hopeful expression in her eyes. "Do you live around here?"

Shit, she wanted to go home with him? No. No way. "Henderson."

"Oh. That's not too far." When he didn't say anything, she looked away chewing on her lip. "You don't have to stay with me. I can book a room somewhere and figure things out."

"Do you want me to leave?" Marco steered her out of the path of a bunch of drunken men crossing the street in the opposite direction.

"No. I don't want you to leave. But I can't expect you to stay."

She turned to face him once they were on the sidewalk again. He saw the spark of interest in her eyes and then she glanced at his lips.

He watched her swallow hard, and then her tongue dart out to wet her lush mouth.

He bit back a groan and his jaw hardened.

You don't want to kiss me, sweetheart.

She had no idea what she was asking. But faced with the naked vulnerability in her eyes and obvious interest, something shifted inside him.

Some of the hardness melted around his resolve, and before he could stop himself he reached out to stroke his thumb down the side of her cheek.

"I'm not going anywhere." Before he could stop himself, he reached up to cup her cheek. His thumb moved to rub across her bottom lip, which parted on a sigh.

That mouth. God, if she didn't have the mouth and those legs.... *She'd be some freak mutant, you idiot. Don't do it. Kissing her will just complicate things. Don't even go there.'*

Her gaze drifted up to meet his, confusion and anticipation in her eyes.

"Ah, shit." He lowered his head towards hers.

For some reason, it seemed perfectly natural for Brandy to lean forward into Marco's kiss. The smell of leather and spice enveloped her senses, just before his arms wrapped around her body.

His mouth closed over hers, firm and confident. It was a hard kiss, nothing hesitant about it. Definitely not the kind she was used to getting from Gordon.

His tongue traced the seam of her lips and a shiver raced down her spine. With a deft move, he slipped inside her mouth and she grabbed onto his T-shirt to keep her balance as the world around them spun.

His tongue rasped against hers. He tasted faintly of beer and all kinds of sin.

He pressed his body harder against her, then moved his hands down her waist to grab her ass. Brandy gasped at the contact and he used it to his advantage, stroking his tongue deeper.

Heat speared down her belly and between her legs, and she curved her body closer to his, wanting so much more of this delicious moment.

He pulled back suddenly and she tightened her grip on his T-shirt to keep from falling forward. Dazed, but not so far out of it that she didn't notice the hard muscles under her fingers.

She groaned. This was insanity. Pure insanity. Or just lust. That was a pretty plausible explanation too.

"We should go somewhere."

Perfect, let's get a room.

The words were on the tip of her tongue, but then she swallowed them. This was all too crazy, too sudden. She should be grieving or at least a little confused about the whole Gordon situation.

But Gordon was the last darn thing on her mind. Instead, all she could think about was that erotic kiss she'd just shared with a perfect stranger.

The thing was, she knew why *she'd* kissed him—he oozed sex and danger. He was attractive. He was like nothing she'd ever experienced before.

The big question was, why had *he* kissed *her*? She was nothing like the Goddess models she'd grown up envying.

She raised her gaze to his and noticed he looked a little uneasy by what had just passed between them.

"Why did you kiss me?" she blurted, the passion bubble starting to deflate. God. Why had she even asked that? But since she had, might as well follow this thread. "Men like you don't kiss women like me."

He shook his head and looked away. "Don't worry, it won't happen again.'

"Oh." Of course it wouldn't. Disappointment bloomed in her stomach but she swallowed it back down and nodded.

Marco turned and began walking again.

Where was he going? Should she follow him? She hesitated a second and then ran to catch up with him. What else could she do? He was her anchor in this crazy storm of a day.

Fuck!

Gordon stalked back into the hotel room and slammed the door behind him.

The prostitute he'd picked up after Brandy had run out on him was still there. Sprawled out on the bed, the remote control was in her hand as she flipped through channels and blew a bubble with her chewing gum.

"Get out," he snarled.

She glanced over at him, her eyes widening. "I thought you wanted me to spank you and then give you head."

"I said get the fuck out!" He grabbed her arm, jerking her off the bed.

"Whoa, hold on there, bucko. You haven't paid me."

"And I'm not going to." He dragged her across the room and flung her into the hallway, tossing her clothes at her and slamming the door shut afterward.

Leaning back against the door he thrust his hands into his hair. Pay her? Hell, he couldn't even afford to buy a burger off the god damn dollar menu.

He crossed the room and tried Brandy's cell phone. It rang twice and then went to voicemail.

Shit, shit, shit!

Sweat beaded on his forehead as he sat down on the bed. He was screwed. One hundred percent screwed.

The money was due by the end of the month. Where the hell was he going to get ten million dollars in three weeks?

Grabbing a pillow, he tossed it across the room with a roar. He'd been so close. So damn close to tripling what he'd come here with last night.

He'd pulled so many damn strings to get into the exclusive high rollers game he was like a damn puppeteer. But in the end, he'd blown it. Lost every fucking penny to his name.

He might have *eventually* had enough to pay back his bookie with his salary on *New You*—not like the bookie would have settled for monthly payments anyway—but that possibility had disappeared when he'd been told earlier in the week that the show wasn't going to be brought back for a second season.

All his fame and fortune was one fucking whirlpool going down the shitter.

And then it had clicked. His only chance at saving his ass. Marry Brandy. Marry her so damn quick she didn't have time to even think of the word *pre-nup*.

Ten million was probably the change in the Summers' piggy bank. They could easily afford it and probably wouldn't have hesitated to lend the money to their new son-in-law.

But the ugly bitch had run out on him. At the god damn altar! His lips curled into a sneer and he threw another pillow across the room.

Hell, she should've been grateful that *any* man had looked her way. But the fact was that *he* had and it barely fazed her....

What the hell was wrong with the woman?

She wanted nothing to do with her tabloid-dubbed title of *Lingerie Heiress*. Had instead gone on to be a choir teacher.

They'd met at a charity event over a year ago, and it was then he'd realized she could be his ticket into one of the wealthiest families in L.A.

He would gain the ability to penetrate the circles her family ran in. Circles that had shunned him his whole damn life.

As a child, he'd been the freak in school—the kid whose dad had snapped one day and killed himself and his wife in a murder-suicide after she'd had an affair.

After playing musical houses with various family members who didn't really want him—he'd gone into foster care.

The rumors and stares had made him a social outcast. And it wasn't like he'd had good looks to fall back on—he'd hands down been the ugly kid in class. It had taken him years and a hell of a lot of surgery to create his new image.

But it hadn't helped. Not really. He was still somewhat of an outcast. To date he hadn't been to more than a handful of parties—Brandy always had an excuse not to go. And the times when she did, her friends had treated him with dubious if polite disdain.

"Son of a bitch." He growled and slammed his foot into her suitcase.

His lips curled into a sneer at the ugly clothes hanging half out of the unzipped case.

Brandy was a disappointment in and out of the bedroom—not that he'd even managed to fuck her more than a handful of times.

He'd been surprised to find a hot little body under her plain attire the first time they'd had sex. Though, she had all the passion of an ice cube with breasts.

But if marrying her was the only way he could save his ass, then by all means he'd do it. She should be more than happy to stay home and play wifey.

And then, as son-in-law to the Summers', he'd be welcomed into the fold of their society. A place that not even his status as a new celebrity had been able to buy.

Gordon stood and walked to the window, jerking the curtains back and looking out over the Strip.

He had to get Brandy back. He would. He just had to find her first.

God, what the hell had made him do it?

Marco shook his head as they walked down the street.

What had made him kiss the choir teacher like he was some teenager in heat? It wasn't as if she was dressed in some sexy outfit that fried his mind.

She was wearing a shirt with a cat on it, for Christ's sake. It was so shapeless he still had no idea what her breasts might be like. He knew what her hips and ass felt like, though.

Do. Not. Go. There.

Damn, what a mess. He'd lost all reason when Brandy had stared up at him with a helpless vulnerability in those wide blue eyes.

Don't make this into something romantic. It's nothing but you needing to get laid.

It was just six months without sex doing this to him. Made him want to sleep with any available woman—didn't matter if she was a stripper or a choir teacher.

Even as he thought it, his gut tightened and he knew he was spouting off bullshit in his head.

Realizing they'd been walking down the Strip with no destination, he steered them toward a restaurant in another casino.

A hostess sat them down in a dark corner, in a booth that was far too romantic for his taste.

He glanced over at Brandy who sat flipping through the menu. Her lips were still swollen from his kiss and her cheeks flushed.

She'd been right when she'd said that she wasn't his type. His type gravitated toward tall, skinny blondes who didn't blush at the mention of sex. Brandy was too sheltered. Too much of a good girl.

She was everything he didn't want. So what had come over him?

The waitress arrived to take their order. His brows drew together when Brandy didn't even bother with real food but went straight for the dessert.

Snickers cheesecake and wine. What kind of dinner was that?

He, on the other hand, was starving. He'd left work without grabbing food, thinking he'd toss a steak on the barbeque once he got home. But Brandy had thrown a kink in that plan.

They sat in silence until the food came. She seemed to be off in her own little world, anyway. Understandable, since she probably had a dozen things occupying her thoughts.

When the food arrived he dug into his greasy burger, his awareness of the woman across from him diminishing some.

He was almost able to stop thinking of her as the woman he'd just shared an insanely hot kiss with, and instead went back to thinking of her as the choir teacher in a cat shirt.

Then she slid her fork into the cheesecake and lifted a bite to her lips. Her eyes closed, and she began emitting the most seductive, orgasmic noises as she ate the bite.

"This is good," she said, her fork diving back down for another bite. "This is *really* good. I needed this."

Did it make him an asshole for thinking she needed a whole lot more than cheesecake? She needed to get laid, and not by some dumb-ass named Gordon.

"Did you want some wine?" she asked.

Marco blinked. "Wine?"

"You were just staring at my wine glass, and I thought you might have wanted some."

Actually, he thought, I was staring at your breasts behind the wineglass. Were they big or small? It was the damn mystery of the night.

"No thanks." He gave her a brief smile and picked up a fry.

"Can I have one?"

He looked down at his dwindling fry supply, ready to protest, but she'd already picked up a fry and proceeded to eat it, savoring each bite as erotically as she had the cheesecake.

Was she doing it on purpose? No. That would have been about as likely as Brandy having actually been a stripper.

"So where do we go from here?" she asked, licking the grease from her fingers.

He ground his teeth and glanced away from her mouth.

"I was thinking," she went on. "Maybe we could go to a show? I haven't had the chance to really do the whole Vegas experience."

He listened to her drone on about the Vegas experience as she polished off the rest of his fries. He hated going to shows. They were a waste of time and money.

And how weird was it that she'd run out on her wedding, and now wanted to go to a show with a stranger?

"I'll pay of course." She drained the rest of her wine and then looked at him, a dazzling smile on her face. "I think the alcohol is kicking in. It should be by now. I mean I had half a bottle earlier, and another glass here. I can tell because—"

"I think a show sounds great," he interrupted, not even wanting to know how she could tell she might be drunk.

"Oh. You are the best. Do you think we could get tickets for Donny Osmond? Does he still perform here?"

Seriously? This was hell. He was fantasizing about a woman that dressed worse than his grandma and wanted him to go see Donny Osmond in concert.

He should have taken her up on the wine.

"He is still here, isn't he? My mom loved Donny Osmond. I had to listen to him when I was a kid. You know that song Puppy Love? I could sing it for you."

Fuck, please don't.

"No, that's cool. I know it," he said so fast he nearly tripped on the words.

Brandy ate the last bite of her cheesecake and gave him a suspicious look. "Okay, let's be honest. I'm guessing you're like every other man out there. You'd rather have a root canal than see that concert."

Marco gave a brief smile. "That about sums it up."

"How about a magic show?" she suggested hopefully. "That's not so bad, is it?"

When? When would this night end? Come midnight he was gone, out of here. Goodbye. Goodnight. Gone. Good Samaritan hat could be hung back up.

"No. That's not so bad," he heard himself say.

Her mouth tilted upward and something shifted inside him; making his breath catch.

"You've got an amazing smile," he told her without thinking. The compliment had her mouth snapping shut and her lips drawing down into a frown. "What. What did I say?"

"I think Gordon only loves me for my teeth," she confided despondently.

"For your...your teeth?"

"Don't look so confused." She sighed. "He's a cosmetic dentist for a reality television show."

"Which show?"

"*New You.*"

He winced. "That's a pretty shitty show. No offense."

"None taken. I agree."

They both laughed and some of his irritation faded. Curiosity arose in its place.

"So, we've known each other a whole two hours. Are you ready to tell me why you ran from your wedding?"

"Oh." Her expression sobered and he almost felt bad for changing the subject. "Umm...I don't really know why I ran. I just know I didn't want to get married in a shrine to Elvis."

"That's it? The location alone?" He raised an eyebrow in disbelief.

She bit her lip and looked down. "And I wasn't so sure I wanted to get married to Gordon. We've been together for a year, but still..."

"So why did you agree to marry him in the first place?"

Marco's curiosity increased as she started to blush again.

"You're going to think I'm ridiculous," she muttered.

"Doubtful."

"I was starting to feel bad because I'm not married. And..." she took a deep breath and folded her hands on the table. "I turn thirty next week."

Marco snapped his mouth shut. She wasn't thirty yet? Hell, in that outfit he'd had her pegged for thirty-five at least.

He cleared his throat. "It isn't so bad being single and thirty."

She rolled her eyes. "Of course being single in your thirties works for you. You're a guy."

"I'm twenty-nine."

Brandy blinked and then shook her head. "I need another drink."

Marco gave her a close look. "What's the problem?"

"You're younger than me," she said with a huff, as if that was an explanation in itself.

"By a year."

"Never mind." She shook her head and waved down the waiter. "I just thought you were older."

"Do you have an aversion to younger men?"

"Like dating a younger man?"

"Whatever works."

"I—I've never really thought about it."

He gave her a curious look. "How old is Gordon?"

"Forty-one."

"Ah, a sugar daddy."

"What?" she yelped. "Gordon is not my sugar daddy."

He gave her a searching look. "Did you grow up without a father?"

"No! What are you, a psychologist?"

"Do I look like a psychologist? I'm just trying to figure out what makes you tick."

"Well don't worry about my ticking," she grumbled. "That's my biological clock's department."

Marco gave a soft laugh. "Did you really want that other drink or would you rather see a show?"

Brandy sighed and glanced down at her almost empty glass. "The show. Alcohol's open twenty-four hours a day here."

With another laugh, Marco caught the waitress's attention and signaled for the bill.

"That was amazing." Brandy knocked back a shot of tequila and covered Marco's hand with hers, giving him an earnest look. "In fact, you know what? You're great, Marco Vargas."

"Er—you're pretty great too, Brandy."

She was completely trashed, Marco realized, as she picked up the bottle of tequila and poured herself another shot. The golden liquid sloshed over the shot glass, but she didn't seem to notice.

He should have cut her off. He'd tried to, seeing as it was second nature to him by now—it was what he did for a living. Seeing people get drunk and push their limits was nothing new to him.

But Brandy had been so adamant that she could handle her alcohol. So after she'd promised to get a room at one of the hotels, he'd driven her to another bar. *Stupid. Real stupid.*

Marco glanced at his watch. *God.* Was it almost two in the morning? What the hell had happened to his midnight cutoff? He needed to get her checked into a room and then head home.

"I don't want to crash your party, Brandy, but I have to be at work by ten tomorrow. I should head out soon."

Brandy's eyes widened and then she nodded. "Oh. Of course. I'll just grab a cab once I finish this bottle of tequila."

Marco's lips twisted despite his fatigue. "I didn't realize a trip to the ER was one of your sightseeing destinations."

"The ER?" She slurred her words now. "Why would I go to the ER?"

"Tell you what. Let me use the bathroom and then I'll drive you to a hotel," he said. "It's after two and we need to get you a room somewhere."

"After two? Already?" Her eyebrows drew into a scowl and then she suddenly grinned. "How about we get a hotel room together, big boy?"

Big boy? What the fuck? And she wanted to get a room?

The blood in his veins rushed south and his mind flickered back over that kiss earlier. Hmm. Get a roo—*No.*

Besides, would she even remember this conversation in the morning?

"I don't really want to be alone tonight." She toyed with the neckline of her shirt and gave him a suggestive look, running her tongue across her mouth.

"Brandy—"

"Please, Polo."

What the hell? "It's Marco."

"That's what I said."

She was trying to be sexy, he could acknowledge that. But she wasn't doing a very good job. In fact she was pretty much failing miserably.

Instead of coming across as a *sex kitten*, she was what she was. A drunken choir teacher in a *cat shirt*.

"It's not a good idea." He stood up. "I'll be right back and when I return we can go. All right, turbo?"

"All right." Brandy frowned, swishing the shot around in the tiny glass.

Marco stood up. Thank god this crazy night would soon be over.

. . .

Tequila was interesting. The color, the taste, the smell.

Brandy frowned. Although she'd never really been a tequila person.

Well, not before tonight. Did she really want this last shot? Her stomach churned and it seemed like such an effort to even hold onto the glass.

Marco was going to take her to get a hotel room soon. Too bad he didn't seem interested in sticking around. She frowned and pushed a wad of curls out of her face.

But what had she expected? That he'd jump at the chance to have sex with her?

Come on, Brandy, you're the drunk one, not him.

He was unbelievably sexy, *and* a younger man. And she was...a dried-up old prune who usually preferred playing the piano to having sex.

She could have been married right now. Married and having more sex with Gordon.

"Yuck." She set the shot glass down on the table and shuddered.

At least when she was drunk she could bring herself to admit sex with Gordon sucked. Always had.

Still, you would've had a husband. Meaning you would've been one step closer to having children.

Brandy shook her head and the movement made her a bit dizzy. Nope. She was completely all right being thirty and single. Besides, she still had plenty of time to get married and have children.

Wincing, she could almost hear the death cry of another egg inside her body.

And this was why she was drunk.

She pushed back the chair, stumbling slightly. How

pathetic was she? She'd forced a sweet man—well not conventionally sweet—to take care of her all night.

It was clear he wanted nothing more than to be rid of her. And then, after practically begging him to go to bed with her, he'd still turned her down.

Her face, already warm from the alcohol, suddenly grew hotter.

Scooping up her purse, she hurried out of the bar area. She didn't really have a plan, only to get far away from Marco and her burgeoning humiliation.

She made her way out of the casino, zigzagging through the gamblers who were still going strong despite the late hour.

Her stomach roiled and the room spun. Leaning against an empty slot machine, she took a deep breath and waited for the room to right itself.

"Hey, sugar, will you pull my lever?"

Brandy turned to look at the leering old man a few machines down.

"Yuck." Her nose wrinkled and she pushed on through the casino, spotting the freedom of the front entrance up ahead.

The automated doors opened, sending a rush of warm air at her full force. She stepped outside and gulped in a lungful of fresh air—then promptly started coughing as she realized someone nearby was smoking.

She kept moving, walked further away from the hotel, and finally onto the sidewalk that ran parallel to the Strip.

What was she going to do? Where would she go?

Cars whizzed past her, the headlights blending in with the bright lights of the city. Dizziness assailed her again and she stood still for a second. Why was it so darn hot? It was the middle of the night for goodness sake.

Swiping a hand across her forehead, she closed her eyes.

When she opened them her gaze landed on the most glorious sight.

The fountains of the Bellagio hotel.

She'd left him. Marco stood and turned in a slow circle, searching every corner of the room trying to find her, but she was gone.

Nowhere in sight. He was completely free of her. So why didn't he feel more relieved?

Maybe because she was alone, drunk off her ass and wandering around Las Vegas without a hotel room.

Shit. He tossed enough money on the table to cover her drinks and then stuffed his wallet in the back pocket of his jeans.

He made his way out of the casino, seeking out frizzy hair and a cat shirt. Letting her out by herself was a bad mistake. She was too sweet and naïve to be out on her own this time of night.

The doors swished open and he bolted through them. He glanced left and then right. The city was slowing down, but nowhere near dead.

How the hell was he going to find her? She could be anywhere.

Though she couldn't have gotten far. Seriously, she'd been out of his sight for a whole five minutes.

How would a drunk person think? He glanced in both directions again. The brighter lights came from the left.

She'd probably headed toward the big-name hotels. He took off running, keeping an even pace as he looked around for her.

Fifteen minutes later he was ready to accept defeat. It was useless. He'd lost her somewhere in the Vegas night.

Anxiety churned in his belly like it was a hot dog from a seedy corner stand.

This isn't your fault. She's not your responsibility.

He could tell himself that all he wanted, but it didn't make him feel any better. Because he'd let her keep drinking, not that he could've stopped her easily.

Time to go back for the bike and head home.

Hell, what else could he do? He glanced at the Bellagio hotel as he passed, vaguely noting the water shows had closed down for the night.

Someone bumped into him, a security guard, who pushed him aside as he ran by. A second later another one went running past him.

What was going on? Marco paused and watched as some kind of activity seemed to unfold at the far end of the fountain.

His eyebrows drew together. "Oh, god."

Breaking into a run, he followed after the security guards who were attempting to pull a woman—Brandy—back from the edge where her feet dangled over.

He spotted the silver handcuffs on one of the guards, while the other one wrestled to get her back from the edge.

"I don't see the problem here. I was just dipping my feet in." He could hear her protest. "My feet are perfectly clean, I just had a pedicure. And it's not like I was actually swimming."

"Excuse me." Marco reached the group and forced a tight smile. "I'm sorry about this, the lady's with me."

"Hey!" Brandy glanced his way and her face lit up. "It's Marco Polo! You followed me. We should swim together. Maaarco. Poooolo."

One of the security guards gave him a bored glance. "Yeah, well pretty soon, Marco Polo, it's going to be a police matter pretty soon."

The hell it was. "No, you don't understand. This whole

thing is my fault. I fucked up—" *think, Marco, think,* "I called her my ex-girlfriend's name during our wedding ceremony. She was so pissed she ran off and I've been trying to find her all day. I guess she's been getting drunk."

"You're an idiot." Brandy snorted and then broke into a fit of giggles as she turned toward the guards. "We're not married, you guys. He's totally pulling your leg."

Fuck? Did she *want* to spend the night in jail? He leaned forward to tuck a strand of hair behind her ear in what he hoped looked like an intimate loving gesture.

"That's because you didn't let us finish the ceremony, princess."

Brandy seemed to think about that really hard like she was beginning to think it entirely possible that they were almost married today.

"I don't know." One of the guards hesitated.

"She's a model citizen who's never gotten into trouble before this," Marco argued with as much conviction as he could muster. "I mean just look at her, does she look like she's used to getting into trouble?"

The other guard shook his head and pursed his lips. "She looks like my mother. In fact, I think my mom has that same shirt, but in blue."

Good sign, a very good sign. Marco waited with what he hoped was an apologetic, patient expression. Finally, he spoke up again.

"Look, can't we just keep this between us? I'll take her home and put her to bed. I'd feel like a complete ass if she ended up getting arrested on what should have been her wedding day."

The guards looked at each other, silently communicating, and then they looked back at him with a brief nod.

"Take her home and sober her up. And then you'd better

work on making things right, buddy." The older guard shook his head. "Hell, I'd have gotten drunk if I were her too."

Relief snapped the tension out of every muscle in his body.

"Thanks, guys. Will do." He stepped forward and slipped his arms beneath her legs, lifting her into his arms.

"Does this mean you'll sleep with me after all?" she asked hopefully, nuzzling her head against his chest.

The guards turned to look at him again.

"It's a long story. I was hoping to wait until our wedding night." Marco gave them a quick grin, not really caring that his excuse had more holes than a golf course. "Have a good night."

He kept walking, and when they didn't call him back he assumed they were in the clear. Thank god.

"Dang, I can't believe you can carry me." She lifted her head, and then let it drop back against his chest. "I'm no lightweight. My cousin Dave used to tell me that all the time growing up. I used to be kind of chunky."

Shitty cousin.

Anger sparked toward a man he'd never even met.

"You're not heavy."

"Ah thanks, Polo. I stopped eating donuts all of the time and so I lost a few pounds since—hey, where are we going?"

Damn good question. Did he check her into a hotel, drunk off her ass? Or did he...just take her home with him?

God, he was a sucker. He should be volunteering at the animal shelter for all the good deeds he was doing.

Lifting his free hand, he waved down a passing taxi. It swerved to the curb and stopped next to them. The driver got out, probably having noticed Marco couldn't open the door himself and helped him get Brandy into the backseat.

"She's not going to puke, is she?" the driver asked, casting a suspicious glance at her.

"She'll be fine." *I hope.*

Brandy scooted over on the seat, followed by the sound of her head hitting the window.

"Ow." She didn't lift her head from the glass.

Marco slid into the cab and helped get her seat belt buckled. He gave the driver his address and then leaned back against the seat. God, how much was he going to regret this in the morning?

Chapter Three

Who the heck was running a jackhammer in her head?

Brandy didn't even open her eyes. She lay as still as possible, hoping the painful throbbing would cease.

It didn't. It kept pulsating, thicker and harder until she was convinced her head was going to explode into a disgusting mess on the pillow.

She needed painkillers. Bad. Opening one eye, she stared at a white ceiling and a poster of a half-naked woman riding a motorcycle.

Where the heck was she? She forced herself to sit up in the bed—god knew whose bed it was—and looked around the room.

Lava lamps, more posters of half-naked women, and some kind of wall hanging decorated with gaudily painted marijuana leaves.

Oh. God. She'd died and gone to a frat house.

Her bladder began to pulse in time with her head. Pressing a hand to the back of her skull, she swung her legs off the bed and attempted to stand up.

The room spun and whatever she'd eaten last night started to swirl heavily in her stomach.

Where was the bathroom? She lurched towards the door, jerking it open as she ran down the hall.

There! She spotted the bathroom and ran inside, throwing the door shut behind her.

She barely made it to the toilet before heaving up more liquid than a human ought to have in them.

Then, after using the toilet for its normal purpose, she went to the sink to rinse her mouth out.

She spotted a bottle of mouthwash and almost ignored it—because god knew whose mouth had been on it—but the urge to get the bitter taste out of her mouth was too great.

A minute later, with a clean mouth, she finally stopped to actually look in the mirror. Her eyes widened.

Oh dear god.

She pressed her palm against the top of her head, hoping it might push the halo of curls down an inch or two. No use, they sprung right back up.

And what was she wearing? Her panties and somebody else's T-shirt.

She pressed her chin against her chest to upside down read the writing on the black T-shirt.

Dante's Place?

Hmm, sounded like some kind of satanic meeting place or something.

Whose shirt was it? Marco's? Or was it Polo?

All she remembered was Marco Polo. What *was* his name?

She lifted the hem of the shirt towards her nose and inhaled. Her fear of getting a contact high from a druggie's t-shirt evaporated.

It smelled clean and a little bit spicy. Closing her eyes she sighed. It was *his* shirt, and it evoked all kinds of visions from the previous night.

They'd kissed. The memory of it spread warmth all through her body and made her legs weak.

Where was she now? In his house? And what, besides that kiss, had happened yesterday?

More memories flickered through her head. Starting from when she ran away from her wedding, to Gordon screwing some prostitute, and then Marco/Polo—god, she really had to figure out his name—hanging out with her all night. They'd drunk a ton...or had that just been her? Then what had happened?

Get it over with. Open that door and find out what kind of mess you got your butt into.

She took a deep breath and went to twist the handle. It squeaked a bit on its hinges until it fully opened. The house seemed quiet. She looked to the left and then the right.

The hall was empty.

Stepping out of the bathroom, she crept out into the hallway and walked slowly as the shag carpet threaded through her bare toes.

The floorboards under the rug let out a loud groan and she bit her lip, glancing around sharply. Still quiet except for a dripping sound that came from what she assumed was the kitchen.

She arrived at the end of the hall and looked out into the living room. Not many furnishings, just a couch and a couple of plastic lawn chairs that were set up in a U around the television.

"Did you sleep okay?"

"Eeeaaw!" Brandy clutched her chest and spun around. "Jeez, you scared me."

"I noticed." Marco/Polo raised an eyebrow and walked past her into the kitchen, flipping on the light switch.

Why? Why did he look so good in the morning?

It should be a crime. His hair was only slightly tussled, and a T-shirt outlined his muscular chest and his flannel pajama bottoms hugged that very nice butt of his.

Her pulse, which had begun to slow down after the fright, sped right back up again.

Stop thinking about his butt, Brandy!

"Are you going to answer? How'd you sleep?"

She sighed. "I slept like someone who drank entirely too much and then passed out. But then I suppose that's exactly what I did do." She narrowed her eyes. "Okay, I'm sorry, but what the heck is your name again?"

What was his name?

Marco stared at her for a moment, trying not to look at the good amount of thigh she showed under his t-shirt. Or imagine what those naked legs might feel like wrapped around his waist.

One thing he could almost distinguish today was her breasts—beneath the thin fabric, he could tell they were full and round.

Miss Choir Teacher was most definitely hiding under the drab clothes, and now he knew her secret.

He lifted his gaze from her chest and met her wide eyes, but not for long.

Christ, that hair. It looked like it was ready to take flight.

Shaking his head, he went to make a pot of coffee. "You don't remember my name?"

She sighed. "Well, it's either Polo or Marco, but honestly it's all kind of a blur."

"Marco." Should he be offended? After loading up the

water and coffee grounds, he flipped the switch up on the pot and turned to face her. "How's your head?"

"Oh, besides feeling like it's been smashed in by a baseball bat? Just dandy."

"Want some painkillers? Or maybe a shot of tequila?"

Her face turned a bit green and he had to laugh. "Hey, don't knock it until you try it, princess."

"Meds, please. I prefer my breakfast in the solid form." She staggered into the dining room and sat down in one of the broken chairs. "Was that your bed I slept in last night?"

"No. It was my roommate's." He grabbed the aspirin out of the cupboard and handed her the bottle with a glass of water. "Here you go."

"Oh, thank god."

Turning, Marco went back and opened the fridge. "Okay, solid food. We've got eggs and bratwursts. You want me to cook you some up?"

"Uh—sure. That sounds fine, thank you. Is bratwurst like sausage?"

What the hell? Had the woman never eaten a bratwurst before? "Yeah, something like that."

"All right. I've always heard sausage is a good hangover food."

Had she been living in a cave her entire life? This couldn't be the first time she'd been hungover.

"So, let me get this straight, I slept in your roommate's bed last night?"

"That's right."

"That's good news. For a minute there I was afraid it might have been your room."

"And that would have been bad because..."

"Well," her cheeks flushed. "Obvious reasons. And, well, you don't look like the type to have ganja wall hangings." She gave him a suspicious glance. "So where is the roommate? Weren't you worried he might come home and possibly climb into bed with me?"

A laugh erupted from Marco's chest before he could stop it, but he did manage to cut it off pretty quickly. If Ben had come home and found Brandy in his bed, he probably would've gotten right back up to go smoke another bowl.

"No, I wasn't worried about that." He pulled a carton of eggs out of the fridge. "Ben's backpacking around Europe and won't be back for another month. He's actually moving out at the end of the summer. I was just giving the kid a break until he felt steady on his feet after college."

"Oh." She seemed relieved by his response and gave him a shy smile. "Thank you for taking me home with you, Marco. I know it probably wasn't something you intended to do."

His stomach shook with laughter again. Damn, if she only remembered half the stuff she'd done.

"You weren't in any shape to be on your own."

"Hey, come on. There's no need to laugh at me. I mean, I wasn't *that* bad."

"Not that bad?" He raised an eyebrow and decided to have a little fun with her. "When you slapped that waitress in the bar, I was laying down money that you could've taken her. But then she called in the bouncer and all bets were off."

The color drained from her face. "I—I slapped a waitress?"

"No. You didn't." He grinned when her face flushed with annoyance. "But you did ask me to go to bed with you."

"I did not."

"Oh yes. You sure as hell did." He waved the spatula at her and then went back to cracking eggs into the pan.

It was quiet. The only sound came from the frying eggs and

the sizzling bratwurst he'd tossed into the skillet. Why wasn't she saying anything? He turned around and found her staring at him with a solemn expression.

"What?"

"Did I really ask you to go to bed with me?"

Something about the fragile tone of her voice made him hesitant to nod. He gave a brief jerk of his head.

"Oh." She swallowed hard and glanced at the floor. "And you didn't want to?"

Fuck? What was this, a trick question? They'd already had the "we're not each other's type" conversation. Though seeing her in his T-shirt this morning, he was having second thoughts.

"Brandy..."

"No, it's probably better if you don't answer that." Her smile was just as unconvincing as her words. "I'm overly sensitive—my friends tell me that all the time."

What was up with her shitty friends and cousins? He shoved a hand through his hair and sighed.

"You don't want to get involved with me, Brandy."

"I know. Of course, I don't," she replied a little too quickly. She glanced away. "I can't stop wondering if my parents would be horrified or extremely proud to know what was going on with me right now."

His brows drew together and his temper flashed. Why did she put so much weight on what her parents thought? She was a grown woman.

"Screw them."

Her mouth opened in obvious shock. "Screw them? My parents?"

"Not literally."

"I realize that." She stared at him for a moment, hard, as if trying to gauge if he was serious or not. "You know what, never mind. You're right, Marco. It's definitely better in the end that we didn't sleep together."

"Right." It was?

He pressed the spatula hard against the bratwurst, taking pleasure in the way the meat spit and hissed. Why didn't he like her admitting that? It was fine when he'd thought it, but to hear her say it was different.

Hypocrite.

Marco scooped up some eggs and meat onto a plate for her and set it on the table.

"How do you like your coffee?"

"I don't. I drink tea."

"I don't have any *tea*, princess." He went back and poured himself a mug of coffee, and then filled one up for her too. "The only leaves in this house are in Ben's room, and I don't think you'll want to use them for tea."

He set the cup down in front of her, and she stared at it as if he were serving her antifreeze.

"Try it, you might like it." He went and dished himself up a plate and then came back to sit down next to her.

She lifted a small bite of eggs to her mouth and chewed slowly. After a satisfied moan, she stabbed a piece of bratwurst and then ate it with a little more enthusiasm.

"You like?"

"Bratwurst is *good*." She grinned and lifted her coffee, sniffing it. "Should I put milk in it or something? Sugar? Does it go down better?"

"I take mine black, but feel free to dump the extra shit in there if you need it."

Brandy pursed her lips and blew on the coffee before taking a tentative sip. Her eyes squinted together and then she sputtered, spitting it back into the mug.

"Oh, god, give me the extra shit please."

Marco laughed, his eyebrows rising as he went to grab the milk and sugar. Was that the first time he'd heard her swear? It sounded about as foreign as if she'd broken into Mandarin or something.

She added the extras to her coffee and they ate in silence for a while. True to her *bratwurst is good* comment, she ate almost the entire plate he'd given her.

The phone rang and he glanced at the clock, his brows coming together. Who'd be calling before eight?

He grabbed his cell and answered. "Hello."

"Marco? Is that you?"

He drew in a swift breath. His fingers tightened around the receiver as the familiar image of his kid sister raced through his head.

"Why are you calling, Elena?"

"I dunno. Me and my friends were gonna come up to Vegas in the next couple of days." There was a pause. "I was thinking maybe I could come to see you."

The idea was tempting. Damn. What had it been, about two years since he'd seen Elena? Even longer since he'd seen his dad.

"I'm not so sure that's such a good idea," he forced the words out past the hurt and bitterness.

"Dad won't have to know," his sister went on quickly. "I'll just drop by the bar—"

"Elena, you're not even old enough to go into a bar."

From the corner of his eye, he saw Brandy glance sharply over at him, and he turned his back to her.

"But I am," Elena argued softly. "I turned twenty-one a few months ago. I've been going to bars for a while now, Marco."

Shit. The knot in his stomach grew. How had he forgotten Elena's birthday? God, he was a real bastard.

He lowered his voice and switched to Spanish.

"*Lo siento, niña. Pero no es buena idea. Feliz cumpleaños. Te amo.*" He closed his eyes. "*Adiós, Elena.*"

Before she could protest, he hung up, aware of a heaviness in his chest that hadn't been there earlier.

"Well," Brandy spoke up with an awkward laugh. "Another reason you probably didn't sleep with me last night. Was that your girlfriend?"

"No." Marco turned around and gave her a tight smile. "That was my sister."

"Ah, I see. Sorry I'm so nosy." Relief and guilt flickered in her eyes before she quickly looked back down. "Is she coming up to visit you?"

He flexed his jaw. "No."

"Oh. But I thought—"

"Look, it's not something I want to talk about."

Her mouth parted and hurt flashed in her gaze. Damn. He could've been a little less abrupt.

Marco shoved a hand through his hair, not willing to admit his own emotions were a bit raw after that phone call.

"How's the breakfast treating you?" he asked with a slight smile, attempting to ease the sting.

Brandy pushed her plate away and sighed. "Oh jeez, I'm so full. Thank you. That was amazing."

He shrugged and lifted an eyebrow. "Hangover food tends to taste better, but you're welcome. And how's the headache?"

"Gone, thankfully." She wrinkled her nose and looked away. "But you know what? I'm feeling a little...gross. Do you think it's possible I could use your shower?"

A shower? All thoughts of his sister faded and were replaced with very alluring ones of Brandy.

A shower would mean she'd be naked. In his bathroom, under running water. A wet, naked female in his house—*you need to get laid.*

"Go for it, the towels are in the cupboard under the sink." The words sounded strained even to his ears.

She gave him a quizzical look but nodded. "Again, thank you."

Marco held his breath until she'd left the room and shut the bathroom door. Sighing he shook his head. What the hell was wrong with him?

This was going way beyond a good deed. Good deeds didn't come home with you and walk around in your clothes.

Before heading into work today he'd drop her off. It was time. She could deal with things from here on out. By now she must have some kind of idea of what she was going to do.

Or so he hoped.

Brandy locked the bathroom door behind her and leaned against it, closing her eyes.

So Marco still had absolutely no idea who she was?

It was probably a good thing.

She didn't really relish the idea of breaking the news to him and seeing the look in his eyes. The look every man gave her when they realized who she was.

Stripping off his shirt, she went to look in the mirror at her body. The lighting was kind of bad and made her skin look blotchy. But it emphasized all her curves, and Lord did she have a ton of them.

Her breasts, in her opinion—and Gordon's—were just a little too big.

She'd considered a reduction for the vanity aspect—since the size of them didn't bother her physically. Then she'd thought about the reaction of the tabloids and had decided against it.

The reporters would have had a field day.

Brandy Summers, heiress to the exclusive lingerie chain Sugar and Spice just got her boobs chopped in half.

She shook her head and unhooked her bra, dropping the $200 scrap of lace onto the bathroom floor.

If she weren't given the lingerie for free, she would never have justified spending that kind of money on it.

It always blew her mind to think that some people did so. Quite a few people actually. Since her parents opened the company twenty-eight years ago, it had become the most profitable lingerie chain in the United States and had recently expanded to Europe.

Turning on the shower, she reached her fingers in to test the temperature. The warm water ran over her hand and down her arm, helping relax her a bit.

The idea of being clean again had her quickly stepping into the small stall and shutting the glass door.

She dunked her head under the water and felt her curls lower an inch toward her skull. After a few minutes, they hung in defeat down her back. Hopefully, Marco had hair gel.

Glancing around the shower she finally found the soap. She picked up the bar and lifted it to her nose to give it a quick sniff.

Ah, and here was the source of *scent de Marco*. It was spicy and woodsy at the same time. Brown flecks dotted the white bar. Cinnamon? Probably.

She wet the bar down in the shower and then began to lather up. Because she knew Marco used this very bar of soap, bathing took on an erotic tinge she hadn't expected. A tremor ran through her body as she ran the slick bar of soap over her skin.

The cinnamon pieces in the soap created friction against her flesh. She passed the bar over her breasts and her nipples peaked in response.

"Oh, god." Brandy dropped her head against the wall of the shower as her knees weakened. This was just stupid. She was a grown woman getting aroused by a bar of soap.

A bar of soap that smells like him.

Why now? Sex with Gordon had been sporadic at best, and more often than not she found herself avoiding it. Which was weird, since she loved the *idea* of sex.

She hadn't even done the self-pleasure thing in god knows how long. So why was she getting the impulse to do it now?

She ground her teeth together, but the urge didn't go away. Her hand moved lower.

Don't do it, Brandy. That is entirely too dirty. It's just wrong. You're not going to masturbate in Marco's shower.

Oh, yes she was.

Brandy closed her eyes, dropping the soap to the floor and slipping her fingers between her legs. She moved her fingers over her clit and bit back a groan.

Oh, sweet Jesus. Why didn't she do this more often?

She rubbed faster, her breathing quickened and it became hard to stand up. Sinking to her knees in the stall, she let out a strangled groan.

The water in the shower grew cooler as it splashed down over her shoulders.

She increased the pressure with her finger as a blessed orgasm raced toward her. Little humming noises emerged from the back of her throat.

"Brandy?" There was a rapid knock on the door. "Are you okay?"

Oh my god.

"Fine," she gasped, the humiliation of being caught not quite overpowering her pleasure. Of course he would have to catch her mid-pleasure. "Just...ah...singing to myself."

"Singing?" he replied, sounding a bit hesitant.

"Yeah." She rubbed faster and started singing You Are My Sunshine.

Her thighs tightened and she forced out the rest of the song in a rushed chant. Her eyes crossed.

"Pleasedon'ttakemysunshineawaaaay.Aaaaay." *Oh my god.* "Heey."

She ground her teeth together, biting back the loud groan as she peaked. Her body shook through the orgasm, and when the tremors finally receded she was in a limp heap on the bottom of the shower stall. Reaching up, she turned off the water.

"Did you hurt yourself?" he asked with concern through the door.

Umm. Almost.

"Nope," she called weakly.

"You're sure you're all right?"

Dandy. Just finished getting myself off in your shower, hope that's okay.

"I'm fine, thanks. I was in the mood for a long shower today." Her voice came out hoarse. "Give me a few minutes and I'll be right out."

"Okay." He was silent for a moment. "Do you need anything?"

What, he couldn't have asked that question ten minutes ago?

She might've been bold enough to ask him to join her then. Of course, if he'd turned her down last night, chances were he'd have turned her down again.

"No, I'm great. Thanks, Marco."

She waited until she heard the sound of his retreating footsteps and then stood up. Yikes, that had been close.

Brandy grabbed a towel from under the counter and wrapped it around her body. Now she had an entirely different problem.

No clean panties. The bra she could do again, but the panties needed to be washed.

She turned on the faucet and washed her pair from yesterday with warm water and soap. Scooping up his shirt and her bra, she set the panties on top and opened the bathroom door.

Peeking her head out, she made sure he wasn't in the hall before dashing back to stoner boy's room.

She hung the panties over the inside doorknob and started to get dressed in yesterday's clothes.

Marco paced the living room, scratching the back of his neck and muttering under his breath.

He could have sworn he'd heard her making sexy little noises in his bathroom. He'd gone to check on her but hadn't actually knocked right away. The little whimpers had stopped him.

Damn, but he'd been about ready to push down the door just to find out for sure. And then she'd started singing the weirdest god damn version of "You are My Sunshine" he'd ever heard.

It all made him think...but no. The idea of Miss Choir Teacher masturbating in his bathroom just wasn't realistic. No, Brandy wasn't that type of woman.

Yeah keep telling yourself that, maybe it'll make your dick less hard.

Glancing at the wall he checked the clock. Nine. He had to be at work in an hour. The plan was still to drop her off at a hotel.

Ben's door opened and he heard her feet padding down the hallway. When she came into the room and for a moment he forgot to breathe.

Damp curls fell around her face and down her back. Her blue eyes, which seemed brighter than before, met his gaze almost shyly.

No, Brandy wasn't classically beautiful, but there was something about her that took his breath away—made him forget about the cat shirt and skirt she had on again.

She licked her lips and his focus slid to her moist and lush mouth. He balled his fists so he wouldn't do something stupid. Like touch her again.

"What's your plan, Brandy?"

Her eyes widened. Damn, he hadn't planned on being so abrupt, but when she was around nothing seemed to come out right.

"Umm. I've been thinking about it...." She glanced away.

Had she? It didn't sound like it with the hesitation in her voice.

"I think I'll just try and keep a low profile for a couple of days while I decide what to do." She bit her lip. "Maybe get a room in one of the smaller motels outside the city. One where no one will recog—Gordon won't find me."

She wanted to stay in some trash motel? His eyes narrowed. That sounded like a shitty plan to him.

"Look, I have to go to work soon—"

"Of course you do. Gosh, I'm so sorry, Marco. I've been monopolizing your life and your time. I mean you obviously have plans." She drew her lower lip between her teeth for a moment. "Look, why don't you just drop me off at a bus stop? I can figure out how to get around."

"No." Shaking his head, he hated the idea already. He didn't want her running around with some half-baked plan.

He wanted her to have a good solid one. One where she'd at least be in a safe place. Where he wouldn't have to worry that he'd thrown her to the dogs.

"Tell you what, why don't you come to *Dante's Place* with me? Hang out for a bit and grab some lunch. There are even places to shop nearby if you want, but don't rush off on your own until you know what you're doing for sure."

Her eyes widened and she looked ridiculously happy at the small offer.

"You're sure you don't mind?" she asked, her tone hopeful.

"I wouldn't have offered if I did. Besides, we make damn good burgers down at the bar. You can't leave Vegas without checking out *Dante's*. We'll just have to catch a cab back to the casino to grab my bike."

"That's right, you left it there." Her brows drew together before she gave a soft sigh. "You've been so nice to me, it's like you've been my guardian angel these past two days."

He laughed, but not because he found her words amusing. His feelings for her were in no way holy.

With a slight smile, he muttered, "I'm no angel, princess. And you should try and remember that."

The parking lot at *Dante's Place* was mostly empty except for a couple of motorcycles out front. So it really was kind of a biker bar.

Brandy followed close behind Marco as he opened the door to the bar and strode inside.

Had she ever been in a real bar? The one in the casino last night had been a first for her, but when she'd been surrounded by the glitz and glam of a Vegas casino it seemed a little different.

This bar was interesting. Like something she would have expected to see in the old west. There weren't swinging saloon doors or anything, but the inside was dim and the wooden floorboards creaked with each step she took.

And it had the smell of new wood, not old. Like it had been built not too long ago.

Marco glanced over his shoulder at her. He was so close his chin brushed her hair.

"You okay?" He lifted an eyebrow in amusement and she flushed, stepping back a few feet.

"Fine, though it's awfully dark in here. Don't you believe in adequate lighting?"

The husky laugh and teasing look in his dark eyes sent those increasingly familiar warm tingles racing through her body.

"There are lights."

"Yes, but not adequate." Okay, so it wasn't that bad. But really, she would have been a lot more comfortable had the place been lit up like a grocery store.

His lips quirked into a slight smile and he stepped forward, closing the distance between them. Her pulse jumped and she took a quick breath in.

"You know, Brandy—"

"Hey, Marco, buddy. How you doing?"

Relief—or disappointment—made her shoulders deflate when Marco turned away to talk to the biker man in the leather jacket and bandana who'd approached him.

With the attention off of her, she took a moment to look around the bar again.

Booths were set up against the walls, with some smaller tables scattered in the middle of the room. There were a couple of pool tables in the back along with dart boards on the wall.

It was pretty much your average bar—well from what she'd seen on television, at least.

Speaking of television... She noticed one was mounted up behind the bar, and turned to a station that made her freeze, her eyes widening as she stared at a flat screen.

Gordon's cherub face and dazzling white smile stared down at her. The volume wasn't up, but his lips were moving as he spoke to a reporter.

This was not *New You*, the reality show she was used to seeing him on. This appeared to be the midday local news. Her blood thundered in her ears.

What was he saying? *Please don't let him be talking about me. Please.*

The screen split, and suddenly in the other corner there was a candid shot of her eating pizza.

Sweet god! Could he have picked a worse picture? It was from a charity event for foster kids they'd gone to last month.

She was eating pizza and there was a line of cheese hanging off the end and down her chin and of course her hair was frizzier than usual.

The picture disappeared and the image switched back to Gordon. Brandy glanced around the bar, certain somebody was about to scream, "It's her!"

But the place was still pretty much empty, and Marco and the biker had kept talking with their backs to her.

She made her way to the bar and pulled herself up and onto one of the stools. Wrapping her feet around the legs, she leaned forward on her elbows and stared at the line of hard alcohol behind the bar.

Oh, god.

She closed her eyes, laid her head on the bar and willed her stomach to settle down.

Never. She was never going to drink again.

"What can I get you, luv?"

Brandy's forehead creased with a frown at the English accent. She lifted her head and stared at the man behind the counter.

Hmm. If she hadn't been so darn hot over Marco, she

might've picked this guy to lust after. He gave Marco a run for his money, but in a different way.

Marco was dark-featured, rugged, and tattooed. This guy had curly blonde hair cropped close to his head.

He wasn't as tall but definitely matched Marco in the broad shoulder aspect. His deep blue eyes were bright and friendly. His only visible flaw was the thick jagged scar that ran down his left cheek, but then, some women would argue that it made him sexier.

She blinked when he waved a hand in front of her face.

"Are you all right, luv?"

"What?"

"Can I get you something? A pint? Food? Tequila?"

Why did everyone keep pushing tequila on her? She let out a pained groan. "Nooo...no more tequila. Just, do you have any sparkling water?"

"Sparkling? Is there a reason why it has to sparkle?"

"What?" She shook her head. "If you don't have—"

"Oh, we have it. I was just having a bit of sport, luv." He winked and went into the back.

Brandy gave a small laugh and watched him walk away. Definitely a cutie. And much friendlier than Marco.

Speak of the devil. Marco sat down on a bar stool next her, his gaze surprisingly hard.

"Don't bother with Sebastian, he's sworn off women."

She wrinkled her forehead. Funny, she really hadn't gotten that vibe off him.

"You mean he's gay?"

"I didn't say that. I said he's sworn off women." He kept watching her. "He's going through a shitty divorce right now and plans to lay off dating for a while. So don't get any ideas."

She narrowed her eyes and swallowed the slow burn of anger that rose in her throat.

"Ideas? What makes you think I was getting *ideas* about him?"

Marco couldn't even figure out that she wanted *him*, yet he'd somehow come to the conclusion she wanted to get his coworker into bed? Men were idiots.

"Everybody's interested in Sebastian. The guy's a fucking chick magnet. It's the accent."

"It's more than the accent. He's hot," she replied before thinking about it.

Marco's scowl deepened.

Eek, wrong thing to say. Change the topic, Brandy.

"I bet you guys get a lot of business from the women. Two hot, single men working a bar?"

"Hmmph. I guess the word hasn't gotten out yet."

"How long has the bar been open anyway?"

"Only about six months, but we're doing okay."

Sebastian returned with her water and glanced at the two of them, his eyebrows rising. He twisted the lid off the bottle and poured it into a cup.

"You two know each other?"

"Yes. I'm Brandy by the way. I hijacked his bike," Brandy answered before he could. She picked up the water and took a sip. "He'll tell you all about it while I run to the bathroom."

She stood, winked at Sebastian, and then made her way to the back of the bar to find the restrooms.

Marco knew he looked about as irritable as he felt. Rubbing a hand across the back of his neck, he waited for the question sure to come.

"Are you fucking with me?" Sebastian asked from behind the counter. "That sweet little lass hijacked your motorcycle?"

"Shut it. She's not as sweet as she looks. The woman's got

balls." His mouth curled into a reluctant smile. "For a choir teacher."

"A choir teacher?" Sebastian's brows knitted together and he looked off towards the bathroom where she'd disappeared.

"What, you mean like that lady in *The Sound of Music*? I always sported a bit of wood over that one growing up."

"You're a sick man, Sebastian."

"Yes. So I've been told." His smile dimmed a bit. "And that's why my Ellen's divorcing me."

Anger drew Marco's mouth tight. "That's bullshit. You need to stop giving that crazy bitch any credence. It was her problem, not yours."

"It doesn't matter anymore." Sebastian gave a loose shrug and grabbed a rag to wipe down the counter.

The hell it didn't. Everyone always harped on Marco to meet a woman and put down some roots, but if anyone deserved a good woman and the picture-perfect life, it was Sebastian.

He just hoped it'd happen someday to the guy.

"So how did you say you picked up the choir teacher?"

"She was supposed to get married yesterday and got cold feet or something. I was on the Strip coming home from work, and she comes running out of this chapel." He shook his head, a laugh rumbling in his chest. "And she just jumped on the back of my bike, man, didn't even ask."

"Ah, that's classic. Sounds like some kind of cheesy romantic movie or something." Sebastian nodded and gave him a curious look. "But let me ask you. You didn't feel the need to tell her to get right back off your bike? Or drop her off somewhere? I mean you said *yesterday*, mate. That's quite a bit of time you've been spending together."

It sounded a little strange when his friend put it that way. Still, he didn't like where the line of questioning had gone.

"It's not like that. I just felt sorry for her."

"Ah, that's quite a bit of niceness for someone who just feels sorry for someone."

"I'm not nice."

"I think the teacher would disagree with you."

"Fuck off." His temper spiked.

"I'm back, did I miss anything?" Brandy approached from behind, climbed up on the bar stool, and grinned at them. "Am I being labeled the crazy psycho hijacking bride yet?"

"Not quite. More like the little lost kitten who needed saving. What are you going to do about your fiancé?" Sebastian asked. "Do you intend to go home soon?"

She hesitated, her smile fading. "No, I don't want to go home. I've been thinking...maybe I should take a couple of weeks away. Give myself time to think." She shook her head. "If I go home Gordon will be all over me and I'm not ready for that yet."

"Sounds like a decent plan. Fortunately, Marco was around yesterday to pluck you from a bad situation."

Her gaze shifted to Marco, and in her eyes shone something close to hero worship that he wasn't worthy of.

He held her gaze and the detachment he wanted to feel crumbled a bit, opening him up at an emotion he didn't want to feel. He didn't want Brandy to fall for him, it could only be trouble.

For both of them.

"Yes, I was very fortunate."

Her smile turned so secretive, he wondered if she'd been remembering their kiss from yesterday.

She lowered her lashes, hiding his ability to read any further emotions in her eyes.

Damn it.

The memory of her luscious mouth under his stirred the blood in his veins.

"So has he been feeding you? Are you hungry?"

Marco shot Sebastian an irritated glance. "Of course I've been feeding her."

"He made me bratwurst and eggs for breakfast." She giggled. "And coffee, I hate coffee though."

"Me too, luv. I much prefer my tea. Would you care for a cup?"

"Of tea?" Her voice rose with excitement. "You guys have tea in a bar?"

"We're not complete heathens. Of course we have tea." Sebastian reached out and touched her hand. "If not for the customers, then for myself."

Marco's blood pounded harder, and the pulse in his neck throbbed with such a force that his jaw clenched.

Was Sebastian flirting with her? Why?

"Sebastian, that is so sweet. I would kill for a cup of tea right now."

And I'm going to kill Sebastian *if he doesn't get his damn hand off you.*

"Are you sure I can't get you a bite to eat?"

"Christ, if she was hungry, she'd ask for something." Marco jumped up from the stool, his movement so abrupt it fell to the ground with a crash.

A heated flush spread up the back of his neck. Ignoring their startled looks, he righted the stool and ground his teeth together.

"You all right there, mate?"

"Just fine, *mate,*" Marco shot back. "I'll be in the back office. There're some things I need to take care of."

He walked behind the bar and slammed through the double doors that led into the kitchen.

Well hell. Talk about losing it big time.

Sebastian was going to really give him shit later. And Brandy must think he was completely off his rocker. What the hell had just happened to him?

He walked through the kitchen, not even bothering to say hi to Dave, the cook on duty. Just bee-lined straight for the small office in the back, then shut the door behind him.

Leaning his head against the door, he closed his eyes with a growl of frustration.

He'd just flipped. Watching Sebastian flirt with her, and then when he'd touched Brandy's hand... How?

How was it remotely possible he was jealous? Brandy didn't do a thing for him. Did she?

"Shit." He banged his head against the door. This was a complication he just didn't need.

Chapter Four

"Was it something I said?" Brandy bit her lip, wrapping her hands around the steaming mug of tea.

Sebastian shook his head and gave her a thoughtful glance. "No, I don't think it was so much that, luv."

She heaved a sigh, leaning down to breathe in the relaxing scent of chamomile. Frowning, she shook her head.

"I don't know, Sebastian. I feel like a complete inconvenience. I've basically attached myself to him for the past two days, and he's just too darn nice to tell me to get lost."

"If he didn't want you around he'd tell you. If you've backed Marco into a corner, then it's only because he wants to be there."

"Hmm." She took a sip of tea.

What did that mean exactly? *He wants to be there?*

"Marco told me you teach music."

Brandy set her cup down and swallowed the tea in her mouth. "Mmm. Yes, I do. I teach choral music at a private high school."

"High school? How do you put up with a bunch of teenagers all day?"

"I have a lot of patience." She smiled faintly and looked at the door Marco had just disappeared through.

Did Sebastian know who she was, beyond a bride on the run? Had Marco told him about Gordon and who he was? Did no one read social media gossip or watch the news?

How was it possible that no one had put all the pieces together yet?

Being the "Lingerie Heiress" made her reluctantly famous, though granted she wasn't in the heiress-gone-wild type of spotlight like others.

The paparazzi had far more interesting people to harass than a boring choir teacher who just happened to be heiress to a lingerie company. But she still got the occasional paparazzi stalking.

Maybe Marco and Sebastian were just normal guys who rarely read gossip sites.

Out of the corner of her eye, she spotted the lone biker in the bar making his way toward the front door.

"See you tomorrow."

"Have a good one, Bubba."

Light flooded in from the outside when he walked out the entrance, but then the door swung shut and the bar once again grew dim. A few seconds later she heard him revving up his motorcycle.

"So when do you guys get busy?" Brandy asked.

"Right around four. People get off work and usually crowd the place. But being a Saturday night, we're likely to get and stay busy earlier."

The phone rang and Sebastian stepped away to grab it, but it cut off in mid-ring.

"Marco must've answered in the back." He turned back to face her, his smile friendly.

"So, Sebastian, I'm going to make a wild guess you're from England. I'm right, aren't I?"

"Indeed you are. County Durham. You ever been there?"

"No." She smiled wistfully. "I've been to London, of course. But when my family and I travel we never take the time to visit outside of the big cities. I'm sure it's beautiful."

"Yes, it's rather lovely, if not rather dull at times. You Americans are crazy bastards, I tell you. That's why I had to come over."

Brandy burst into laughter, her attention sliding beyond Sebastian to Marco who now stood in the doorway. And surprise, surprise, he still didn't look pleased.

Sebastian followed her gaze and his grin faded.

"Hey. What's going on?"

Marco stepped out of the doorway and went to stand beside Sebastian behind the bar. He picked up a straw and twisted it around his fingers.

Marco had really nice hands. Brandy's gaze followed the movement, watching his long tan fingers working the straw.

Imagining what else those hands were capable of. She swallowed hard and ignored the heat that spread through her body.

"That was Val on the phone. She's got food poisoning and had to call in sick."

"Well fuck me."

"Who's Val?" Brandy asked since they both looked like the world was coming to an end.

Marco tapped the straw on the counter next to where her hands rested. "Val is our waitress. She single-handedly runs the floor during the night shift."

"Oh. You don't have another waitress who works here?"

"Ginger quit last week to become a showgirl. We haven't found someone to replace her yet."

"Oh my. That does leave you in a predicament. I wish there was some way I could help."

The men exchanged glances.

"Have you ever waited tables, luv?"

Her eyes widened. Oh no, she hadn't meant that.

"Me? Wait tables? No. I've never had a real job before."

"What?" Marco and Sebastian both spoke at the same time.

"Oops, sorry, that came out wrong. I mean I have a real job —I'm a teacher."

"Teaching was your first job?" Marco's surprise was evident.

"Yes." She'd done volunteer work, actually a ton throughout the years.

"Not even at a burger joint or coffee shop?"

"No." Jeez, if he knew who she really was, this line of questioning would have been a joke.

All annoyance she'd seen building up earlier in Marco was now being directed fully at her.

"I just...never really needed to work."

"Hmm, must have been nice." His tone was hard as he looked away and shook his head. "I knew it the minute you opened your mouth yesterday, princess. Pampered through and through."

Brandy's jaw dropped. Had he really just said that? Out of left field? Anger finally bubbled past the shock and she blinked.

"Is that why you call me princess? That's so..." she broke off, furious at herself to find tears of frustration and hurt stinging the backs of her eyes. "That's so harsh, Marco."

Sebastian cleared his throat. "Marco's a bit of a jerk—"

"That's what I've been trying to tell you this whole time. You don't want to like me, Brandy. I'm not a nice guy."

"You know what? You don't know the first thing about me. I'm not pampered."

She knew she sounded like a kid throwing a fit, but she was upset. Really upset over a stupid comment. It was just one man's opinion. It didn't mean anything.

"I know your type."

"Okay, enough. Let her be, Marco." Sebastian placed himself between her and Marco. "Brandy, luv, aren't you on summer vacation? Are you teaching right now?"

Grateful and somewhat confused by the change of subject she shook her head. "Yes, it's summer break. So, no, I'm not teaching."

"Champion. How'd you like to take a job here for a week or two, just to help us out—"

"No," Marco cut it emphatically.

Sebastian glared at him and lifted his hand in warning. "Would you be willing to learn how to wait tables?"

Wait tables? That sounded a bit harder than it looked, and it looked downright chaotic at times.

"I'm not sure I could—"

"Forget about it." Marco's voice had gone flat again. "She can't handle it."

"What?" How dare he just write her off so easily. What an *idiot*. "I can handle it. Train me."

Irritation flashed in Marco's eyes. "Why? You wonder what it's like to go slumming with the boys who run a bar?"

"Marco, for fuck's sake, shut the hell up." Sebastian glared at his friend. "Our arse is screwed if she doesn't agree to help us out tonight. Now take your bloody pride out of the equation and think about this logically."

Marco's jaw flexed, but fortunately, he took Sebastian's advice and shut up.

A tremor of emotion ran through Brandy. What the heck had brought on his anger? It seemed so left field.

"What—" her voice cracked. "Do I need to do? I really do want to help you out."

"That's wonderful. Thank you, Brandy. Well, first we need to make it legal. Marco will take you in the back and help you fill out the necessary paperwork." Sebastian glanced at Marco. "Can you handle that?"

Marco glared at his friend. "Of course, I can handle it." Standing up, he jerked his head. "Follow me, princess."

Having him call her princess wasn't as cute as she'd thought it was this morning. Not now that she realized why he said it. He knew she had money, and resented the heck out of it.

Her teeth snapped together, but she jumped off the stool anyway and followed him behind the counter and into the kitchen.

"Have a seat." He led her into a small office and gestured to a hardback chair on the other side of a desk.

She sat down, folding her hands in her lap. "Why are you treating me like this?"

He stopped searching through a file folder and glanced up. A flash of guilt flickered in his eyes before he quickly masked it. Ah, well at least he knew he'd been acting like a complete jerk.

"How am I treating you?" He went back to searching.

Okay, so he knew but apparently would deny it. Irritation flicked through her hurt.

"You know how you're treating me. Last night you were nice and patient, this morning you made me a wonderful break-fast. And now you're treating me like something you found on the bottom of your shoe. Why are you mad at me?"

He slapped a few papers down on the desk in front of her. "I'm not mad at you. Fill these out, please."

"Liar."

Frustrated with the conversation more than she wanted to be, she picked up the pen and forced herself to fill out the paperwork. Well aware of Marco watching her, she tried to keep the pen in her hand from shaking.

She scribbled in her social security number and hesitated. Was she nuts? Taking a job in a bar? Her parents would really flip over this one.

They'd been trying to get her to work for Sugar and Spice since the day she'd turned eighteen, ultimately gearing her up to take over the company.

But working for the lingerie giant—let alone running the corporation—had never appealed to her. Up until this point, she'd only been interested in doing a job that gave back to the community.

"And now I'm going to work in a bar," she muttered under her breath.

"Second thoughts?"

She glanced up at Marco and found him still watching her.

He'd love that, wouldn't he? If she changed her mind and ran out on him.

"Not at all. Actually, I'm excited. This will be something new, a little bit fun. Wild even."

"You think being a waitress is wild?"

"Being a waitress, in a bar, on a Saturday night? I'm sure it is." She lifted her eyebrows and then looked down at the paper.

She signed the final line and then slid the papers back to him, looking up at him again.

He held her stare, accepting the papers, then picked them up and tapped them on the table so they lined up in a neat stack. The look in his eyes softened a bit.

"Look, Brandy. I'm—"

"How's our newest waitress doing?" Sebastian strode into the backroom, rubbing his hands together. "We have a customer and he wants lunch. Are you ready to start training, luv?"

What had Marco been about to say to her? Had it been an apology? He spun the wheeled chair away to face the wall.

She bit her lip and sighed. Well, apparently her curiosity wasn't to be appeased—not now anyway.

"Sure, Sebastian. I'm ready." She stood up, glancing at Marco one last time before giving a brief nod. "Let's do it."

The bar was crowded as all hell. Marco kept half his attention on Brandy while working behind the counter taking money and making drinks.

She held her own, though just barely. Running around like her ass was on fire, eyes bright with excitement.

Fortunately for her, half the crowd came to the bar and ordered drinks directly from the bartenders; she only had to worry about the customers who were seated at the tables or people who came up to her.

Even with those it was strictly drink orders since the kitchen had closed two hours ago.

"Hey, I'll take a light beer." A regular sidled up to the counter and grinned. "So what's with the waitress in the cat shirt? You pick her up at a library convention or something?"

Marco bit back a smile and slid the beer toward the man. "Something like that."

"Yeah, she's kind of cute. Got that whole innocent look about her." He leaned across the bar. "But you know those are the same girls who've got a kinky streak a mile wide. Probably has one of those dominatrix outfits at home or some shit."

"You think so, huh?" His lips twitched and he glanced past the customer to see Brandy making her way back to him.

"How's it going?" Marco asked her.

She gave a weak smile and shook her head. "I'm so tired. But I'm having a great time."

"How are you doing on tips?"

She shrugged. "I've gotten a few dollars here and there. But it doesn't matter. I'm not here for the money."

Valerie usually scored big on tips, but then again she was a seasoned flirt and dressed hot. Brandy struck out on both of those counts.

He'd actually been kind of worried about the backlash from some of the regulars. Thought they might get annoyed with an inexperienced waitress dressed like she was attending a church picnic. But besides a couple of comments, no one seemed to care much.

"You've got two more hours, princess. Think you can make it?"

"Sure." She didn't protest or seem the slightest bit annoyed by the princess reference this time. A yawn popped her jaw and she raised a hand to cover her mouth, giving him a guilty smile. "So I'm a little sleepy, I can make it."

"You want an energy drink?"

She wrinkled her nose, but before she could turn him down he pushed on.

"It'll wake you up."

She narrowed her eyes and gave him suspicious look. "Do you even have an energy drink?"

He gave a deep laugh and shook his head. She didn't have a clue what was in half of the drinks she was serving.

"Of course we do. Though usually, we're mixing them with Vodka." He grabbed one of the drinks and cracked the can open. "Pound it. It'll wake you up a bit."

She glanced over her shoulder at the tables.

"They're good for now. You can take a minute to drink this."

"Okay." She snatched the can out of his hand and slammed it back, swallowing a bunch of times before she dropped it back on the counter.

Damn, she'd taken pound it seriously. His eyes widened with admiration.

"Yikes." She blinked and shook her head. "I think I'm going to get a sugar high."

"And then some. Good, that's what you need to get through the night. Now get your butt back out there now."

Giggling, she spun away and went back to check on the tables.

"That was nice of you."

Marco glanced down the counter at Sebastian who was filling up a pint of beer.

"What are you talking about?"

"What with the way you were treating her earlier, I would have thought you'd be thrilled if she keeled over from exhaustion."

Marco scowled. "I might be an asshole, but I'm not that big of one."

"Really? Where's she staying tonight?"

The same question had crossed his mind a few times throughout the evening. Where would she be staying? They hadn't talked about it since breakfast.

This morning—before she'd become the newest employee at *Dante's Place*—he'd just assumed he'd drop her off at a hotel in town.

Now the entire game plan had changed. It was going on one in the morning, and now her idea of getting a room in a small off-Strip motel didn't seem like such a good idea.

But he didn't want to admit his thoughts to Sebastian. The guy already thought he'd slipped off the deep end.

"I don't know where she's staying, and it's not my business." The words left a bitter taste in his mouth.

You're an asshole.

Marco spotted the flicker of surprise and annoyance in Sebastian's eyes, but he didn't say anything and just shook his head.

An hour later they booted out the last customer and locked up. Brandy sat down on a bench in one of the booths and laid her head on the table, making little moaning noises every few seconds.

Marco glanced over at her, his sympathy level kicking up a notch. That energy drink had barely gotten her through.

"I'll go cash out. Be back in a few." He grabbed the till, glancing again at Brandy before heading into the back.

Hell, he couldn't send her to a motel. His conscience wouldn't let him—actually, there were probably other reasons, but he hesitated to acknowledge them.

He counted down the till in record time and locked the deposit in the safe to be dropped off in the morning.

When he headed back up front, he found Sebastian sweeping the floor as he chatted with Brandy. After turning the lights off in the kitchen, he walked out to where they were.

"Hey, we all about ready to head out?"

"I think we're set." Sebastian went to return the broom. "So what do you say, Brandy?"

The hairs on the back of Marco's neck rose. "Say to what?"

Brandy looked away from Sebastian and gave a hesitant smile. "Sebastian offered me his couch tonight. That way I wouldn't have to check into a motel this late at night."

Marco's vision blurred as the blood pounded faster through his veins. "What?"

Sebastian's innocent smile didn't fool him for a second.

"That's right, mate. I have that big living room with a comfy couch. Tomorrow we can—"

"No." Marco folded his arms across his chest.

Sebastian and Brandy both turned to look at him.

"Marco, there's no need for her to waste money on a motel room this late at night."

"She's staying with me." The words were out and he wasn't sure he'd take them back even if he could.

Sebastian's expression turned to pure satisfaction. Damn it. Marco knew he'd walked right into that little setup.

The muscles in the back of his neck bunched with tension as he glanced back at Brandy. She seemed hesitant, and maybe a little relieved by his statement.

"Really, mate, are you sure?" Sebastian persisted. "I don't mind her staying with me."

"Her stuff is already at my house."

"Oh." She patted her smiley face tote bag. "But I only have my purse—"

"You're staying with me."

Her eyes widened. "Okay...if you think that's best."

Sebastian lifted his palms in the air, his smile broadening. "Well, now that that's settled, shall we call it a night?"

"Sure. Thank you, Sebastian, for the offer. And thank you Marco for letting me crash again." Brandy took a few steps towards the door and hesitated. "Hey, what time do I work tomorrow? I'd like to try and swing by the outlet mall and buy some clothes."

"You don't have any clothes?" Sebastian raised an eyebrow, then teased, "Now, luv, waitressing naked might also be an option."

"You'd better quit with that shit, Sebastian." Marco walked towards the door and opened it, gesturing for the other two to follow him out. "It's amazing your ass hasn't been slapped with a sexual harassment suit yet."

Sebastian stepped outside and glanced back at Brandy. "Women know I'm just a big harmless flirt. Don't you, luv?"

"You are the king of flirts." She giggled and followed him out the door.

Sebastian's outrageous flirting with the women had never bothered Marco before. Why the hell did it tonight? Marco set the alarm and then locked the door behind them.

"You can start in the evening again. The lunches are slow enough that we can run on a fewer amount of employees."

"Wonderful. I'm sure I'll do better tomorrow, guys. Now that I know what to expect."

"You did splendid, luv. You should be proud of yourself. Besides, tomorrow is Sunday. We'll not be nearly as busy."

Sebastian patted her back and Marco clenched his fists to avoid slapping his hand away.

Every move Sebastian made was deliberate at this point. Set to egg him on. Marco wasn't an idiot. It was a little game they'd always played, find each other's weakness and then needle it until one of them broke.

Brandy yawned and took the helmet that Marco held out to her, but didn't put it on. "Well, I'm proud that I didn't drop anything or spill any drinks. And everyone was rather nice to me."

"That's because you're a sweetheart." Sebastian winked and headed across the parking lot to the only car left in it. "Good night, kids. I'll see you tomorrow."

Marco watched Sebastian climb into his car and drive out of the parking lot, honking his horn as he passed. Then he turned his gaze back to Brandy.

She climbed on the back of his bike, looking like she'd been riding for years. She looked good on it, like she belonged there. Cat shirt and all.

He stepped closer to her but didn't climb on in front of her just yet. There was something about her. Even with the just-ran-over–by-a-truck mask of exhaustion on her face. Reaching a hand up, he tucked back a curl that had fallen free from her ponytail.

Her eyes widened and he watched her throat move as she swallowed hard.

"You did great tonight, Brandy."

He could smell his soap on her. His soap mixed with her apple perfume gave it a spicy, sweet, feminine smell. It stirred his blood to think about her using his soap this morning. Running it over every luscious curve on her body.

"Do you think so?" Her gaze locked on his.

"Do I think so what?"

She gave a soft laugh. "Um... think I did great tonight. Like you just said."

"Ah right. Sorry. Yes, I do think so." He paused. "I'm sorry for the way I acted earlier. I was being an ass. I misjudged you." He wasn't about to admit that he'd been jealous.

"Yes, you were being a butt. Apology accepted."

"Good." He leaned a little closer and breathed in her scent again. "You know, I can smell my soap on you."

The words came out in a low rush

Was that guilt flickering in her eyes? And under the street-lights, he could swear her cheeks turned pink.

"Oh. You can?"

"Yeah, I can. And I like it."

She inhaled swiftly. "You do?"

Maybe it was because it was so late and he'd worked an abnormally long shift. Or maybe it was the full moon, but, damn it all. He wanted to kiss her again.

"I do."

He cupped the back of her neck and pulled her forward.

"Are you...are you going to kiss me?"

He nodded. She just had to put it into words, didn't she?

"Is that okay?"

"Oh, yes." She gasped. "It is, it really is. I mean that first kiss we had was unbeliev—"

He closed his mouth over hers, stopping her breathy prattle. Her words died on a soft sigh and her arms slipped around his neck.

Chapter Five

The softness of her lips parted to give him entry into her mouth. Needing to taste her, he slipped his tongue inside to find hers.

She made the sweetest little moan and her hands moved over his chest. Her tongue rubbed against his, almost hesitant at first, and then became more confident.

He angled his head to give him deeper access to her mouth, delving deeper. The taste of her and her scent had his blood roaring, his jeans fitting tighter.

Pulling away, she gasped for air. Her pale throat gleamed in the moonlight and he lowered his mouth to kiss the pulse that beat like crazy in her neck.

"Marco..."

She lifted her hands to his shoulders and dug her nails into him.

More. He needed more. He slipped his hands to her waist, moving them under the hem of her shirt until they encountered the warm softness of her skin.

The sound of her heavy breathing aroused him further.

And when she squirmed on the bike, giving him better access to her body, he took advantage of it.

He slid his palms up the slight swell of her stomach, towards the curves of her breasts.

Closer. His fingers skimmed her ribs and then came to rest on the underside of her breasts. A lace bra? On Brandy?

The idea didn't seem to mesh with the outfit she was wearing. He'd imagined white cotton.

"Lace?" he muttered.

"Mmm." She groaned as if she hadn't even heard his question.

His line of reasoning disappeared, and only the fullness of her curves at his fingertips mattered. The lace wasn't so sexy anymore, the fabric wasn't as nice as her silky skin.

Lifting his palms to cup each of her full breasts, he groaned when her nipples tightened in his hands.

"Marco."

He caught her gasp in another kiss, closing his mouth over hers while he kneaded each big breast.

Her body trembled and he pressed closer, making their bodies mold into one, so anyone passing by on the street wouldn't see fully what was happening—that he was losing all control with Brandy in the parking lot of his bar.

That he was about to bend her over his bike and take her, even if anyone driving by would see.

His thoughts slowed him down.

What the hell was he doing? Making out with Brandy like a teenager, a rock-hard dick pressing at his jeans.

Idiot.

It hadn't been a good idea yesterday, and it still wasn't any better today.

He lifted his head, his breath ragged. "We should stop."

Her breath feathered warm on his face. "Should we? Why?"

"We're in a parking lot."

"Okay."

"And it's late."

"Yes, yes it is." She glanced up at him, her gaze foggy with arousal. "But I was really into that, Marco. I want to make love to you tonight."

Everything inside him stopped. His hands that cupped her breasts slipped away.

Make love.

Phrased like that it put sex in a whole new context. And it went beyond making out like horny teenagers. Making love sounded so much more serious, so committed.

He hadn't had a woman in months. And now here was a woman who'd just run from her wedding, offering herself to him. Sober this time.

Every part of him—and one in particular—wanted to accept her offer.

"Brandy..."

"Oh, that's a no. The tone gives it all away." She pulled back a bit and pulled her shirt back down. "Is this that 'You'll regret it' stuff? Because if it is, I can promise you I won't."

"You might."

"Come on, can't I decide that? You're acting like I'm some halfwit." She went quiet and he wasn't sure what to say either.

"I'm sorry."

She shrugged. "Don't be. Like I said, I really enjoyed what we were doing. And I..." Her words trailed off into a long yawn.

"And you're tired," he finished for her, unable to resist trailing a finger over her swollen bottom lip.

"Yes, I am." She yawned again and then sighed. "Oh, who am I kidding? It's after two in the morning and I'm exhausted. I won't try and talk you into going to bed with me tonight."

"You won't?"

"Nope. When we sleep together, I want to have buckets of energy. Because something tells me I'll need it. You are an outstanding kisser, Marco. And your hands will give me sweet dreams tonight. But right now, I'm too tired to do anything besides go to sleep."

Marco blinked. Go to sleep? What the hell kind of transition was that? She'd gone from wanting to go to bed with him, to wanting to go to bed.

Stop it, this is what you wanted.

"Ugh...okay." He shook his head and climbed on the bike, telling himself it was better this way.

The sound of someone knocking on the door woke her. Brandy blinked her eyes open, spotted the half-naked woman poster on the ceiling, and remembered everything.

"Yes?" she croaked and pulled the sheet up to her chin.

"You awake?"

"Define awake."

Marco's soft laughter on the other side of the door slid over her senses, sending warm tingles through her. She touched her lips, remembering the kiss from last night.

Lord, the man knew how to knock a girl's socks off with just a kiss. And he'd done it twice now.

"Are you hungry?"

For?

She bit her lip to stop the naughty taunt from spilling. Jeez, what was wrong with her?

Calm the hormones, Brandy.

"Yeah. I'm a little hungry."

"Great. I need to go into the city this morning. I thought we could grab breakfast if you want."

He was inviting her to spend more time with him? Surely he should be nearly sick of her by now. The idea he wanted her to come with him again spread warmth throughout her body.

Her stomach rumbled and she scrubbed a fist over her eye. "I'd love to. When are you leaving?"

"Can you be ready in a half hour?"

"Sure." Brandy winced and climbed out of bed.

So much for getting herself off in the shower again. Between that mini-make-out session last night, and the sensual dream she'd just woken up from, a little relief would've been welcome.

But now she'd be lucky to have time for a shampoo. Though, she somehow doubted she'd be willing to settle for taking matters into her own hands anyway.

No. Next time, she wanted it in his hands.

"I washed your clothes last night," he called out from the other side of the door. "I know you wanted to shop before your shift, but I figured you'd want clean clothes for this morning."

She froze, halfway to the door, her eyebrows rising. The man did her laundry? Amazing.

It might not have fazed her if she'd led the same life her parents did. But she'd been in her own condo since she'd graduated college, and she refused to hire a housekeeper.

So she knew full well how laundry could suck the life out of someone's day.

Grabbing the door handle, she suddenly stopped. She tugged the T-shirt he'd lent her further down her thighs self-consciously, then twisted the handle to open the door.

Marco stood on the other side, leaning against the door jam and watching her with a lazy smile.

"Your hair's cute in the morning," he said.

She blinked. Was he serious? She knew darn well what her hair looked like, and cute was not the adequate adjective.

To test her reasoning, she patted the top of her head. Sure enough, the curls were a good couple of inches in the air.

"Thanks for washing my clothes." She took the small stack from him, and her cheeks warmed a bit when she saw her bra and panties folded neatly on top.

"No problem." His smile widened. "That's a pretty hot underwear set you've got going on there."

Her face went from slightly warm, to burning up. "Seriously? You just had to comment on those?"

"Yes. 'Cause I'm dirty." He gave her a roguish look. "And so are you, so go get your butt in the shower."

"Nice." She rolled her eyes and walked past him towards the bathroom. "You go from a backhanded compliment on a girl's underwear, to telling her she stinks? How do you even get a date?"

Marco laughed, a low sexy sound that sent hot little shivers through her.

"Getting a date, or anything else from a woman has never been a problem, princess."

Brandy wrinkled her nose at him and then shut the bathroom door, blocking out his amused smile.

She closed her eyes and pressed her forehead against the door.

Of course, Marco never had issues with women. The man was a walking sex symbol. Confident, sexy, and had that dangerous edge most women flocked to. He was the type of man you had a wild, uninhibited fling with but never married.

So what did that mean for her? Did it mean she really wanted to get involved sexually with him? That was if she could even convince him to go to bed with her.

There were times when she was thoroughly convinced he

wanted her. Would take her in the middle of a freeway during rush hour traffic type wanted her.

But then there were other times...an arctic breeze could be warmer than his attitude towards her. He was such an absolute puzzle.

I'll bet he wouldn't be so quick to say no to me if he knew who I was.

She sighed. Which was why she still avoided telling him.

If he was going to be interested in her, she didn't want it to be because she was the Lingerie Heiress. She wanted it to be because she was some girl named Brandy, who taught music, who he just happened to fall for.

"Enough already. You don't have time to overanalyze all this," she muttered to herself. "Just get your butt in the shower."

It'd all work out. Whatever fate intended.

Brandy pulled off her shirt and climbed into the stall. She tilted her head and pursed her lips.

Then again, maybe people created their own fate.

"A buffet?"

"I'm starving." Marco grinned and gestured for her to go into the restaurant first. "I tend to avoid the Strip at all costs. But if I'm coming down here anyway and plan to eat, I occasionally swing by one."

He gave the cashier his credit card and ignored Brandy's protests. Maybe she did have money, but that didn't mean he'd let her pick up the tab when they went out.

"I'm buying next time," she said, folding her arms across her chest.

"Deal."

The hostess led them to a table and gave them instructions on how the buffet worked. Brandy seemed to be hanging on her every word, and her gaze would continually dart over to the numerous food counters.

Had she never been to a buffet? His brows drew together as he watched her. He got the feeling this would be another first for her.

When the hostess walked away, Brandy turned to him her eyes round and her mouth parted slightly. Clearly, she was a bit overwhelmed.

"There's so much food," she finally said.

He laughed. "I'm going to take a wild guess here. You've never been to a buffet?"

Her expression relaxed into a smile and she gave a slight shrug. "No. I've never been to a buffet."

"Come on, it's easy." He grabbed her hand and led her over to where the plates were stacked high. He picked one up and handed it to her. "First you take one of these."

She rolled her eyes. "Thank goodness you're here. I never would have figured that part out on my own."

"Sarcasm becomes you." He picked up his own plate. "And next..."

"Next?"

"You fill your plate with everything and anything you want to eat." He waggled his eyebrows. "And then you do it again. And again and again. Until you need a forklift to get out the door. Or you barf."

"Holy crap. No wonder my mom said these places were the devil." She walked past him, eyeing the food with open excitement.

Christ. What kind of person had never been to a buffet?

He didn't know whether to pity her or roll over in shock. Maybe both. And interesting that she'd dropped a diluted curse from her lips.

Leaving her to explore on her own, he went to load up his own plate.

Meat. Meat. Eggs. More meat.

He started to head back to the table and hesitated at his one weakness. Grabbing a gooey chocolate doughnut, he squeezed it onto his plate.

Their table was still empty, and he glanced back at the various food stations to see Brandy still eyeing all her choices with the same intensity and consideration as a girl picking out a wedding ring.

Wedding ring.

His thoughts sent a sharp reminder through him of exactly who she was. A rich runaway bride. Meaning he still needed to tread carefully.

Funny how quickly she'd grown on him. Quirky habits and bad clothing be damned.

He settled at the table and ordered a coffee from the waitress when she came by, then asked for tea for Brandy.

"Okay. I did it."

He glanced up, a bite of ham dangling from his fork. Brandy stood before him, grinning as if she'd just won an Oscar.

"Good job. What did you get?"

She slid into her chair and set her plate down. One waffle covered in strawberries lay on her plate.

He lifted his gaze to hers. "That's it?"

"That's all I wanted." She grabbed her knife and fork and sliced a piece, lifting it to her mouth.

She closed her eyes and made a small moan of approval. The same kind of moan he'd bet she'd make if someone was going d—

"This is so good." Her tongue swept across her lip before she took another bite.

His grip on the fork tightened and he forced his attention back to his own plate.

"So did you always want to open a bar?" she asked.

The sudden question threw him. It brought him back to his life and what it had been just a couple of years ago.

His throat tightened and suddenly the food he was eating didn't seem quite as awesome.

"No. The concept for a bar was more of a recent idea..." Became the way out.

"What were you before? A tattoo artist or something?" She grinned and nodded her chin at his arm. "I love your dragon by the way."

"Thanks."

A tattoo artist? If she only knew.

Maybe that's why she didn't seem in any hurry to go off on her own. Maybe the sweet, conservative choir teacher considered herself to be exploring her wild side by slumming with the guys who owned a bar.

Lord if she only knew that just two years ago most of his days had been spent in a suit and tie.

"Your tea."

They both glanced up as the waitress set down a steaming cup of tea in front of Brandy.

"Oh. Thank you." Brandy glanced over at him, the surprise and pleasure on her face evident. "You sure are figuring me out."

Relieved that the subject had shifted from his past, his lips twisted and he offered an amused shrug.

"You made it pretty clear yesterday morning you weren't a coffee girl."

"No. You're right. I'm certainly not." She went back to her waffle and glanced over at his plate. "Okay. You've thrown me. You've got every edible animal on your plate. No hashbrowns, toast, or pancakes. I mean, I'd guess you were doing low carb or something—"

"Or just a guy."

"Okay or a guy. But, what's with the doughnut then?"

At the mention of the sweet treat, he picked it up and licked a bit of chocolate from the side.

"I mean donuts are so..." her words trailed off and her gaze slid to his mouth as he licked the donut again. "Sweet."

Interesting. Was she still a bit hot and bothered this morning? He allowed a slight smile. It'd be nice if she was, so they would be on the same level.

"Comfort food," he finally answered. "When I was a kid my dad used to bring us doughnuts for breakfast every Saturday morning."

"Ah, that's sweet. I was given protein shakes by my nanny."

He started to laugh and then realized she was serious. How awful.

There was a flicker of sadness in her eyes before she glanced down at her plate. A wave of sympathy swept through him.

What had her childhood been like? What had Brandy been like pint-sized?

"Do you have any brothers or sisters?" he asked.

She shook her head. "No. Just me. Which is why I'm the..." She bit her lip, obviously deciding not to finish what she'd been about to say. "It's just me. How about you?"

"I have a younger sister."

"Oh, that's right." Her expression turned wistful as she ate the last bit of her waffle. "That must've been great."

"It was."

It had been great in some ways. His family had been close, but then they'd lived in a two-bedroom apartment in the bad part of town. Money had been tight, but the love had flowed freely.

He drew in a slow, unsteady breath and closed his eyes for a moment. God, he missed them.

The need to see his dad and sister again came on so strong that it replaced every other urge. But he tapped it down. Just like he always did.

It just wouldn't happen. Things had changed when he had. When Marco told them what his future plans were, the disappointment in his dad's eyes said it all.

"You know, I almost want another waffle."

He lifted his head, tearing his thoughts out of his painful past. "So go grab one. Get your money's worth."

She rubbed her stomach and grimaced. "I'd better not. I'm pretty much full. Besides, later today I want to try one of those burgers at your place."

"Yeah, you sure as hell do," he agreed, finishing off the rest of the doughnut and then grabbing his last piece of bacon.

Good thing he didn't always eat like this.

"So what do you have to do in Vegas today?" she asked, sipping her tea.

"I promised I'd drop off a final check for the waitress who just quit. She doesn't do bank accounts."

"That's awfully nice of you. You're such a good boss."

"Careful, you've only worked for me for one day. And I wasn't nice to you for most of it. Let's see if you're still saying that in a week," he teased, even though he knew the chances of her being there in a week were slim.

"Are you ready to head out?" she asked a few minutes later. "Or were you going to get more to eat?"

"I'm done." He tossed his napkin on the table and stood up.

"Thanks for breakfast. That was probably the best waffle

I've had in my life," she said as they walked out of the casino and moved down the Strip.

"You're welcome. I'm glad you enjoyed it."

"I did. I—oh my god!" She gasped and turned around, grabbing his shirt. "Hurry and kiss me."

"What?" His eyebrows rose.

"Oh for god's sake." She tugged on his shirt, pulling him forward as her mouth slammed against his. "Gordon." The word came out muffled between their tightly pressed lips.

Surprise rendered him immobile. It took a second for him to realize she hadn't been calling him Gordon, but warning him that the man was nearby.

But even that took a lot of thought. It was hard to focus beyond the caress of her soft lips against his.

"Grab my hair. Bunch it up in your fist so it isn't recognizable," she whispered against his mouth.

He complied, eagerly delving his fingers into her soft curls and tugging her head back. The move gave him deeper access to her mouth, and the soft little moan she made had him silently applauding her acting skills.

Her tongue seemed hesitant as it slipped into his mouth, but her arms were confident as they slid around his back to clutch him to her.

He took over, deepening the kiss. The sweetness of her mouth was beyond tempting. The taste of strawberries and syrup was intoxicating against his tongue.

The kiss may have started as a way to disguise Brandy, but it turned into something completely different. It was the hottest kiss he'd experienced in god knew how long.

He wanted to slide his hand up her shirt again. Touch that lace bra. But damn they were in public.

Again.

Tonight. After work, he'd have her. No more excuses or

denying it. They wanted each other, so why the hell fight it anymore?

"Brandy," he lifted his mouth slightly but didn't pull away from her.

"Mmm." She didn't open her eyes, instead brushed her lips against his more.

"I think he's gone."

"What?" Her eyelids fluttered open and she looked around. Her cheeks turned pink. "Oh yes. Yes, he is."

He knew he should release her and step back, but somehow it seemed so right having her in his arms, holding her like this. Even if they were standing on the sidewalk in the middle of Las Vegas. Hell, worse sins had probably occurred.

"You need to talk to him, Brandy."

He wanted to kick himself the minute the words were out. The last thing he wanted was for her to chat it up with the reality star ex-fiancé.

"You don't know Gordon." She shook her head. "He's too persuasive. He's got the charisma of a snake charmer. He'd have me saying *I do* before I know what I really want."

"How long were you engaged?"

She laughed and pressed a hand against her forehead. "Like three hours."

Interesting. "Spontaneous Vegas wedding, huh?"

"To say the least."

He let go of her hair and her arms unwound from his waist. He immediately missed the warmth of her soft body against him.

Christ, she was so sexy. A ball of fire and passion, an untapped, undiscovered treasure of a woman buried beneath some profoundly bad clothing.

And I found her.

Never had he considered himself romantic, but tonight, he

wanted it to be special. He'd bring home a bottle of wine, maybe put on some sexy music—

"Sorry about that," she said and then sighed. "I didn't mean to drag you into all this."

"You're fine." He smoothed a stray curl off her forehead. "Don't worry about it. Anyway, we should head out. We've got a lot to do today."

She nodded, disappointment flickering in her eyes. Did she think he wasn't interested? Wouldn't she be surprised tonight.

Watch it, buddy, you're acting like a teenage boy with a crush on his teacher.

Which, in a way could be kind of an adequate description. She was older, barely, and she did teach.

He stepped back and drew in a deep breath. "Let's head out."

Gordon sped walked down the sidewalk, his manicured nails biting into his palms. Sweat beaded his forehead and he shook his head.

God damn it, nothing had helped. Going on the local news had produced no results. It was like Brandy had upped and disappeared off the fucking planet.

A second ago, he'd almost been convinced she'd been across the street. Making out with some tattooed guy, but then he'd realized he'd just been seeing what he wanted to see.

She's gone. And you have to find out where.

Obviously, she was a bit traumatized after seeing him with the hooker, but hell, he hadn't thought she'd go into hiding this long.

Her cell phone had been turned off and she hadn't gone to her parent's house. He'd driven back to L.A. and passed by their house multiple times.

No sign of her there or at her own place. And he'd gone to her place—used the key she'd given him and searched for any trace that she'd been there.

Had even hit redial on her landline phone to see the last person she'd called. It had only been the local library. Boring little bitch.

The last thing he wanted to do was get her parents involved, but hell, if he couldn't find her soon he just might have to.

Unfortunately, Brandy's parents had never been one hundred percent thrilled by his presence in their daughter's life.

Smart parents. Too damn smart. But then that was why they were billionaires and he wasn't.

Like it or not, though, he was going to have to employ them for help in finding her. He'd still keep the details of what had preceded her running off quiet.

There'd be no mention of the attempted wedding or the shitty events that had unfolded in the hours after.

They'd go straight to the media, and maybe if she saw her parents on television she'd come up for air.

And when she did...fuck. He'd think of something. But he'd get her down the damn altar if he had to carry the fat bitch.

Chapter Six

"Are you hungry?"

Brandy looked up from the bar stool and frowned. "Didn't we just eat?"

Marco wiped down the counter with a rag and glanced up at the clock.

"Three hours ago. And you just had that waffle."

"Give me a few more minutes to get my stomach up to speed again."

"Whatever you want." He moved to the other end of the bar, organizing and cleaning.

Hmm, she still had five hours before her shift. What was she going to do? Shopping had been on her agenda originally.

If she had to wear this recycled outfit one more day, she was going to chuck it into the nearest dumpster. And this was her favorite shirt, so it would have killed her to do it.

But then part of her was more than content to just sit and stare at Marco for those five hours. Just being in his presence made her palms a little damp and her knees a little weak.

No, she'd be perfectly content to watch the man who had

her heart and hormones going into overdrive. Of course, she hadn't confessed that last part to him. Though he'd have to be blind not to have realized it.

What had happened last night had been a first for her. The desire she'd felt when he'd touched her, kissed her. It was totally new.

Even being beyond exhausted by the end of the night, she'd lain in the marijuana-scented bedroom of Marco's roommate and thought about Marco and those amazing moments on the bike.

She glanced up, snapping out of her reverie, and watched Marco walk around the bar checking in with the few customers that were there.

It was barely noon and there weren't many of them. Just a few that came in for the lunch more than the alcohol.

Brandy swung her feet against the stool at the bar she sat on, watching as he walked back towards her.

His expression turned surprisingly gentle. "You didn't have to come in this early with me, you know."

"I know. You told me last night and again this morning. And as I told you before, I don't mind hanging out. So long as you don't mind me here," she rushed to add.

He gave a soft laugh. "I don't mind in the least. I've kind of gotten used to having you around."

"You're not just saying that?"

"Not at all."

Her stomach warmed ridiculously with pleasure. "Okay. I'll take that burger now."

He smiled and shook his head. "I'll have Dave whip you up one. You want cheese on it?"

"Yes, please, and lots of mayonnaise."

"All right, princess. Be back in second."

He disappeared into the kitchen and she braced her elbows

on the bar, humming along to an old Steve Miller song that filtered out from the speakers in the bar.

The front door to the bar swung open, letting a band of light in. Brandy glanced towards the entrance and saw the body of a woman silhouetted in the frame.

The woman glanced around and then stepped inside, letting the door slam shut behind her. She strode across the floor with a purpose, and Brandy stared at the woman with open amazement.

She had Betty Page styled hair, only it was dyed purple. Her nose was pierced and she wore the shortest excuse for a dress Brandy had ever seen. The lace neckline somehow managed to make it look demure and crass at the same time.

She was like a slutty Stepford Wife.

"Hello," Brandy called out.

The woman stopped for the briefest second to say hi and give her a curious look. Then she continued walking and disappeared behind the bar and into the back.

Hmm. Who was that? Could it be that Valerie girl they'd been talking about?

Somehow when they'd said the name Val, she'd gotten more of a cute little co-ed image. But this worked too. In fact, it was a whole lot more interesting.

The back door swung open again a minute later and the girl came back out, sitting down on the bar stool next to her.

She looked Brandy straight in the eyes. "I'm Val. I hear you're working here now?"

She couldn't have been more than twenty-three, and the girl had more confidence than Brandy had ever possessed.

"Hello. I'm Brandy, and yes, I just started yesterday." She smiled. "I hope you're feeling better today."

"Feeling better?" The girl raised a pierced eyebrow that Brandy had just now noticed.

"Yes, they said you had food poisoning yesterday?"

"Oh yeah." Her eyes danced with amusement as she leaned close. "I didn't really have food poisoning. I was just having the best fuck of my life with my boyfriend, if you know what I mean. But don't tell the boys. They love me, but I know that'd piss them off to no end. Especially if they realized I was getting some and they weren't."

Brandy's eyes went wide, and she pressed a hand to her chest. Okay, so her parents owned a lingerie chain, but the people who ran in her circles just didn't talk like that.

"Ah, shit. I shocked you. Sorry, kid."

Kid? She was calling *Brandy* the kid?

"Nice shirt, by the way, it's almost retro."

Brandy glanced down at her shirt. "Thank you. I need to go shopping. I have no clothes."

"No clothes? Damn, now that is a problem. When are you going?" Val blinked and popped a mint into her mouth. "I don't work until five, can I come?"

Shopping with Val? Her glance fell to the dress she was wearing again. Was that such a good idea?

"I can help you pick out some cute outfits." Val narrowed her eyes. "How'd you do on tips last night?"

"Oh..." She mentally counted the amount on two hands. "About eight bucks."

"Eight bucks? Total?" Val's eyes widened and she shook her head. "You poor kid. I'll help you pick out some outfits that'll get you an eight-dollar tip with just one drink on the tab."

The kitchen door swung open again and Marco came out holding her lunch.

"What's going on?"

"Val wants to go shopping with me."

Marco glanced at the other woman with obvious concern.

"You should be taking it easy, Val. You were just sick yesterday."

"Ugh. I know, it was pretty horrible." She pressed a hand to her stomach and made a face. "But I feel a ton better today. I think it's all out of my system now."

Brandy blinked in astonishment. The girl was a great actress. If Val hadn't confided in her that she'd been getting fu—er—making love, she'd have believed the girl had actually been sick to her stomach too.

"Well, don't push yourself." Marco shook his head and set down the burger in front of Brandy. "Do you want something to drink with that?"

"I'll just have a diet soda, if that's okay?" Brandy picked up a fry and took a bite. "Thank you, Marco."

Marco filled up a cup with ice and then went to the soda machine.

Brandy never took her eyes off him, thinking about that kiss last night while eating one fry after another. God, when was the last time she'd eaten so much junk food? She never indulged.

"He's pretty hot, huh?" Val asked quietly next to her.

"Hmm?"

"Marco."

Brandy opened her mouth to answer, but Marco turned around just then and made his way back toward them.

"One diet soda. I'm going to run some numbers in the back. Let me know if you need anything."

She waited until he'd disappeared behind the kitchen doors and then sighed.

"Yes, he's a hottie."

"He's single you know." Val stole a fry and gave her a curious glance. "Are you?"

"Umm. Sort of?" She wasn't about to go into the details of

running away from her wedding yesterday. "But I'm not really his type."

Val laughed and stood up, walking behind the bar. "You'd be surprised just how much his type you actually are."

What? What did she mean by that cryptic remark? How could a guy like Marco possibly be her type?

Brandy shot Val a disbelieving glance as she picked up her burger.

"Don't give me that look. You've known the guy for, what, a few days?"

"Two." She took a bite of the burger and closed her eyes. *Heaven.*

"Right. And I've known him for over a year. So trust me on this one." Val poured herself a soda and then came back to the barstool. "Hurry with that burger, Brandy. I'm getting the urge to max out my credit card."

"Oh. Is that wise?"

She'd never maxed out a credit card in her life. And not because her parents had given her one without a limit, but because she never shopped. Never made big purchases.

Well, besides her Lexus. That was the only time she'd dropped an obscene amount of money. And every now and then she had major twinges of guilt on that one and considered trading it in for something cheaper.

"Wise? Hell, you'll never hear me claiming to be wise. But I'm a damn good shopper." Val glanced around the bar. "Did you meet Sebastian yet? Was he here last night? He's our resident Brit."

"Yes, he was here last night. He's very...charming."

"Charming?" Val snorted. "The guy flirts with anyone who has breasts. But he's a good guy."

"Yes, he is a bit of a flirt."

"He's single, too, or soon to be. But has a big ol' mess of a love life. The guy should open a luggage shop, he's got so much baggage."

Marco had hinted about something along those lines as well. What had happened to Sebastian? She finished off her burger and considered the possibilities.

"You ready? Here I'll take it to the back." Val stood up and reached for the basket of food.

"Thanks." Brandy grabbed one last fry before she could take it. "Let me use the bathroom and then we can go."

Marco started to shut down his computer and glanced up when Val came into the back.

"Hey, try and be back by four if you could, around when the rush hits."

"Yeah, we'll be back by then." She sat down on the edge of his desk, crossing one skinny leg over another. The familiar scent of patchouli oil followed wherever she went. "I figure we'll hit some thrift shops."

"Thank god. See if you can get her to burn the cat shirt."

"Ah, don't you like pussy, Marco?"

He rolled his eyes, used to her crude behavior by now. "I like it fine, Val, just not on a T-shirt."

She laughed and shook her head. "I'll pick her out something cute."

He waited for her to say something more, or maybe get off his desk, but she just kept looking at him with an amused little smile.

"What?"

"Nothing."

"Bullshit. I know that look on you and you're hiding something."

She chewed on her lip and narrowed her eyes. "You have absolutely no idea who she is, do you?"

"Who? Brandy?"

"Yup." She folded her arms across her chest.

"She's a bride who ran from her wedding."

"Okay, maybe so. But do you know *who* she is?"

Should he? He stared at Val, his brain whirring through the past twenty-four hours and all the little things Brandy had said.

"Think lingerie."

Lingerie? What the hell did lingerie have to do with anything?

"Damn it all, Val, just tell me already."

"Oh no. This is too great." She slid off the desk and shook her head, laughing outright. "She's been sleeping in your house for two days and you had no idea she's—"

"All right." Brandy pushed through the swinging doors and came into the back. "Are we ready, Val?"

"Sure, Brandy." Valerie closed her mouth and her smile widened.

Christ, Val was just going to leave him hanging like this? Without telling him who the hell Brandy was? She was loving it too, judging by the blatant delight on her face.

"We'll see you in a few hours." Valerie winked and headed for the swinging doors.

"Thanks for lunch," Brandy murmured.

She stayed behind, even after Val went up front. Offering a shy smile, she twisted her hands in front of her.

"You were right, it is the best burger I've had. I'll be sure to spread the word."

"Thanks, I'd appreciate that." He didn't want to hear about the burgers now, he wanted to know who the fuck she was.

He couldn't imagine her being anyone but a badly dressed

choir teacher who could somehow tie his hormones and emotions into a knot.

"Okay, guess I'd better go shopping. You're probably as tired of this outfit as I am."

More so.

He smiled and lied, "I don't even notice what you're wearing."

Her expression fell slightly and hurt flickered in her eyes. Shit, he'd just unintentionally insulted her.

"That came out wrong. I'm—"

"I'd better go. Val's waiting for me." She gestured behind her, and then spun around and practically ran out of the back office.

The door swung shut behind her and he sighed.

Damn.

She'd rushed out before he could even apologize. Not like it would have helped much once the words were out.

He slammed his fist on the desk.

Who the hell was she?

"I'm going to have a smoke. Want one?"

Brandy wrinkled her nose and shook her head. Her feet hurt like crazy from all the walking and shopping they'd done.

"I'll go back and grab an iced tea at the Starbucks we just passed."

"Cool. Meet me inside the shop across the street when you're done," Val grinned and pulled out her pack of smokes. "I saw the cutest corset in there that I think you should try on."

Brandy swallowed hard and tried not to wince. "Right. A corset...sure." She forced a slight smile, craving that tea now. "See you in a few."

Inside the shop, she let out a sigh of relief for the small

respite. She'd just accepted her iced tea from a perky barista when a hand closed over her shoulder.

She turned, expecting Val's face to swim into view.

"You owe me one hell of an explanation."

Brandy stumbled backward, her stomach rolling as she eyed Gordon in shock.

Damn. Double damn.

"Gordon." Her fingers crushed the plastic cup, and the cold beverage leaked a bit over the side onto her hand.

Her gaze darted to the door, seeking a way out. The urge to run was just as prominent as it had been on Friday. Maybe even more so.

He must have sensed her intent because he wrapped long fingers around her wrist in a move that guaranteed he had no intention of letting go until they talked.

She licked her lips and tugged on her hand. "Gordon…"

"Why don't we go somewhere private to talk." He jerked his head toward the door. "I've got a rental car parked just down the street."

Her pulse jumped and she tugged at her hand, but he made no move to loosen his grip.

She leaned forward and said in a low voice, "Gordon, I need time."

"The hell you do."

Her brows drew together in surprise at the anger in his voice.

Since he wouldn't let go, she walked toward the entrance to the store before he created a scene—tugging him along after him.

Outside in the overwhelming heat, she turned on him with a determined glare.

"Listen to me. I said I need time to think." She held up her hand when he began to argue. "And if you love me like you say you do—" *and god help me if you do,* "then you'll give me this time."

"Okay, you're not making sense. I think we should go back to L.A. and see Doctor—"

"No. God, why aren't you listening to me, Gordon? I need time." Sweat beaded on her forehead and she took a few steps away from him. "I'm going to be real honest, you're scaring me a bit."

"Is this about the girl in the room? I promise—"

"No. Though that had to be the most screwed up thing I've ever seen in my life." She shook her head and made a face. "I'm not sure we can fix this, Gordon. But if you even want one iota of consideration from me you'll back the heck off and give me space."

His face contorted into a shocking mask of rage before he wiped his hands down it and he made an obvious attempt at patience.

"Listen, love muffin. You're going to get your ass—"

"Everything okay, Brandy?" Val came jogging across the street and paused in front of them. She grinned and dropped her cigarette onto the ground, snuffing it out.

"Val." Relief washed through her and she gripped the other woman's hand. "We need to go. To those other shops across town."

Val gave her a scrutinizing look and then nodded. "Let's go."

"Hold on a minute." Gordon reached for her, but Val stepped between them.

"She'll give you a call later, buddy. Maybe." Leaning forward, her voice took on an edge. "But obviously right now she's not in the mood to chat."

Good lord, how embarrassing was it that she needed this petite little thing to defend her? But darn if she wasn't grateful.

Val ushered her away from the store and back to her car.

"You know that guy?"

"Yes," Brandy muttered. "I was dating him...think that's over now."

"Good call." Val looked over her shoulder back at Gordon. "He's creepy. And I'd bet my last cigarette he's going to try and follow us. But don't worry, I'll lose him."

Brandy gave a soft laugh, some of the tension dissipating. But she had to admit Val probably hit the nail on the head. Something wasn't right with Gordon, and she really didn't want to stick around to find out what.

Marco finished mixing up a Red Headed Slut and set the drink down in front of the woman standing at the bar.

"Thanks, hon." She winked, tossing her platinum hair, and went back to join her friends who'd come in for lunch.

She was cute, and a week ago he probably would have gotten her number. But today she did very little for him, she seemed too overdone. Too plastic.

He glanced over at the table of women again and had to pick out which woman had just come to the bar. They all looked the same in their various styled black clothing, long fake lashes, and matching haircuts.

Which wasn't exactly a surprise. It was like half the women in Vegas were just clones of one another.

Now Brandy. Brandy was like the anti-norm. She was original, sort of like Val, but in her own conservative way. Maybe that's why he was somewhat stuck on her. Whoever she was.

The earlier conversation with Val had been running through his head all day.

Who the hell was she?

He glanced at the clock at the end of the bar. Three-thirty, they should be back any minute now.

The door swung open and he looked up to the entrance, hoping it would be them. No such luck.

Sebastian strode in and came straight to the counter, swinging one leg over a stool and sitting down.

"And how are things today? Is Val sick again?"

"Nope. She's better today and came in here earlier to pick up her sneakers she left."

"Champion." Sebastian glanced around the bar. "Ah, look at the table of chits over there. Don't they look lovely?"

"Go for it. You're not on the clock yet."

"Ah, but you see even if I was," Sebastian murmured, his accent coming out more. "I own the bar. I can do whatever the fuck I want, mate."

"Co-own the bar. I believe that hole in my mass money market account would indicate that part of this place belongs to me."

"Ah, right you are, my friend."

Sebastian smiled at the group of giggling women who were watching them both at the bar.

"So where's Frauline Maria?"

Marco narrowed his eyes, refusing to be needled. "Brandy is out shopping for new clothes."

"Ah, by herself?"

"Nope. With Val."

"Are you shitting me? Val and Brandy?" Sebastian's mouth twisted and he gave a short nod. "Interesting."

"Val said something to me before she left."

"Ah, she wants to shag you, doesn't she?"

Marco laughed and shook her head. "No, you idiot, she doesn't want to shag me."

"But Brandy does." Sebastian gave him a knowing look.

Marco's humor died and his smile faded. "Yes, I'm pretty sure Brandy does."

"So why is that such a problem?"

Good question. And the only answer he had seemed pretty flimsy. "She's vulnerable. Forty-eight hours ago she was standing at that altar ready to get married."

"If the lass wants to shag you and you want to shag her, then I fail to see the problem."

"It's not that simple."

"Sure it is." Sebastian leaned forward, steepling his hands on the bar. "You know what this is? This is your conscience coming out."

Marco's blood rushed faster and sweat broke out on the back of his neck. "No. I really don't have a conscience. Never have. Which is why I made such a damn good defense attorney."

"Everyone has a conscience, Marco. If you think about it, that conscience is exactly why you left your other career." Sebastian shrugged. "Not that everyone you defended was actually guilty. You have to realize that deep down inside you're not as big of a badass as you'd like to believe yourself to be."

"I don't want to have this conversation. Not today, not tomorrow, and not even yesterday," Marco grumbled, uneasy about going down that past emotional path. "In fact, I did have a point before you steered this talk toward sex."

"Ah, well then I apologize. You know I'm an activist for a healthy sex life."

"Yes, I'm well aware of that." Marco went to pour himself a glass of water.

Sebastian's comments had gotten under his skin, like it or not.

A few years ago he'd thought he'd known what he wanted

in life. Had finally reached a place where he'd convinced himself he wanted to be.

But he'd been fooling himself. Himself and his family. And he doubted his dad would ever forgive him for his choices.

"So what was your question then? Before I so rudely changed the subject."

"Right. My question." Marco took a drink of water and set the glass down on the counter. He leaned forward, resting an elbow on the counter. "Does Brandy look familiar to you?"

"Familiar? Well, she worked here all last night, so I'm fairly certain I'd recognize the lass if I saw her walking down the street."

"That's not what I meant."

"Right. Well, just having a bit of sport. No, I'd never seen her before last night. Not that I'm aware of anyway."

"Hmm."

"Why, what's the deal?"

Marco shrugged. "No clue. Val made some kind of comment about me having no idea who Brandy was. Seemed to think it was the funniest thing in the world."

"Are you serious?" Sebastian's eyebrows rose. "Like we should know who she is or something?"

"Apparently."

"Hmm." Sebastian pursed his lips. "Who the hell is she?"

"That's what I've been asking myself for hours. And I've got no clue. A choir teacher, I thought."

"Well, you could just ask her." Sebastian's smile turned wicked. "Or lock Val in the walk-in freezer until she promises to tell you all she knows."

"I'm liking that second option." Marco stood and headed towards the back. "I'll be back in a few. I'm going to check with Dave and see if he needs anything in the kitchen for the evening."

Chapter Seven

"Try this on, too."

Brandy dodged the shirt that flew over the door of her dressing room and then scooped it up off the floor. It was tiny, black, with the word *Bitch* in silver glitter.

"Um, Val, I'm not sure this is my style," she called weakly from the safety of her room.

Her idea of going shopping at some trendy retail outlets had died a painful death. After that unsettling run-in with Gordon, Val had dragged her into every thrift shop and funky store in Vegas.

Despite protesting every item Val had tossed her way, the girl continued to bring them to her to try on.

In two hours of shopping Brandy had only purchased one long plaid skirt that she'd found on the clearance rack at a thrift shop.

She'd also begged Val to stop at *Sugar and Spice,* and had made a lightning-quick trip inside to pick up a good amount of panties and bras to get her through the next few weeks. Or however long she'd be hiding out. Fortunately, the girl ringing her up hadn't even batted an eye when she'd told them who she was.

She fingered the newest top Val had brought her and sighed. Why try it on when there was absolutely no way she planned to buy it?

Her dressing room door flew open and she shrieked, covering herself with the tiny excuse for a shirt.

"Okay, here's the deal."

"Shut the door! I'm naked!"

"You're not naked." Val rolled her eyes but obediently closed the door to the dressing room. "You've got a bra and underwear on."

"That's pretty much naked!"

"In my world that's considered overdressed."

Brandy jerked the shirt on, her cheeks burning with a blush.

"Okay, Brandy, we need to talk."

"About what?" She gave Val a suspicious look while pulling on a short skirt from the stack of clothes she hadn't yet tried on.

"You and this matronly image you insist on presenting to the world."

Brandy hesitated in zipping up the skirt. "What do you mean by matronly?"

"The way you dress, Brandy. My grandmother has a better fashion sense than you do."

The air left her lungs and she blinked in disbelief. "I'm sorry, but I think this Bitch shirt might be better suited to you."

"Very well put." Val laughed and her smile appeared a little more apologetic. "I like this side of you. I knew you had a little bit of fire buried under that perfectly polite personality."

"Val! I have fire." Oh god, had she just said that?

"Yes, you do." Val folded her arms across her chest. "You

wear undergarments that would make a hooker blush, yet cover yourself from head to toe in the frumpiest clothes."

Her blush deepened. And now they were going to talk about her underwear? Oh god, this had gone from bad to worse.

"Well, the undergarments I can explain," she muttered, raising a hand to her forehead.

Val's gaze softened. "I know you can, Brandy. Actually, let's just get that out. I know."

Brandy hesitated. How much did Val know? "You...you know?"

"Yes, I know."

"Oh." She bit her lip and looked away.

"Yes, Brandy, I know exactly who you are," Val went on seriously. "And I was hoping you could hook me up with that purple satin and lace garter belt that just came out in the summer collection. That shit is hot, but way out of my price range."

Relief flooded through her. Relief that someone knew who she was, and hadn't messaged the trashiest gossip site to cash in on her.

"I'm sure I can get you one," she promised with a smile and sat down on the lone chair in the room. "So you know my little secret. Did you...did you tell Marco or Sebastian?"

"No. They don't have a clue, but they'll figure it out. You're all over the local news." Val went to the mirror and toyed with her hair. "So, you're kind of hot and bothered for Marco, aren't ya?"

She gave a weak laugh. "Am I that obvious?"

"Yes. And then some." Val tweaked her purple bangs and then turned back around. "Unless you guys are already boning?"

Brandy's shoulders sagged. "No. I wish. He's kissed me a couple of times, and..." She bit her lip. *I will not tell her about him grabbing my breasts.* "And fooled around a bit, but he never seems to want to take it further."

"Well, that doesn't surprise me. Nobody wants to sleep with a woman who reminds them of their grandma."

"Okay, will you *stop* with the grandma reference already? I get it. Nobody likes my shirt."

"It's not just the shirt." Val sighed. "You've just got to realize something. Marco is a bit rough around the edges. He likes his women a little more…"

"Bad girl?" She wrinkled her nose.

"No, you don't have to be bad necessarily. But you are going to loosen up a little." She reached down and picked up Brandy's cat shirt. "I was kidding about the grandma comment, but it has a little bit of truth to it. He's going to feel like he's taking advantage of you when you've got such a pristine demeanor."

"Do I come across as prissy?"

"You could've been a cast member of The Brady Bunch." Her smile twisted. "But that's easily changed—if you let me play dress up with you. I mean, check yourself out in that outfit, Brandy."

Brandy chewed her lip and looked at herself in the mirror for the first time. Really looked at the outfit she was wearing. Her jaw went slack and the air exhaled from her lungs in a rush.

"That's right. You look hot. You have a great rack, Brandy. That shirt will make the boys go nuts. Marco especially."

"Do you think so?" She twisted to the side and glanced over her body. "My breasts don't look too…?"

"Big? Honey, they are what they are. You've got big knockers. Stop hiding them."

Brandy couldn't tear her gaze away from the curves she'd never allowed herself to accept. Yes, her breasts really did look big under the shirt, but they didn't look bad. They looked...sexy.

She had curves. Curves she'd always tried to hide under the baggy shirts. Curves she'd resented after growing up watching the tall, stick-thin Sugar and Spice models.

"Here," Val kneeled and adjusted the denim skirt, pushing it a bit higher. "And you've got great legs, too. Show them off a little instead of covering every square inch."

She stood back up and they both stared at her new outfit in the mirror.

Val squeezed her shoulder. "Well, what do you think?"

"It's amazing. I think I like it. I do look a little sexier."

"A little? Honey, that eight dollars in tips yesterday will be a joke when you clock off tonight. You are going to be a popular girl at the bar."

Brandy gave a quiet squeal, a little excited about Marco's reaction. She sobered quickly when she looked at the shirt again.

"Although, Val, I'm not sure how I feel about the profanity on my shirt."

"So we'll find you one without it. There're plenty of options." Val grinned. "In fact, now that I know you're up for a makeover, let me pick out a few more outfits."

A makeover?

Brandy's mouth parted in surprise, but she closed it. Yes, that's essentially what this was. And surprisingly, she wasn't too bugged by the idea. In fact, it would aid her in the effort to stay low profile.

Everyone would be looking for the old Brandy. Nobody would recognize her if she went all out and got made over.

"Val?" She stopped the other woman before she could open the door.

"Yup?"

"Do you think we have time to get my hair cut too?"

Val laughed and winked. "You read my mind, kid."

Marco pushed through the swinging doors that led from the kitchen to the front of the bar.

Glancing at the clock up front, he hoped like hell the ladies were back by now. He was considering a quick chat with Brandy before she clocked in.

Sebastian must have turned the music up because classic rock blared from the speakers throughout the bar. It helped add to the relaxed end of the weekend atmosphere that lingered throughout the room.

Marco walked around the floor, checking just how full up they were. He caught sight of purple hair and breathed a sigh of relief.

Well, there was one less worry off his back. Although he didn't see Brandy anywhere.

He glanced around again. No Brandy, but there was Sebastian flirting with some young sexy woman of course.

He shook his head. Although, he had to give Sebastian credit for straying from his usual blondes.

This woman was all curves and had no fear of showing them. In fact, she was probably the sexiest woman in the bar hands down right now.

This was the type of woman he used to lust after before his tastes had changed to the more drab look Brandy sported. Marco let his attention linger on her.

Long legs clad in fishnet stockings stretched out from beneath a tiny black mini skirt. Her profile was to him and he could see her full breasts pressed against the tiny white tank top.

A hand rested on her hip and she tucked a curl of her short

hair behind her ear. Sebastian said something and she giggled in response.

The sound sent a frisson of unease through him. That laugh....

"She looks hot, huh?" Val came up behind him and elbowed him in the side.

No. It couldn't be.

"Who looks hot?" The words were just a formality.

The woman, still laughing, turned and looked toward the bar where he and Val were standing. Those familiar blue eyes, now heavily outlined with makeup, narrowed slightly.

Blood rushed through his veins and pounded in his head, causing his vision to blur.

No way.

But he knew who she was. It was impossible to deny.

"So what do you think? We shopped all..." Val was trying to speak to him, but her words sounded distorted and slow in his ears.

Without realizing he'd taken a step, he moved closer to them until he could hear her and Sebastian's conversation.

Brandy giggled. "I know, I look—"

"Like one of those teachers that a teenage boy wants to shag," Sebastian finished for her.

Her mouth rounded and Marco watched a blush steal up her cheeks. Which was probably the only thing that convinced him it was truly Brandy.

"I was actually just going to say that I look a little different." She gave that familiar shy smile. "But thank you, Sebastian. I think."

Sebastian leaned forward and whispered something into her ear and her smile turned hesitant.

Total, unwarranted jealousy exploded inside Marco and he strode the last few steps toward them.

Brandy's gaze drifted his way and her eyes grew wide. She must have seen the fury in his eyes because she gasped and took a few frantic steps backward.

Sebastian stepped in front of his path, placing himself between Marco and Brandy.

"Hello, mate. Brandy was just about to start her shift. Why don't you let her be for now?"

Marco's jaw went rigid. "Why don't *you* step aside."

"Marco."

"Step aside."

Sebastian hesitated, his eyes narrowing. He cursed and spun away, leaving Brandy wide open.

"We need to talk."

"Oh. Now? Are you sure? I already clocked in." Her tongue darted out and ran over glossy red lips. "Perhaps you should wait for my break?"

"Perhaps not. Now, Brandy." He reached out to grab her wrist and then cursed, fisting his hands against his side so he wouldn't touch her. "I want to see you in the back office."

He waited for her to give a hesitant nod and then she walked past him toward the back. He glanced down at the tight leather skirt and cursed.

That ass. That ass could not belong to Brandy.

"Damn, Marco, where'd you find that sweet little thing?"

"Watch it." Marco turned a fierce glare on one of the regulars.

The man lifted his hands in the air with a laugh. "Sorry, buddy. Didn't realize she was off limits."

Marco bit back a growl and set off after Brandy. He slammed through the double doors that led to the back, sending them smashing into the wall.

Dave shot him an alarmed look and nearly dropped the burger he'd just lifted onto a spatula.

Ignoring him, Marco strode back to the office and shut the door behind him. Still steaming, he went behind the desk and sat down in the refined leather chair.

Brandy sat on the other side of the desk, her hands folded primly on her knees and a confused expression on her face.

"Marco? What's going on?"

He closed his eyes for a moment, picturing her again in the cat shirt, hoping it would settle his blood pressure. Make his dick a little less hard.

"Marco?"

He opened his eyes. Short, glossy curls framed her face. The makeup she had on made all her features more defined. Why hadn't he noticed how pretty her pale blue eyes were before?

Her cheeks seemed to have a glow to them, and her lips... What before had been the one exotic feature on her face was now downright sinful.

She was utterly gorgeous.

"Val gave me a bit of a makeover." She shifted in her heels as if she still weren't quite used to them. "Do you think it's too much?"

"Yes." The word erupted from him.

Her expression crumpled into complete devastation. "Oh."

"Why did you do it, Brandy?"

"I wanted to be..." She bit her lip, looking like she wanted to say more. Her eyes lowered and she gave a stiff shrug. "Because I thought it was time for a change."

He ran his gaze over her outfit again. Not only did she wear the tiny leather skirt, but the tank top was so thin that it clearly showed her peaked nipples beneath her bra.

If she walked back out there, with all those curves barely covered up, she'd be like the last beer on Super Bowl Sunday. She'd have every man in the joint fighting over her.

He shook his head, knowing and not caring that he was about to get seriously out of line. "I can't let you go back out there looking like that. Where's the cat shirt?"

"The cat shirt?" Her cheeks filled with color and uncertainly flickered in her eyes. "I thought you hated it."

"No. It's fucking great. Put it back on."

She hesitated and then lifted her chin. "I think this new look gives me a sexier image. Which should be good for business. Val said—"

"I don't really care what Val said."

And damn it she did look sexy. But who the hell was she trying to look sexy for? Was she having second thoughts about Gordon? Had she done this big makeover to impress him?

The blood started pounding in his veins again. The thought of her leaving....

No, she couldn't go back to Gordon. She wouldn't.

He shoved a hand through his hair and bit back a groan of frustration, not understanding his irrational thoughts.

"Look. I just don't understand," she said and her eyes suddenly narrowed. "I'm not dressed any differently than Val. Why the double standard?"

"Because on Val it's normal," he sputtered. "But you're different. You wear cat shirts and skirts to your ankles."

Her mouth thinned. "So? I decided it was time for a new look. Why are you suddenly so uptight?"

"Because you look like a two-dollar whore," he ground out.

She reared back and her face drained of color.

Oh fuck. Why the hell had he said that? Regret ate a bitter hole in his gut. She'd called him uptight and it had pushed him right over the edge.

"Ah, shit. Brandy, I didn't—"

The door swung open and Sebastian stormed in, his mouth drawn tight and his eyes narrowed with rage. Val stood in the doorway, her eyes wide and a hand pressed to her mouth.

Hell, they'd probably heard half of the conversation.

This wasn't going to be pretty. Sebastian looked ripe and ready to rip him a new one.

"Brandy, go back up front with Val," Sebastian said with a jerk of his head.

Marco tried to catch Brandy's gaze, to convey a silent apology for his reckless words, but she refused to look at him. She just kept her eyes diverted as she stood up and walked from the office, her body rigid.

Val waited for her to leave and then shut the door behind them, giving Marco one last searing glance that silently declared him a bastard.

He took a deep breath, braced his hands on the desk, and faced Sebastian.

"If you weren't my friend I'd be knocking you out cold, instead of trying to rationalize with you." Sebastian folded his arms across his chest. "You are out of line, Marco."

The anger that had lowered back down to a simmering level, flared right back up.

"Yeah? Well, why don't you tell me what the hell you were doing hitting on her?"

"Hitting on her? I wasn't hitting on her. We were having a bit of a chat."

"Bullshit. You couldn't take your eyes off of her—"

"Because she looks amazing, Marco. And I'll wager you didn't even take the opportunity to tell her that."

The words died in his mouth and his jaw hung slack. What could he say? She did look amazing. He just resented like hell that other men were noticing it.

"I was treating Brandy like I treat every woman, mate. I'm a bit of a flirt. It's common knowledge."

"You were whispering in her ear. That goes beyond your usual level of flirting."

Awareness dawned in Sebastian's eyes, and his smile turned amused.

"Ah, I see." He nodded. "You know I could be a nice bloke and tell you what exactly I was whispering into her ear, but I don't think I will. You're being a complete ass and deserve to fester in your jealousy."

Son of a bitch.

Marco ground his teeth together and fisted his hands.

"You're enjoying this, aren't you? What this is doing to me?"

"You're doing this to yourself, mate. Nothing is any different from yesterday about who she is as a person." Sebastian turned and headed for the door.

"*Everything's* different." He wasn't even sure if he was talking about the makeover anymore.

"And be warned," Sebastian continued. "If I hear you refer to her as a two-dollar whore again, I will hit you next time. She's a nice lass, Marco, and you'd better treat her as such."

Sebastian gave him one last pissed-off look and then left the office.

Damn.

Marco spun the chair around and stared out the window. He'd completely lost it. With Brandy and with Sebastian.

And over the stupid fact that she'd put on new clothes, makeup, and got her hair cut.

Closing his eyes, he shook his head. He should apologize, but he'd probably get within an inch of her and kiss her senseless.

He thrust a hand through his hair and groaned.

Getting through this night without touching her was going to be hell.

. . .

"He hates it." Brandy rushed behind the counter up front and grabbed a cocktail napkin to dab her eyes.

Val came up beside her and gently turned her away from the customer side of the bar.

"You don't want the customers to see you cry."

"Thank you." Brandy sniffled. At least someone was still thinking like a professional.

She'd completely lost it. Thank god she'd managed to stay somewhat composed when she was in the office with Marco.

"He doesn't hate your outfit, kid."

"Yes, he does." Brandy gave a watery laugh and looked over at her. "And why do you keep calling me kid? I'll be thirty the day after tomorrow."

"Wow, really?" Val's eyebrows rose. "You're younger than I thought. See, I told you it was the cat shirt."

Younger than she thought? Dear god, was it really that bad?

"Well, apparently I should have kept the cat shirt. Marco won't even let me work tonight."

"He has no choice. He's hard up for wait staff, and you're not dressed any differently than me."

"Yeah." She wrinkled her nose. "And I told him that."

"Oh, I gotcha. Is that when he called you a two-dollar hooker?"

Her shoulders quaked as she dragged in a quick breath. "He called me a whore, not a hooker."

"Same thing." Val laughed. "Hey, kid, look at me."

Brandy looked to the left, not wanting to see the amusement in the other woman's eyes.

"No, no, look at me. I want you to understand something." Val grabbed her chin, turning her back until their gazes were leveled. "What just happened in the office is a good thing."

Brandy's brows drew together and she shook her head. "I'm sorry, how could any of that have been a good thing? I did this whole makeover thinking it'd blow his mind." She shut her eyes and curled her fingers until her nails bit into the palms. "I just can't get the whore comment out of my head."

"Okay, yeah, the whore line was way out of line. And he did go a little caveman on you for a few minutes, which you should make him grovel over later. But do you realize why?"

"Because maybe I do look like a whore?" She opened her eyes.

"Don't you say that. Don't you ever say that. You look like me." Val grinned. "Sure, it's a little sexier than you're used to, but around here you fit right in."

"Then why was he just so mean to me?"

"Because he's realizing he likes you. And I'm not talking a little bit. I think Marco like you a lot. He's terrified, and his natural instinct is to be an asshat."

"He likes me because I got a makeover." Brandy harrumphed.

"That's just it." Val paused, her expression gentling. "Marco was falling hard even before your makeover."

Chapter Eight

"No." Brandy's pulse slowed and then sped back up to double time. "Do you think so?"

"Of course. That's why he flipped out on you. He liked you before when you weren't flaunting your goods to the world. But now that you threw on some clothes that say 'hey I'm sexy', he knows other men are going to figure out what he saw before you changed."

Brandy shook her head, but some of what Val said actually made sense. Though she still wasn't one hundred percent convinced he liked her before or after the makeover.

"So what do I do?"

"Just go to work as usual with the knowledge that you look totally hot. And then at the end of the night you reap the rewards in tips."

It sounded simple enough. "Okay. I can do that. I hope."

"You can. And be prepared for men to flirt, because they're gonna be on you like flies to honey." Val gave her a teasing frown. "Just don't take all my tips."

"I won't. I promise." Brandy sniffled again, a little less

shaky now, and dabbed her eye one last time. "Thanks, Val. I needed that."

"Good." Val patted her shoulder and turned back towards the floor.

"Wait!"

Pausing, Val turned back around and lifted an eyebrow. Brandy hurried over to her.

"But, I mean, what do I do about Marco?"

Val gave a slow smile. "Let him come after you—and he will. But don't let him off the hook too easily. The man did call you a slut."

"Whore."

"Right. Make him grovel. And be sure to flirt with other men. That'll really get his boxers in a knot."

"Oh..." Brandy's cheeks warmed.

The image of Marco in boxers, with no shirt on flitted through her head. Not that she'd ever seen him in such a state, but the idea of it was quite...sexy.

"Ahh, look at that, I see where your mind went. You dirty girl." Val grinned and nudged her in the ribs. "Yeah, you two are perfect for each other. I gotta get out on the floor. Those people are beer-guzzling, nacho addicts."

"Okay, thanks, Val. I'll be out on the floor in a minute." She pressed her hands against her cheeks and took a deep breath.

The door to the kitchen swung open and Sebastian strode out. His gaze immediately sought hers and then he came over to her.

"How are you doing, luv?"

"I'm fine." She gave him a less wan smile. "Thank you, Sebastian. Is he still...?"

"Being an ass? Very much so. But he'll get over it." He winked. "Are you okay to work tonight?"

"Okay? What do you mean?"

"If you're too upset, I completely understand—"

"No, not at all. Val had a nice little chat with me, and I feel much better."

"Male jealousy is equivalent to PMS in my opinion. So just go about your business until his cycle passes."

Brandy burst into laughter and pressed a hand against her belly.

"You're a funny guy, Sebastian. Why are you single again?"

She glanced up just in time to see Marco coming upfront. His jaw hardened and he turned right around and returned to the kitchen.

Sebastian glanced over his shoulder. "Ah, the man has terrible timing"

Her smile faded. Sebastian was right about Marcos' timing. She never flirted, and he'd caught her doing it twice with Sebastian now. But the man was practically a professional flirt. A woman got in his presence and couldn't help herself. It certainly didn't mean anything. Sebastian didn't make her blood heat the way Marco did.

Sebastian turned back to the counter where a customer waited. "All right, luv, time to get to work. If you need a few minutes, please feel free to take them."

Maybe she should take this time to call her parents. She had yet to even check in with them. And if Gordon contacted them first they'd probably flip out.

Her phone, where was it? She glanced back at the office and groaned. Or right. Back with *him*.

Taking a deep breath, she pushed through the double doors and walked back toward the office. She kept her head held high and her stomach sucked in—she still wasn't quite used to how tight the new clothes were.

She pressed her lips together and tiptoed inside. Maybe she could grab her purse and leave, without alerting him to her presence. Kneeling, she slipped her hand into the straps and lifted it onto her shoulder.

"If you insist on flirting, could you not do it with Sebastian?"

Crap.

He hadn't even turned around. Damn. Her reflection was glaringly obvious in the window.

"I wasn't—"

"I should have been clearer about the rules we have at *Dante's*. We don't encourage dating amongst the employees."

Seriously? He was seriously going to throw that comment at her? She braced her hands on her hips and glared at his back.

"Oh really? It sure didn't seem to matter to you last night when you were feeling me up in the parking lot."

"Yes. About that." He turned around, his expression cool and unreadable. "A mistake. It won't happen again."

Her stomach felt as if it sank into the floor. How could he sound so calm about what had happened between them? Stare at her as if they'd never even met.

"Funny, you keep saying that. And yet...."

His scowl deepened.

This was absolutely ridiculous. Ever since the makeover today, she'd felt a little different. A little more confident and daring. With the conversation with Valerie still fresh in her mind, she lifted her chin and decided to gamble.

"Also, bullshit."

He blinked, obviously shocked. "I'm sorry?

"I'm calling bullshit on you." She stepped forward and jammed a finger into his chest.

"You're doing what?"

"Bullshit on everything." She took a deep breath and plunged on before she lost her nerve. "You don't think I look like a whore, you think I look hot. And it pisses you off."

His eyes narrowed. "Now hold on—"

"And you know what else pisses you off?" she went on, gaining more confidence. "The idea that other men are going to be hitting on me tonight. Because they will."

"Brandy—"

"So here's the deal, buddy." She slid her finger up his chest and then placed it against his lips. "Either step up to the plate or accept the fact that others will."

Before he could respond, not that he could with his jaw hanging open, she turned and left the office with her purse in hand.

Her heart pounded double time, and she hoped to god she hadn't just made a major mistake.

She started to head outside, to call her parents real quick, when Sebastian waved to her from across the bar.

"What's up?" she called out, heading towards him.

"I lied. We're about to get slammed. I know I said feel free to take a few minutes, but can you start now?"

The phone call would have to wait. She slid her cell back into her purse and nodded.

"No problem. Let me just drop my purse in the backroom again and I'll be right out."

She took in a deep breath, wishing she didn't have to go face Marco so soon. She'd wanted to leave him to stew in those parting words.

Tiptoeing back through the kitchen she peeked around the door, saw Marco's back was to her, tossed her purse on the floor, and ran back to the front like the devil was on her heels.

True to Valerie's prediction, she was a popular girl.

The realization came not even an hour into her shift, and Brandy had already made a couple of hundred bucks in tips.

"How about another beer, cutie?"

Already on her way back to the bar, she stopped and smiled at the customer leaning against one of the pool tables.

"A Corona ,was it?"

"Yes, ma'am."

"You got it." She grinned and resumed her trip to the bar.

Sebastian was busy serving up a customer, but she squeezed her way in and set down her tray.

"I need a Corona and two Cosmos."

He glanced up and winked. "Sure thing, luv."

"Thanks." She put her hand on her hip and glanced around the bar.

The place had slowed a little but still held a few dozen people. Not bad for a Sunday night, she assumed.

"How are you doing out there?"

She glanced back at Sebastian and smiled. "I'm doing great. Although my feet are starting to hurt a little."

Sebastian leaned forward to glance over the counter at her feet. "I do not envy you in those heels, luv. Though they look mighty sexy on you if I do say so myself."

"You're good for my confidence, but stop flirting and make my drinks," she said and gave him a big grin.

"I think your confidence is doing just fine without my help." He lifted an eyebrow as he started mixing the drinks. "Have you seen Marco since...?"

"No. I think he's keeping his distance. I told him he needed to step up to the plate."

"Step up to the plate?"

She wrinkled her nose. "It's a baseball term. Don't you watch baseball?"

"Can't stand the stuff. I only watch football—ours, not that thing you Americans call football."

"Soccer?" She rolled her eyes. "You're going to have to convert, buddy. You've been in America for how long?"

"Five years." His smile dimmed some.

"What brought you over here again?"

"My wife. Well, she's in the process of becoming my ex-wife," he said, and she didn't miss the way his jaw tightened. "In any case. I'm here now."

Nice job pushing him into that emotional minefield, Brandy.

She cleared her throat and tried to back peddle from an obviously sore subject.

"Well, Sebastian, if I didn't want to sleep with Marco so bad, I'd probably seduce you."

Her attempt at shocking him worked. His eyes widened and he threw back his head and gave a huge belly laugh.

"Thanks, I needed that." He set the beer and the cosmos on the tray.

"Me too." She grinned and took the tray from him. "Thank you."

"Behave out there, luv."

"I can't make that promise, but thanks for trying." Her lips twisted as she turned away.

Her stride back onto the crowded floor had a confidence-induced swing. She could feel her butt doing that ultra-sexy swish she'd always seen on other women, but never seemed to be able to mimic before tonight.

She did enjoy this. Allowing herself to loosen up a little and explore this new part of herself. This embracing of her femininity and sexuality.

After dropping off the Cosmos to a couple of rowdy twenty-something women, and collecting money and tips from another table, she headed back to the pool table to drop off the beer.

"Well thank you, cutie." The middle-aged man took the

beer from her and handed her a twenty. "If I tell you to keep the change will you give me a kiss?"

He had several friends sitting around him, all of who laughed and poked each other at his comment. Obviously, the man was trying to impress his buddies.

"Well, I can't show customer favoritism, can I?"

The group of men laughed harder and the customer pushed the money back into her hand and shook his head with a sheepish smile.

"You keep the change. You earned it. What's your name anyway? Are you new?"

"Brandy. And yes, I'm new. Enjoy yourselves, boys." She spun away, congratulating herself on earning her biggest tip of the night so far.

The next two hours passed in a blur, and her tips grew steadily higher.

By last call her eyelids felt as if there were dumbbells attached to them, and her feet were swollen around the strap of her heels. She was relieved when the last customer left a short while later.

She lifted one leg and jerked off the heel, rubbing the arch of her foot.

"The price of looking sexy." Val sat down across from her and started counting her tips. "The longer you wear them though, the easier it gets."

Brandy winced and glared down at the offensive shoe. There was no way that vicious heel was going back on her foot tonight.

Thank god Val had helped her pick out some comfortable clothing to just relax in during the off hours. Because flip-flops and those pink joggers sounded positively orgasmic right now.

"So Brandy, where are you staying tonight?" Val asked, rubber banding her wad of cash together.

Wasn't that the question of the hour? Ignoring the sinking of her stomach, Brandy glanced towards the kitchen.

Marco had remained back there most of the night. No doubt avoiding her.

Way to step up.

"The past couple of nights I've stayed with Marco." She sighed and set her foot back down on the floor. "But it's probably time for me to just check into a hotel."

"Nah. Don't check into a hotel. Come crash at my place. Slasher pretty much lives there now, but he'll stay out of your way."

Brandy's hand fluttered to her throat. "Slasher?"

"My boyfriend. His real name is Stan, but he gets all pissy when you call him that."

"Oh right. The great sex guy who inspired you to call in sick to work."

"That'd be Slasher." Her smile turned wistful. "The man could fuck his way out of a murder rap."

"Oh. He sounds like...quite a fucker." She smiled and rubbed her foot harder. "I think I'm going to have to wait tables on my knees tomorrow."

Val grinned. "Well, men do love a woman who's on her knees."

"Who's on their knees?"

Brandy glanced up and found Marco crossing the empty floor towards them.

"Brandy's going to be tomorrow." Val stood up and stuffed her tips into her purse. "Or maybe tonight if you get back on her good side. Running to the bathroom, be back in a few."

Brandy watched the other woman hurry to the back and then turned to face Marco.

His eyes were locked on her, his expression lacking the

anger that had been there earlier. Instead, there was something else, a flicker of heat that gave her hope.

Her pulse quickened. The tiredness disappeared, leaving only a buzz of anticipation. She licked her lips and lowered her feet back to the ground.

She waited for him to say something. Felt the heavy, strain of the thick silence between them as the seconds ticked by.

Say something to me. Say you're sorry.

He was thinking She could see he wanted to say something. He would open his mouth and then shut it again.

Finally, "I'm going to have you start working the day shift tomorrow. You'll be working with me."

And, obviously, he had no intention of apologizing tonight. Her jaw clenched so hard she felt the promise of a tension headache come on. She looked at the clock.

"Okay...and what time does the day shift start?"

"Eleven." His gaze moved over her, from head to toe. As if he wanted to touch her, but realized fighting was the safer route.

"Well, then I'd better get some sleep." She slid out of the booth and walked past him. Unable to resist muttering, "Asshole."

"What did you say?"

She ignored him and pushed into the back of the bar. All the lights were off except the office.

The door swung open and banged against the wall.

"What did you just call me?"

"I didn't call you anything," she said calmly, scooping up her bags and her purse. "My inner whore did."

He knocked the bags and purse from her hand, and backed her up against the wall. His hands slammed on either side of her head and her pulse sprinted to life.

She dragged in a quick breath, inhaling his spicy scent.

His lips moved in to hover just above hers, and her knees went weak.

"Well your inner whore is right." He slid a hand down the wall until it connected with her hip, his fingers curled around her flesh possessively. "I am an asshole."

"Yes." In the moment of weakness, she couldn't keep the hurt and vulnerability out of her voice. "You are, Marco."

"I'm so sorry." Regret flashed in his eyes before his mouth slanted across hers. Shock and pleasure combined to send tingles of pleasure through her body.

She gasped and pulled away slightly. "What are you doing?"

"Stepping up to the plate."

His mouth came down again, harder this time. His tongue slid deep to find hers. The tingles turned into waves of heat and desire.

His thumb swept under her tank top, stroking the bare skin above the waist of the skirt. Each stroke of his thumb sent arrows of heat between her legs.

Part of her wanted to shove him aside, not let him off the hook right away as Val had suggested. But the other part, the turned-on side, was begging her to say to hell with it and go full throttle.

Screw it. The sexual side of her had been in lock-down mode for way too long.

She grabbed the front of his shirt as he curled both his hands around her hips, grinding his pelvis against her.

"Brandy, are you going to stay with me—oh shit." Val's laughter faded. "Guess that's a no." The door swung shut again.

Neither of them came up for air or bothered to acknowledge Val's brief presence and ensuing disappearance.

Marco pulled her away from the door and they stumbled

across the office, tripping over her bags before finally making it to his desk.

She heard the sound of papers and objects being brushed off, before he lifted her onto it.

"What did Sebastian whisper in your ear earlier?" He caught her earlobe between his teeth.

"Oh." She gasped and squirmed against him. "J-just that you wouldn't be able to keep your hands off me tonight."

"He was right." He yanked her tank top over her head. "Damn. For a choir teacher you have some of the hottest underwear I've ever seen."

"About that...oh God." Her impulse to confide who she was died a quick death when his hands covered her breasts.

"Pink lace." He shook his head, pinching her nipples through the bra. "And a white set yesterday."

He stepped between her legs, spreading her thighs wider. Even through his jeans, she could feel the hard length of his erection pressing against her panties.

"If you don't want this, tell me to stop," he said as he unfastened the back clasp of her bra and tugged the lace from her breasts.

"Do I look that stupid to you?" she asked.

"No." He traced the circles of her areolas with his fingers. "You look like a woman who's about to have sex in the back office of a bar."

"Promises, promises." She gave a breathy laugh and arched into his touch. "I'm beginning to think you're all talk."

"I'll show you all talk." He growled and lowered his head to suck one of her nipples into his mouth.

Her teasing mood fled as his touch sent fire racing through her blood. An ache grew between her legs.

He switched his mouth to the other breast, licking the

nipple while his cock ground against her through the layers of clothes they both still had on.

Off. She wanted all the barriers gone.

Blindly, she reached for his zipper and tugged it down, then unbuttoned his jeans.

She had her hand inside his pants a second later, exploring and touching the impressive erection she found inside.

Marco pulled back with a groan, pushing his jeans and boxers down his body and all the way off. He tugged his shirt over his head and another hot ripple of desire shot through her.

His shoulders were broad, his chest defined and sprinkled with dark hair.

"Come here," she whispered, already reaching for him again.

He grinned and shook his head. "I showed you mine."

She didn't miss the reference to what she'd said to him the first day they'd met, she just was too turned on to dwell on it.

Sliding off the desk, she unzipped her skirt in the back and wiggled out of it and the fishnet stockings. Good lord, the skirt was tight, how had she gotten into it in the first place?

They finally slid over her hips and down to the floor.

"Wait."

He grabbed her wrists to stop her before she could slide out of her panties too. She stood awkwardly in just the pink lacy thong.

"Let me just look at you like this for a second," he said hoarsely. "Jesus, Brandy. You're amazing."

A blush heated her cheeks. "I'm not."

Amazing? No the models for *Sugar and Spice* were amazing. She was just an average woman who could stand to lose fifteen pounds.

He glanced up at her long enough to let her know he clearly thought she was insane.

"You're absolutely beautiful," he reiterated and then went to his knees in front of her.

She gasped. "What are you doing?"

"What do you think?" His large hands wrapped around her thighs, and then his warm breath nuzzled her curls through her panties.

"Marco," she gasped and gripped his shoulders. "Val told me to make you grovel, and I'm thinking this is what she meant."

He laughed softly. "Sweetheart, I was going to eat your pussy tonight even before I was an asshole earlier."

Her breath caught and she tightened her grip on his shoulders.

He glanced up, his smile knowing. "Does that word freak you out?"

"Sort of," she whispered, staring at his dark head between her legs. "But it's also super hot. I think... I think I like it."

"Yeah?" He traced his tongue over her slit through her panties. "You're going to really like it when I'm licking you without these on."

Her cheeks warmed, both at his words and the anticipation for what he was about to do.

"Marco, please," she whispered, desperate for him to make good on that promise.

He made a small groan, before curling his fingers into the lace and tugging it to the side.

The next instant his mouth was on her and her knees buckled.

"Oh my god."

The three words seem to be on repeat as he parted her labia and licked her slit from top to bottom.

With a murmur of pleasure, he backed her up to the desk again. He took a second to pull her panties free from her body and toss them aside. Then eased her onto the edge of the desk.

It must've been just a few seconds, but it felt like an eternity before he lowered his head back between her legs. This time his focus was all on her clit.

Each flick of his tongue brought her deeper into that world of pleasure. Closer to that impending climax closer to the horizon.

It was impossible to think, only feel. Feel the pleasure his talented mouth created.

He slipped a finger inside her and she cried out. When he sucked her swollen clit and added another finger, she came with a ragged cry.

Waves of pleasure rocked her body and she ground herself against his mouth as he continued to pleasure her.

When he stood she couldn't have moved from the desk if she'd wanted to.

"One second, sweetheart." He walked to the other side of the desk and pulled out a condom.

Did he do this often?

The question flitted through her mind, leaving a trace of unease before he came back and parted her legs again.

The head of his erection pressing against her pussy wiped away all doubts she had that this might not be the best idea.

She sighed and pressed herself against him until the tip of his cock slid just a bit inside her.

"Please, Marco," she begged, gripping the edge of the desk.

His gaze, so hot and yet so controlled, met hers and then he thrust deep inside her.

Her body welcomed his intimate invasion—his thick length—and she dragged in small, shallow breaths.

"Brandy." He groaned, his eyes closed and he stayed buried inside her for a second.

She let her eyelids flutter shut as well. Each breath she took in just accentuated how wonderfully he filled her.

He tightened his hands around her thighs and then he began a slow rhythm. With each thrust, the pace increased, and the deeper he moved inside her.

The blood roared through her veins, and sweat gathered on her body. Her hips moved against him, meeting each thrust as if it would be the last.

He released one of her legs to reach between them to rub her clit again, and she came almost instantly.

"Marco." She cried out. Squeezing him with her inner muscles as the waves of her orgasm rolled over.

"Oh god." He thrust hard, his hips wedging her legs open even further as he came inside her.

His hands slid down to the desk and he supported his weight as he made shallow thrusts through his climax.

Her pulse slowed a little and her vision became less hazy. She watched his face, saw the pleasure and the naked emotion there.

Reaching up, she ran her hand down his cheek.

"You okay?"

"I don't think I can walk." He grunted and nuzzled her breast.

"Neither can I. And I only blame half of that on the heels."

He laughed, the movement shaking her breast and causing her nipple to stand at attention again. His tongue slipped out to give it a light flick.

"Marco." She groaned. "This is the first time I've ever had sex on a desk, and though it's been fabulous, I can't see it happening again right now."

"No?" He lifted his head, a wicked grin on his face that sent warmth through her. He was so damn sexy—lethally so.

"No." Her lips twitched and she gave him a light push. "I'm thinking pillows and a mattress next time."

"You know what? I just happen to have some of those at my house."

"Is that so? Does that mean...." She pulled his head down towards hers. "I don't have to sleep in the ganja lounge tonight?"

"No, I think you've inhaled enough stale smoke. Tonight you get to sleep in the Marco lounge." He brushed his mouth across hers and then stood.

"I like the sound of that." She took the hand that he offered her and climbed off the desk. "Now where the heck did you throw my clothes?"

Chapter Nine

How the hell that purple-haired bitch had lost him on the road this afternoon was beyond his comprehension, but the fact that she had seriously pissed off Gordon.

Something had happened to Brandy. She'd changed. Though the fact that she'd run out on him at the altar had been a big clue on that in the first place.

At least the fact that she hadn't left Vegas was a big relief. She had to be staying somewhere nearby. And who was the ballsy girl who'd been with her? Shit. He needed to get Brandy back. And fast.

Wandering around the drug store, he grabbed a candy bar and tossed it into his basket. Then after a moment of hesitation, added a second one. Almost out of the aisle, he grabbed some gummy candy that he'd always warned his patients would rip their fillings right out.

Damn. What was wrong with him? He hadn't had a sugar binge like this since he'd been a kid.

But each day that he didn't get Brandy back, he seemed to

sink further and further into a desperate funk. The usual stuff didn't matter.

Who cared whether his shirt had a designer label? Hell, even if his hair was combed. He just wanted to eat junk. Eat and fuck. Damn it he had one hell of a hard-on. He needed to get laid—something to take the edge off right now. Not that it would help much.

Standing in line at the checkout stand, of course, he wound up behind a young red-haired twenty-something. Tiny shorts that barely covered her ass and a tank top that hugged her tits. And he had no trouble checking her out.

She glanced over her shoulder, probably catching his blatant leer.

"I see you've got a sweet tooth," she said, suddenly and then giggled. "My friend saw you earlier. She said you were famous. Are you?"

He gave her small breasts a pointed glance and answered with a brief nod.

She placed a hand on her hip and adjusted her body so her chest stuck out further. "Nice...so what are you doing later?"

Watching you suck me off. He didn't say the words aloud but knew she wouldn't have any doubts when she looked into his eyes.

He was all too familiar with the little fame whores. Women who'd sleep with anyone who might even be remotely famous. They got off on it. And he just got off. He had no problem taking what they were so willing to give.

Especially since Brandy was about as fun to fuck as peeling potatoes.

"Wait for me out front," he told her as she paid for her six-pack of beer.

Excitement flickered in her eyes and she nodded. "I'll do that. Let me just bag out of my plans with my friends."

After she'd disappeared out the door and his dick was pounding with the promise of sex, his phone began to ring.

Cold sweat beaded on his brow as he jerked his cell from his pants pocket to check the id. Caller Unknown.

"Fuck." A chill ran down his spine and he shoved the phone back into his pocket.

It had to be him. The bookie who'd been stalking him like he was a god damn turkey on Thanksgiving.

He paid for his stuff and headed outside. Someone touched his shoulder and he spun around with a curse.

The girl from inside giggled and stepped back. "Oops, scared ya, did I?"

His teeth snapped together and he bit back a growl. God, she was annoying. But she was a woman who wanted to screw him, so he'd take it.

"My name's Anna, by the way—"

"I don't need to know your name."

He watched her. Waiting to see if his cold bluntness would deter her, and doubting it would.

"Oh." She gave a slow nod, understanding dawning in her eyes. "Okay. So where's your car."

Smothering a laugh, he didn't answer and just turned to walk toward it. He knew she'd follow.

He'd have her suck him off in the car down some dark street, and then drop her back off at the drugstore. It wasn't much, but at least she was free—unlike that whore he'd brought to the hotel after Brandy had ditched him. Stress made him horny though. It was a weakness he despised in himself.

There wasn't time for a hotel. It was too risky with time running out. No, tonight he'd get his things and go back to his home. Not for long though, it wasn't safe.

He should've never let the gothic bitch whisk Brandy away. One thing was certain he wouldn't make the same mistake twice. In fact...maybe it was time to enlist outside help in locating her.

Waking up next to Brandy was an interesting experience. Marco braced himself up on one elbow and watched her as she slept.

She'd hogged the bed. She'd rolled to the very middle and had one arm thrown across his side of the bed. And she lightly snored.

And yet she was the sexiest, most interesting woman he'd ever woken up next to.

He touched one of her curls, which, with the new haircut, wasn't as wild as it had been the other morning.

She did look good with the makeover Val had done. But she'd looked good to him before, too.

"Why are you staring at me?" she muttered and buried her face into the pillow.

"Because you're a woman in my bed."

"Hmm. You're that easy?" She yawned and pulled the sheet up to her chin.

"So I've been told." He grinned and reached out to tickle her side.

She gasped and rolled away. "No tickling!"

He followed her across the mattress, pinning her down with his weight.

"Beg for mercy?" He moved his fingers to the sides of her ribcage.

"Mercy!" she squealed. "Please, I'm begging you. Mercy!"

"I like it when you beg." He grinned and released her.

She climbed out of bed and stuck her tongue out. "We'll see who's begging later."

He watched her walk naked across the room. The curves of

her body jiggling in all the right spots. He felt himself getting hard again and bit back a groan.

Jesus. How many times could he fuck this woman silly before he got tired of her? They'd gone at it two more times after returning from the bar last night.

He cleared his throat. "How do you feel about grabbing a hot beverage and something to eat?"

"Do we have time?" she called over her shoulder.

"It's only eight-thirty, we don't have to be in until eleven."

"Sounds good to me."

"Great. I'm going to get on the computer for a second and then I'll get ready."

She gave a little wave of her hand and then disappeared into the hallway.

Marco groaned and leaned back against the pillow. He needed to get control of his hormones. She'd turned his brain to mush the past few days.

Going to bed with her had at least taken the edge off, giving him a clearer head. Just barely. He climbed out of bed, thinking about the number of emails he probably had in his inbox.

Brandy narrowed her eyes and stared at her naked body in the mirror. Full breasts with a couple of love marks that could be covered with a bra, the flare of her hips gave her a provocative all too feminine look.

Usually, she looked at her body with something close to disappointment—even annoyance. But not today. She'd woken up this morning with an entirely different outlook.

Today only one word came to mind while staring at herself naked. Sensual.

She lowered her gaze to the mass of curls between her legs and new words popped into her head. Jungle. Yikes.

Glancing at the bathroom door she wondered just how much time she had before Marco wanted to run and grab some tea and coffee.

Hmm. She probably had a few minutes.

She shook her head, staring at the curls between her legs. Lots of women got waxed down there. Maybe it was time for her to take the plunge.

Oh! She knelt and opened the cabinet under the sink, remembering the shopping trip with Val yesterday. They'd picked up some necessaries at the drug store, including a bottle of hair remover lotion and a razor.

Might as well make use of this stuff and trim things up. But which one?

She glanced at the bottle of lotion and the razor. Sweat broke out on the back as she stared at the razor.

"Absolutely freaking not." There was no way that blade was going anywhere near her private area.

Which meant...the lotion.

She grabbed the bottle and squeezed a good amount into her hand, then began to liberally apply it on every piece of hair in her pelvic region.

Recapping the bottle she set it down and sighed. Okay now what. Just wait a bit?

She heard footsteps walking down the hall and tensed. He wasn't ready yet, was he?

"Give me a few more minutes, Brandy. Sorry, Sebastian called."

"Not a problem," she yelled back and stared at the lotion.

She was kind of excited to see what it felt like to be all silky and smooth down there.

She closed her eyes, envisioning Marco's strong hands. Long fingers, calloused hands. Those hands on her...in her.

A blush swept to her cheeks and she giggled.

"He is going to be so shocked," she whispered. "Hopefully in a good way. When this stuff comes off—oh." She blinked, shifting her stance. "Wow, that kind of hurts."

She glanced down at the lotion and how red her inner thighs were turning. The slow burn intensified.

"Wait, no 'kind of' about it. That hurts." Had she not grabbed a bottle that was safe for this area of the body?

She reached for a towel and started wiping it off, gasping.

"Oh my god, it burns. It burns!"

She shrieked and waddled over to turn on the shower, her eyes watering. The sound of footsteps came from the hall again, this time he was running.

"Brandy? What is it?" The doorknob turned, but he couldn't open it since she'd locked the door.

"Nothing—ow! Damn! Shit!"

"Are you actually cursing? What's—"

"Ouuuuch!"

Wood splintered as he broke the lock and the door swung open. Marco rushed in, his frantic gaze seeking her out.

"You broke down the door?" Her eyes widened and her own pain was momentarily forgotten.

"Well, you were screaming in pain and not really answering me." He rubbed his shoulder and stared at her, looking slowly up and down her body. "What's all over your..."

"Don't worry about it." Her cheeks burned with humiliation as she moved under the spray of water. "I was trying to do sexy stuff for you and made some poor life choices."

"Were you trying to get rid of...?" His gaze lingered between her legs.

"Yes."

"Sweetheart, you're sexy no matter what the hair situation is like down there." His eyes darkened and a slow smile curved his lips. "Don't worry about trying to please me. I'm a guy, it's what's inside that counts."

Her brows shot up. "Was that a dirty joke?"

"Yeah. It really was."

She groaned. "Terrible. Also, I'm embarrassed as heck."

"You're hot."

"Are you insane? I have lotion burning the hell out of my crotch and legs right now."

"I see it differently. I see a naked woman in my shower." He stood up and pulled off his shirt, then began to take off his pants. "That's pretty sexy in my book."

Most of the lotion had rinsed off her body and the sting had begun to fade to a dull throb. She grabbed a bar of soap to wash away any remaining traces of it.

He stepped into the shower with her and took the shower head off its hook. Then, with utter gentleness, he directed the spray between her legs.

"Let me help you," he murmured when she started to protest.

"What are you doing?" Her pulse quickened and she swiped her tongue across her bottom lip.

His lips nuzzled her neck. "I figure you might need help easing that burn."

And then he nudged her feet apart and tilted the shower head in a way that directed the spray right toward her clit.

She gasped and reached out to hold onto his shoulders.

"Okay, I'm not going to complain if you want to help out."

With one hand occupied on the shower head, he used his other to cup her breast. His thumb stroked her nipple, sending a different heat through her body.

"Good girl." His mouth covered hers, before his tongue speared deep.

She kissed him back, her body responding to the spray and the way he stroked her nipple.

Good Lord she wanted him again. Even after all the times they'd done it last night.

A heavy ache pooled between her thighs as Marco pressed himself closer. His cock brushed against her belly and she reached down to wrap her fingers around his thick length.

He groaned and abandoned the shower head, replacing the water with his thumb.

While she explored him with her hand, he made quick strokes over her clit that sent her into a vortex of pleasure.

Before she realized it, she was climaxing. Leaning into him and gasping in steamy air as he easily brought her to release.

Her grip on his cock tightened until he groaned.

"Princess, if you keep touching me...."

His words registered as she floated back down from Mount Orgasm, and she glanced down to his hard flesh in her hand.

"Yes? If I keep touching you...?" She smiled. "What then? Because actually, I had it in mind to do a whole lot more than just touch."

He drew in a swift breath and his eyes darkened. "Is that so?"

"Mmm hmm."

Her heart sped up as she decided what she wanted to do. What she usually hated doing with Gordon.

Before she could second guess her decision, she slipped to her knees in the shower stall.

With his cock still in her hand, she leaned forward and drew her tongue across the tip.

"Brandy," he choked. "You don't have to do this. I came in here to help you."

"And you did. In multiple ways." She tilted her head to look up at him. "Now I'm thanking you."

"I see." He gave a ragged gasp when she kissed the head again. "Then by all means...keep on thanking."

She parted her lips and let him slide into her mouth. The taste and feel of him were amazing. The sounds he made when she sucked were even more incredible.

For once, she realized she was loving this giving head stuff. She was committed, ready to see it through, but then he pulled out at the last second.

Her cry of protest ended with a sigh as he came on her breasts. While still on the floor, she lifted her attention to his face.

"Not yet," he mumbled, staring down at her, his gaze soft and hazy from release. "I want you to make sure you're ready for that."

She laughed and rose to her feet. "I think I would've been okay."

"Maybe." He reached out to massage her slick breasts. "Or maybe I just really wanted to come on your incredible tits."

This time, she wasn't shocked. She was getting used to it. Starting to love it. The dirty talk. The things they were doing.

Marco had opened a door to a whole new world, and she wasn't sure she ever wanted to leave.

"Now for real," he murmured, grabbing the bar of soap again. "Let's get washed up and ready for the day."

"You're not pulling a double again are you?" Sebastian asked, sliding his shades up onto his head as he walked into the bar.

Marco glanced up from his task of straightening up some of the tables.

"I figure I'll stay until six. I'm thinking of sending Brandy home, we've been slow all day."

"Mondays sure seem to be." Sebastian pulled out a chair,

spun it around, and sat on it backward. "We do great during the weekend, but I think we're losing money during the week."

"I agree." Marco scratched the back of his neck and pursed his lips. "We need to find a way to bring in more people on weekdays."

"You guys should do karaoke," Brandy came up behind them. She pulled out another chair at the table and sat down. "Seriously, though, I think it would bring in a lot of business."

Her glance drifted up to him and when their gazes held, he watched as her cheeks filled with color. Was she remembering this morning? He was. It was hard not to remember Brandy on her knees, her breasts slick with his cum.

Karaoke. She'd mentioned karaoke. Get it together.

His brows drew together. "Karaoke's been done more than a two-dollar—" He broke off and winced. "Sorry."

"Yeah, watch it, buddy." She wrinkled her nose at him. "I'm starting to understand that it's a favorite phrase of yours, but you're still not completely off my shit list yet."

"Yes, mate, you'd better watch it," Sebastian piped in. "Though I do agree with Marco. Karaoke's overdone."

"Hmm. Well, what else could you do?" She drummed her nails on the table and pursed her lips. "I've got it. What if we brought in live music once a week? Feature local Bands. That way you could even charge a small cover fee if you wanted."

"Local Bands?" Marco asked, a little dubious about the idea.

"Sure. I have a couple of students, seriously talented, who went on after high school to form bands. They would love this kind of opportunity."

"Are they even old enough to be in a bar?" he drawled raising an eyebrow.

"Well let's see. Eddy graduated in..." Her brows drew

together in the cutest *I'm thinking* way. "Yes. He should be about twenty-three now."

"It might be a good idea." Sebastian gave a slow nod. "Or maybe we could even do some kind of Battle of the Bands."

"Exactly!" She snapped her fingers. "Like, we bring in a bunch of bands, let them all perform, and the audience decides."

Marco finally pulled out a chair and sat down. The bar had emptied again, and there was no point in standing around.

"People do love this stuff." Sebastian nodded. "I say we do it."

"I'm in. I'll make up some fliers and we can go distribute them. How about next Wednesday?" Brandy stood up and stretched. The tiny t-shirt she wore over her jeans rose a couple of inches, exposing her belly button.

Marco dragged in a quick breath and looked away. How many times last night had he kissed that tiny crater before moving lower to—

"Works for me. Marco?"

He blinked and jerked his head up. "Huh?"

"Are you cool with that?" Sebastian asked, amusement in his eyes.

"Yeah. That sounds great." He gave a brisk nod and thrust his fingers into his hair. "Thanks, Brandy."

He watched her scribble notes onto a pad she usually took orders on.

Damn. Had it only been four days since she'd jumped onto his bike and into his life? It was hard to fathom the idea of not having her around.

And she seemed to be enjoying herself—in no hurry to get back to her normal life. To Gordon.

He bristled in the chair at the thought of the other man.

She's been in your bed, not that shmuck's.

But was she feeling guilty about leaving the fiancé? Well, probably not as much after finding him getting ready to nail some prostitute.

The door to the bar swung open.

"Well screw me backward. Is it dead in here or what?" Val walked in swinging a skull and bones purse clutched in her hands.

"It's dead," Sebastian agreed and leaned back in the chair so it lifted onto its back legs.

"Well, there's no need for all of us here." Val sat on the table and looked around. "You guys should clock off and Sebastian and I can handle it."

"You're sure?" Brandy pushed back her chair and tucked the pad into the pocket of her short denim skirt. She glanced at Marco. "That would give us time to go print up those Battle of the Bands fliers now."

"Battle of the Bands?" Val quirked an eyebrow. "Did I miss something?"

"I'll explain it to her," Sebastian said after a yawn. "You two go ahead and go."

"Thanks, guys." Marco slapped Sebastian on the back and winked at Val. "See you both tomorrow."

"Have fun," Val called out, "that's an order."

"Yes, ma'am," Brandy agreed before her gaze met his. "Let me just grab my purse in the back and clock out."

She turned and left for the office. Marco hadn't missed the message in her eyes, she wanted him to follow.

He cleared his throat. "I need to grab something in the back, too."

Sebastian chuckled. "Sure you do. Like her ass."

Ignoring his friend, he followed after Brandy who'd disappeared into the office.

Pushing open the swinging doors, he met up with her in the back where she was scooping up her purse.

She turned around and her eyes flashed with pleasure when she saw him.

"Hi," she said hesitantly, her mouth curving into a smile.

"Hey." He shut the door, closed the distance between them, and then dragged her against him.

She wrapped her arms around his neck, already tilting her head up to offer her mouth to him.

With a groan, he covered her lips with his. She parted for him and he slipped his tongue inside, surprised at his possessiveness and need for a quick taste of her.

The kiss deepened. Only her sweet cry pulled him up from the tidal wave of desire that threatened a repeat performance from last night. And hell, it'd taken him a good half hour to get his desk back in order as it was.

He lifted his head and dragged in an unsteady breath.

"Thanks." She nuzzled her forehead against his shoulder. "I needed that."

"Not as much as I did." He breathed in the scent of apples and the scent of his shampoo in her hair. "Maybe we should skip the fliers and just go straight home."

"Oh yeah?" He could hear the smile in her voice.

"Yeah."

"And what would we do there?" She traced a finger over the tattoo on his arm.

"The same thing we did last night. And this morning."

"As much as I love the suggestion, we should save that for later. Besides," she lifted her head and looked at him. "I want one of these."

"One of what?" He brushed a few curls away from her cheek.

"One of these." She traced a nail up and down his arm again.

His gaze dropped to where she was touching his ink.

"A tattoo?"

"Yeah."

He frowned and for the first time, he started to wonder how far she was going to take this whole makeover thing.

She sighed. "Stop it."

"Stop what?"

"Thinking that I'm crazy for wanting a tattoo." She gave him a chiding look.

"You're just so..."

"Straight? Narrow? Innocent?" She shrugged. "Maybe I was. Maybe I still am? But I want to try new things, if that's so wrong then sue me."

He flinched at the *sue me* line, but fortunately, she missed it as she stepped away and slipped her purse back onto her shoulder.

Still the smiley faces tote bag, he realized with a small amount of surprise. The bag was something that hadn't yet changed about her, and it sent a bit of warm relief through him.

"But first let's do the fliers, and then distribute them at some businesses around town." She gave him a firm look. "Including some tattoo shops—one where I'll get that tattoo. Today."

The air whistled from between his teeth and several beats passed before he could answer her. The makeover he could understand, but a tattoo was permanent.

"Brandy—"

"Don't talk me out of it, please." Her words were soft, her lips pursed.

Marco bit back a groan and thrust his fingers through his hair. *Shit.*

Like he could anyway? Chances were if he refused to take her she'd just take a ride share to the nearest shop and do it herself.

"You're sure about this?"

"Completely."

So this is what the inside of a tattoo shop looks like.

The flyer dropped from Brandy's limp fingers and fluttered to the floor.

"Long time no see, man."

Brandy stepped out of the way just as the employee inside the shop reached past to slap Marco across the back.

"No shit." Marco returned the slap and then pumped the guy's hand.

"So what have you been up to?"

Brandy let them have their guy talk, and eyed the tattoo designs on the wall. So many choices and possibilities.

Of course, it probably would have been a good plan to have some kind of idea of just what she wanted to have permanently imprinted on her body, but then this whole thing was spontaneous.

She jumped as Marco touched her shoulder. "So anyway, Jack, I'm bringing you a virgin today."

Heat flooded into her face and she swallowed hard, lifting her head to look at the other man.

Tattoos and piercings decorated every inch of his body that was exposed.

"Hell, you know I love me a virgin." He grinned, his teeth shining white against his tan skin. "What's your name, kitten?"

She licked her lips. "Brandy."

"I've never met a Brandy I didn't like. Nice to meet you,

any friend of Marco's is a friend of mine. So what are you thinking?"

"Thinking?"

"Where and what?"

"Oh." She glanced back at the wall of art. "Umm..."

"Still deciding?"

She gave a brisk nod and glanced over at Marco. His mouth had curled into a smirk, his thumbs hooked into the belt loops on his jeans.

"Hey, Jack, we were also hoping you'd let us put up a flyer. We're trying something new at the bar. A Battle of the Bands."

"Sweet. Go for it. I know a lot of my clients would be all over that. A lot of musicians come in here."

Music. Brandy blinked. Jeez, why hadn't she thought of it earlier?

"Can you do a treble clef?"

"What the hell is a treble clef?" Marco asked.

"Sure can." Jack nodded. "Where do you want it?"

"What the hell is a treble clef? Is it dirty? It sounds dirty."

"It's a symbol in music," Brandy explained and then turned her attention back to Jack. "How about on my upper back, shoulder area?" She reached over her shoulder and patted the spot. "Here."

"Sounds good to me." He went behind the counter and grabbed some papers. "Fill these out and we'll get started in a few minutes. I'm going to run into the back and get some things set up."

Brandy took the papers from him and went to sit down to fill them out.

"Are you sure you want to do this?" Marco asked, kneeling beside her.

She glanced up and smiled, her heart pounding with nervous excitement. "Yes. I am."

"Why?" He shook his head, his browns drawn together. "Look you already did the makeover, which was drastic enough. But a tattoo is permanent—you can't change your mind about it. I just don't want this to be about you having a rebellious streak."

"It won't be. I'm a music teacher, and getting a music-related tattoo is totally in line with what I love. Whether you realize it or not, you and Val both have done me a favor." She bit her lip and spun the pen between her fingers. "You've helped me realize I've been smothering a side of me that I didn't want to admit existed."

"I understand."

His gaze took on a new light—something flickered in his eyes that made her think there were still things she didn't know about this man. Things she hoped he'd share someday.

He gave a slow nod. "You sure you won't regret this?"

She reached out and grabbed his hand, giving it a squeeze. "I promise you this is something I won't regret."

As she spoke the words she realized the double meaning to herself. No. She would never regret getting a tattoo or getting involved with Marco.

He seemed to almost read her thoughts. His eyes darkened and he reached out and squeezed her hand. "Okay. Then I'm behind you one hundred percent."

His words sent a calm through her, even while a shiver ran through her at his gentle touch.

"You ready, kitten?"

Both she and Marco swung their heads to look at Jack as he came back out front.

Drawing in a deep breath, she gave a small nod. "Ready."

"I'll come in with you."

Relief seeped through her as they walked back to the tattoo

chair. As much as she wanted this tattoo, she didn't really relish the idea of doing it alone.

"All right, I'm gonna need you to take your shirt off," Jack instructed.

Brandy gulped and wrung her hands together. "And my bra, too?"

Jack grinned and gave a loud laugh that cracked through the air in the tiny room.

"Only if you want to, kitten. Otherwise, you can just lower the straps."

Her cheeks burned as embarrassment swept through her. Before she could look like any more of an amateur, she gripped the bottom of her shirt and tugged it over her head.

Chapter Ten

M arco's blood rushed through his veins at the sight of the bra she wore today, a purple, satiny-looking thing. He snuffed out the irritation that came with the knowledge that Jack was also getting an eyeful.

"So how big are you thinking you want the tattoo to be?" Jack asked, all business.

"Umm. Not too big. No more than a couple of inches."

"Okay. And how well do you tolerate pain? Personally," he rushed on. "I don't think a tattoo is painful, but some people straight up lose it."

She didn't answer right away and by the way her eyes widened and her face paled, Marco could tell she was freaking out a bit inside. Maybe she hadn't thought the pain part through.

But she straightened her spine and said, "I do all right."

"That's a good girl." Jack cleaned the area and then put down the small transfer design that had the treble clef on it. Next, he smeared some Vaseline-like substance over her skin and then turned on the needle. A soft buzzing filled the room.

Marco held his ground, telling himself not to step forward and grab her hand for support. She probably resented the fact that he'd followed her in here as it was.

Jack dipped the tip in ink and then brought it just above her shoulder. "Here we go. I'm just going to do a small line first, okay?"

"Okay," she whispered.

Marco kept his eyes on her face, watching her closely. The minute the needle made contact with her skin she flinched, but her jaw hardened.

Jack moved the needle down to draw the tattoo and her jaw became more rigid, even as her face drained of color.

Swearing under his breath, he stepped forward and took her hand. Her fingers immediately wrapped around his in a death grip.

"You doing okay?" he asked quietly.

She gave the tiniest of nods and after a few minutes asked, "Are we almost done?"

Marco shook his head and grimaced. "We just got started. Just try to relax, princess. The pain will fade."

The fingers around his hand tightened. "Okay. I can handle this."

And she did, he realized thirty minutes later when Jack was finishing up and taping gauze over the new tattoo.

Her cheeks were flushed from the combination of adrenaline and pain. There was a hint of pride in her eyes. A pride he knew was mirrored in his own gaze.

He leaned down and brushed his lips across her ear. "You did great, princess."

Her responding laugh sounded a bit manic. "Are you kidding me? I kept hoping I'd pass out because it hurt so darn bad." She winced. "Unfortunately it never happened."

Marco gave a soft laugh and helped her to her feet. She pulled her shirt back on and then turned to face him.

Damn, this chick was amazing. Incredible. So sexy. A constant surprise. His blood pounded hard through his veins and he had the same kind of rush as if he'd been the one getting ink. Brandy did this to him.

Maybe she felt it too, because she stared intently at his mouth for a moment, then asked huskily, "Could I use the bathroom?"

"You'll find it out front."

Jack's comment was another reminder they weren't alone, bringing Marco right back to reality.

"Thanks, I'll be back in a minute."

After she'd hurried back up front, he glanced over at Jack and smiled.

"Thanks for doing that, man."

Jack's lower lip moved over the top one as he shook his head and shrugged. "Not a problem. She handled it pretty well."

"I thought so." He glanced back up front and gave another quiet laugh.

"So... what's going on? You getting serious about the chick?"

Marco's brows drew together as he thought about the question. And a helluva question it was too.

"We just hooked up a few days ago," he replied ambiguously, not ready to admit he was in way over his head.

"Yeah, I hear ya." Jack went back to cleaning up the room but kept up the conversation. "That's how Trish and I started. Met at a bar, had a complete fuckfest for a couple of days, and next thing I knew we were getting married while parachuting."

"I remember that. I'm still a little pissed you didn't invite me to the wedding."

Jack guffawed and slapped him on the back. "Yeah. Like you'd jump your ass out of a plane."

"No. I wouldn't. I'm not *that* crazy."

"Not crazy, man, it's called living life." Jack's attention slid past him, and Marco turned to see Brandy in the door.

"So how much do I owe you?" she asked, reaching behind her to brush her fingers over the makeshift bandage.

"I got it."

She turned to Marco, her eyes widening. "Oh, you don't have to—"

"I got it," he insisted and caught her chin between his fingers. He lowered his head to drop a soft kiss across her lips.

Her eyelids, which had fluttered shut the minute his mouth touched her, blinked back open. The blue of her eyes seemed extra bright, her pleasure and desire for him making her gaze sharper.

Jack cleared his throat. "You can come up front and pay when you're ready, Marco. I'll be up there."

"Thank you," she finally said quietly.

"You're welcome."

"We still have an entire stock of fliers to distribute."

"Ah, yes we do." He touched her cheek. "Wanna grab some lunch first?"

"Mmm. Yeah." She wrinkled her nose and smiled. "I'm kind of craving one of those burgers from *Dante's* actually."

He laughed and led her upfront. "Nice. Way to keep the profit in our pocket."

The ringing of the phone woke him. Marco slid his arm out from under Brandy and rolled over to answer it.

He blinked at the clock, which read seven-thirty in the morning. "This better be good," he muttered.

"Hey, it's Val."

"Val?" He yawned and ran a hand through his hair. "You don't have food poisoning again, do you?"

"Er, no. I just wanted to give you a heads-up."

"On?"

"On Brandy's birthday."

"Yeah? When is it?"

"Today."

He sat upright and glanced over at Brandy who was sprawled out over more than half the bed and snoring.

"Shit, really? How do you know?"

"Yesterday we were discussing the stigma of being thirty and not being married. She mentioned the big day was today for her."

"Damn."

Brandy had mentioned something about that, the night they'd first met. But hell, remembering birthdays had never been his forte.

"Don't sweat it. Sebastian and I ordered lots of food and a cake and we'll give her balloons and shit."

"And shit, huh?" He gave a soft laugh. "Thanks, Val. I owe you."

"Hell yeah, you do. Anyway. She's a little vulnerable about the thirty thing, so make her breakfast in bed or something."

"I can probably do that." He yawned. "Okay, see you in a bit."

He clicked his phone shut and swung his legs out of bed.

Brandy stirred next to him, but didn't wake. She thrust one leg out from under the sheets as she snuggled her cheek deeper into his pillow.

Moving as quietly as possible, he pulled on his jeans and walked into the kitchen. He dragged his hands over the stubble on his face and opened the fridge.

Shit.

The view that met him showed his food supply was in serious decline.

He could always cook her another bratwurst. She'd seemed pretty thrilled by it the first time. But it didn't really seem like a very special birthday breakfast. Not to mention that he only had coffee—no tea.

Hell. Maybe he ought to just run down to the small store on the corner. He could pick up something and maybe even get a card. Chances were he couldn't get much, but at least he could get *something*. Dust off his creative gene a bit.

The desire to please her, to surprise her, came on suddenly and strong. To see the happiness in her eyes and have the reward of her curled up in his arms afterward. She deserved this. This and so much more.

He grabbed his keys off the banister and headed out the door.

Brandy woke alone in Marco's bed. She pushed the sheet off her and sat up and looked around, her brows drew together as she yawned.

Her mind was still foggy, but something pricked in the back of her head. Something she should be remembering. The fog cleared and she leaned back against the pillows, staring at the ceiling.

Today was her birthday. The big 3-0. She waited for the panic and disappointment to sweep through her. The near desperation she'd always felt when she thought about hitting that landmark age and not being married.

She waited for the familiar emotions to come, but they didn't. In their place was a strange sense of relief. An unusual calm. Thirty. It was just a number.

So what?

When she thought about her options—being married to Gordon, or having what she had right now with Marco, it was all too clear which side of the coin she preferred.

She climbed out of bed, more resolute with every passing second.

"From now on everything changes," she muttered. "How I view myself, and my life. If I want to have a little fun, then, darn it, I will."

"Are you talking to yourself?"

Marco came down the hall, a tray in his hand and an amused grin on his face.

"Yes, and I do it quite often." She stretched her arms above her head and eyed the tray curiously. "What have you got there?"

"Breakfast," he closed the distance between them and dropped a kiss on her mouth. "But not just any breakfast, your birthday breakfast."

Lightheaded from his kiss, it took a second for his words to penetrate. She stepped back in surprise.

"You knew it was my birthday?"

He opened his mouth and then shut it again, giving her a rueful smile. "I remembered you said it was coming up, but I admit, Val had to tell me that it was today."

"I'd hardly expected you to know the date." She looked down at the tray in his hands and grinned. "What is all this?"

He shrugged. "Some of the foods that I know you like. Now back in bed, princess. That's part of the deal."

Brandy giggled and hurried back to bed, sitting up against the headboard and putting a pillow on her lap.

Marco set the tray on her lap and her breath hitched as she noted the single rose on the tray, and the card beneath it.

She hadn't heard him leave, but Marco must have left the

house to get this. She found herself momentarily choking up at the simpleness of the gesture. The sincerity in it.

She picked up the rose and breathed in the sweet scent, closing her eyes.

"I know the food is a little random..."

Food? She hadn't noticed the food with the rose and card. She opened her eyes again and really took note of what was on her plate.

"Bratwurst and a waffle. Yummy. You've been busy." She laughed and reached for the card, pulling it from the envelope.

She scanned it and then giggled, glancing up at him again. "Happy Birthday, Mom?"

He gave a guilty grin and pointed to the card. "No, you see what I did there? I crossed out the mom part and put your name." He gave a chagrined laugh. "Sorry, it was the only birthday card they had left at the mini-mart."

But he'd still bought it for her and had made her breakfast. Over the years she'd been given just about any gift possible for her birthday. There was nothing she hadn't been offered, nothing she couldn't have had.

And yet this...this beat it all. Tears pricked behind her eyes. She blinked rapidly and drew in an unsteady breath.

"I'm so...touched. Thank you, Marco."

"I know it's not much—"

"Stop it." She lifted her head and met his hesitant gaze. "It's everything."

Pleasure and relief flickered across his face and then he leaned down to cup her cheek.

"Happy Birthday, Brandy."

· · ·

"I've been eating all day." Brandy pushed aside her half-eaten slice of cheesecake and groaned. "You guys have been spoiling me."

Marco glanced over from where he'd just filled a beer for a customer. The bar crew had just done a few small things, and yet she still seemed pleased.

More than pleased. She was on cloud nine. Her smile hadn't dimmed all morning, her eyes as bright and eager as if it were Christmas.

"You love getting spoiled by us. Admit it." Val scooped another bite of cheesecake into her mouth and grinned.

"You're right. I do. Though I should probably invest in some treadmill time or something after this."

"Exercise is overrated." Marco walked back over to her, smiling slightly. "Especially on your birthday."

"Hey, I like the way you think."

He touched her shoulder. "You about ready to clock off?"

"Clock off?" Her eyes widened and her tongue darted out to catch a crumb from the corner of her mouth. "Didn't I just get here?"

"You've been working all morning, princess."

She looked up at the clock above the bar and she gave surprised laugh. "Wow, you're right. My entire shift has passed." She slid off the bar stool and placed her hands on her hips. "Are you staying late?"

"A little bit. I promised Val I'd stay later so she could take you out."

"You're taking me out?" she turned back to Val had just finished off her cheesecake. "Where?"

"Another little educational day." Val waggled her eyebrows. "It's called waxing 101."

"Waxing?" Brandy repeated a bit uneasily. "Like ripping out the hair on my body waxing?"

"One and the same."

"Oh. Well then."

"I had nothing to do with this and if you want to say no, I'll totally back you." Marco's grin widened.

She tilted her chin and made a face. "If I could handle a tattoo yesterday, I can certainly handle a little eyebrow waxing."

"That's right." Val hurried over. "I totally need to see your tattoo."

Brandy spun around and tugged her shirt down in the back, showing Val.

"Sweet. It looks good." She glanced up at Marco with a raised eyebrow. "And she didn't faint?"

"No, she did great." Marco laughed and shook his head.

His gaze connected with Brandy's and she gave him a soft, intimate smile.

"Real great," he repeated gruffly.

"Good." Val looked from one to the other, a speculative look in her eyes. "Well, she'll do just fine with the wax I'm guessing."

Marco turned back to the bar. "Sebastian and I can hold down the fort. Go on and get your wax on, ladies."

"I'll be out in the car," Val said, and hopped off the bar stool, striding out the door.

Brandy hesitated and then approached him on the other side of the bar. "Thank you, Marco."

"No problem. Just come back when you're done and we can head out." He set down the bar towel. "Maybe go out for a nice birthday dinner if you want."

She hesitated and then shook her head. "You know what?"

"Hmm."

"Just ordering a pizza would be perfect. I could use some downtime."

His eyebrows rose. She didn't want some fancy dinner? To be wined and dined on her birthday? He gave a brief nod.

"Pizza it is. See you soon, princess."

"See you soon."

"Hang on." He came around the bar to her. "You forgot something."

"I did?"

"Yeah." He cupped the nape of her neck and lowered his mouth to hers. Stealing a quick, but all too thorough kiss.

He lifted his head, the blood in his veins pounding twice as hard.

"There, now you're set."

"I want your help with something," Brandy murmured to Val who sat in the corner chair of the waxing room while the Esthetician continued to spread warm wax over Brandy's eyebrows.

"Oh yeah? With what?" Val asked, turning the page to a magazine.

"I want to do a strip tease for Marco."

Val shut the magazine in a rustle of pages. "No kidding?"

"No kidding."

"You will close your eyes now," the woman who was about to rip out her eyebrows commanded with an unfamiliar accent.

Brandy shut her eyes. "I thought it would be a fun way to be...umm...well, thank him so to speak."

"That's one helluva thank you."

"Isn't it though?" Brandy's lips twitched. Jeez, this was like the epitome of bold for her.

The Esthetician pressed some kind of paper over the wax and patted it down.

A strip tease. The idea had hit her as they'd driven past

some of the casinos and she'd stared at the billboards of sexy showgirls.

"So is it something you can help with? Or should I go download a video?"

"Good lord, don't find a video," Val pleaded. "I can help. I used to strip a few years ago."

"Now," the lady interrupted. "It may hurt since it is your first time waxing."

Brandy drew a deep breath in. Nothing could hurt as much as the—*holy hell*! She jerked against the reclined chair, half convinced the woman was ripping her face off.

"There. Not so bad?" The woman frowned. "Oh wait, there is blood. One moment."

Val stood up and walked over, looking down at her. "Oh yeah there is. But damn, check out that arch. It looks great. Your eyes just pop now."

"You used to be a stripper?" Brandy gripped the edge of the chair and forced herself to take deep breaths in.

"Yeah. The money was fantastic." Val looked down at her brows, a small frown on her face.

"So is that it? Are we done with that side?" Brandy asked hopefully.

"Usually they get the tweezers out and pluck. Now that's the part that hurts a little," she warned. "But you'll do great."

That's the part that hurt—the tweezing? So what the heck was that she felt with the waxing? A tickle? Brandy closed her eyes and sighed.

"So when did you want to do this striptease?" Val asked.

"You have much eyebrow. Like cousin Mildred." The muscles in Brandy's body went rigid as the Esthetician descended upon her with the tweezers.

"Tonight." She grunted as the first hair was jerked from her eyebrows. "Is that even—ouch—possible?"

"We can do it. Suck it up, Brandy. If you got a tattoo you can do this," Val said with little sympathy. "Besides it only gets worse from here."

"What gets worse? The waxing?"

"Yeah. If you really want to do this striptease thing then I have one word for you, kid."

Brandy opened her eyes and swallowed hard. She wasn't too thrilled by the wicked gleam in Val's eyes.

"And what would that word be."

Val tossed her hair back and grinned. "Brazilian."

Marco pushed through the door to the front of the bar and glanced around.

"The girls back yet?" he asked, though not seeing them in the bar was a clear indication they weren't.

The place was still dead. They hadn't had a customer in almost two hours.

"Nope." Sebastian looked up from the flat screen where the weather forecast flashed across. "Hey did you ever find out who Brandy was? You know, after that little comment Val made yesterday?"

Marco blinked and shook his head. How the hell could he have forgotten about all that?

Oh yeah. He'd been too busy getting a hard-on over Brandy and then screwing her silly.

"Hmm. There's got to be a way to find out. If it's really that obvious."

"True." The back of his neck tingled with a premonition as if he were better off not looking it up.

Sebastian slapped his hand on the counter. "Did you try and Google her?"

"Google her. Why the hell didn't I think of that earlier?"

He shook his head. "Just type in her name? You think?"

"Of course." Sebastian gave him an incredulous look. "Have you no brains in you at all? You have all her paperwork in the office. You could have done a background check on her by now."

"Damn, you're right. I've obviously been thinking with the wrong head." Marco dumped a water glass into the sink. "You are a genius."

"Yes, I quite think so myself."

"I'll go grab the paperwork and hop online to see what I can find."

"Whoa. Hold on a minute."

"What?" Marco stopped, halfway to the door to the back and turned around. Sebastian was staring up at the TV again.

"I don't think that'll be necessary," Sebastian murmured quietly.

At his friend's tone, the hairs on the back of Marco's neck lifted. He turned around, almost afraid of what he would see, and then lifted his head to the screen.

Chapter Eleven

I t was Brandy. She was on TV.

She was leaning against Gordon who had his arm draped possessively around her.

She was wearing that same damn cat shirt! No, wait, it was different. This one had a cat playing the piano.

"She went back to him." The words fell from his numb lips, and he gripped the bar so hard his knuckles turned white.

"Is that the fiancé?" Sebastian gave him a quick look. "She couldn't have gone back to him. She's been with you the whole time. Besides, as of yesterday, she looks nothing like that woman on TV."

Marco stared at the screen, watched Gordon lean down to kiss her and his blood pressure shot through the roof.

"Let me just check something." Sebastian walked around the bar and reached for the remote to adjust the volume. "There, now you can hear. No, she didn't go back to him. This is old footage."

Old footage.

Marco sat down on the stool and continued to stare at the screen, listening to the reporter.

"Brandy Summers disappeared Friday in the late afternoon from this restaurant," the reporter stated and gestured to the restaurant behind her. "Reports of her being abducted by a man on a motorcycle are unconfirmed at this time."

"Abduct—" Marco broke off, his voice shaking. "Abducted? What the hell? They think *I* abducted *her*? And it wasn't from a restaurant, she came running out of that shithole chapel!"

"Shh!" Sebastian waved his hand, his wide eyes glued with obvious anticipation to the television. "I'm trying to hear this."

Gordon snatched the microphone from the reporter and the cameraman zoomed in on him.

"I'm making a plea for anyone who may have seen or heard from Brandy. She is a sweet woman, but she's a bit unstable."

"Ah, shit." Sebastian shot him an amused glance. "I didn't get the impression she was unstable, mate. Did you?"

"She's not unstable," Marco snapped and shoved a hand through his hair. Christ what a mess.

He should have insisted that Brandy call Gordon to tell him not to worry. That she'd needed time. Instead, he was harboring her like a god damn fugitive.

The news switched to a different image. A good-looking couple, probably in their late fifties, clutched each other's hands as they sat on a white, leather couch.

"Brandy," the woman spoke to the camera. "Your dad and I are terribly worried about you."

"Do they look familiar to you?" Sebastian asked, casting him a quick glance.

"No." Marco hesitated. Hmm. Now that Sebastian had mentioned it. "Wait. Maybe they do. I can't tell."

Well, it was obvious where Brandy got her legs from. He

watched as Brandy's mom crossed her legs in the surprisingly short skirt she was wearing.

"Brandy is extremely dependable. She's never done anything spontaneous in her life. And that's why we're so worried," the dad told the reporter. "This isn't like her at all. Today's her birthday, and for her not to call or come over...."

"If you could just at least call us and let us know you're okay." The woman took a shaky breath and pressed her hand to her chest. A sparkle of diamonds caught the light and reflected into the camera.

"Holy hell." Sebastian gave a long whistle. "Will you look at the size of that rock on her finger?"

"I see it." Marco narrowed his eyes.

Her parents obviously were the ones with the cash. This must be the money she'd been referring to when she'd jumped his bike on Friday.

The cameraman focused again on the reporter. "As you can see this is a trying time for both Gordon Perry and the Summers family. If anyone has any information on Brandy's whereabouts, please contact..."

"So what, her parents are utterly rich?" Sebastian asked as the announcer went on to give the details.

"I knew she must have some money, but this... damn." Marco shook his head. He could understand her getting cold feet and needing time to herself. But why hadn't she bothered to call her parents? They were obviously stressed out over her disappearance.

"Well. First off we'll insist the lass call her parents when she gets back." Sebastian started back around the bar and reached for the remote control again.

"*Wait.*" The screen changed and up came a snapshot of Brandy, with a nice little caption under it. Marco blinked, his pulse slowing and then speeding up again. "I don't believe it. There's just no way in hell...."

"What? What am I missing?" Sebastian ran back around the counter where the screen was more visible. "Shite! How did we miss that?"

It had to be a mistake. There was just no way—

"Brandy's *The Lingerie Heiress*?"

Marco glanced over at his friend. Sebastian's eyes were wide with excitement, and a huge smile spread across his face.

"Have you even heard of *The Lingerie Heiress*, Sebastian?"

"No, mate, I haven't. But it sure sounds impressive."

The tabloid name seemed vaguely familiar to Marco. He'd heard it in passing but never bothered to pay much attention. Why the hell would he?

The Lingerie Heiress.

They listened to the rest of the report on who she was and where the title Lingerie Heiress originated. Apparently, her parents owned *Sugar and Spice*, the massive lingerie chain.

After the report was over, Sebastian changed the station to a sports channel and set down the remote.

Marco shook his head, his mouth still half open. How was it even possible that someone like Brandy would be heir to a lingerie company? But more so, why hadn't she told him? Didn't she trust him?

Obviously not.

A sense of dread formed a heavy knot in his stomach and he swallowed hard. After everything that had happened between them in the past four days, and she'd never once even hinted at who she was.

"Well," Sebastian said brightly, casting him a quick glance. "This certainly puts a spin on things."

He couldn't even respond, just gave a grunt of acknowl-edgment.

There had always been clues. He'd just been too caught up to pay attention. From the first day he'd met her, to the first night when they'd ended up in bed together.

The sexy as hell garter belt he'd seen when she'd pulled out the key to the hotel. And then the parade of sinfully hot bra and panty sets—and those breasts in them.

Don't even go there right now.

He squeezed his eyes shut, taking a deep breath.

Why wouldn't this compute? That Brandy equaled Lingerie Heiress? And why hadn't she told him? The hurt and unease built in his gut.

"Are you upset?" Sebastian's quiet question cut through his turbulent thoughts.

"Wouldn't you be?" He got up and paced behind the bar. "I mean she's been living in my house since Friday, and I had no idea who the hell she really was." His lips twisted. "And for some reason, she didn't think it was important to tell me. Not only that, the damn media thinks I abducted her."

"That can be straightened out," Sebastian said with a wave of his hand. "And as to the rest, well, maybe she had her reasons."

"It'd have to be a pretty good reason," he muttered, not completely convinced.

"Well, you have to admit," Sebastian said quietly. "That you haven't been completely honest with Brandy about who you are either, Marco."

Marco's head jerked up and his eyes narrowed. "Because who I *was* is in the past. It's completely irrelevant and has nothing to do with who I am now."

"I'm not so sure about that." Sebastian sighed and looked away.

"*Drop it.*"

"It's dropped." Sebastian cleared his throat. "It is a little hard to believe, though. That she's...who she is."

Marco grunted again and then shook his head. "I knew she had money. She never hid that. But to find out she comes from a famous family and is actually dubbed the Lingerie Heiress—shit, Sebastian, that's just a little harder to swallow."

"It is," his friend agreed. "I'm just surprised nobody else figured it out. If they had, we'd have those bloody paparazzi all over the place."

"Val figured it out from the get-go. But apparently, she was just interested in tormenting us, not outing Brandy. She should have told us."

"Yes, but it's Val. She lives to torment us." Sebastian sighed. "You okay there, mate? You still look a bit shaken up. Would you like a shot of whiskey?"

"No, I don't want any whiskey. I want..."

Brandy.

With her clothes off so he could see that damn lingerie again. See the heiress in her element, kiss every inch of her body while demanding why the hell she hadn't confided in him.

Sebastian gave him a considering look. "You look a bit stressed. What's this really about, mate?"

Marco massaged the back of his neck, his brows drawn together. "We slept together."

"I figured as much."

"And we've done it a bunch of times since."

"Ah. Well then." Sebastian went silent for a moment. "That certainly puts a new light on things. You like the lass. Quite a bit it would seem."

"We're having sex. It hardly equates to a serious relationship." His response was unconvincing even to his own ears.

"Why not? It certainly could if you'd let it."

Irritation pricked deeper and Marco shoved away from the bar.

"I don't want to have this conversation. I just want to know why the hell she didn't tell me."

He headed towards the bathroom, seeing a few customers walk in, but knowing Sebastian could handle it.

He splashed water on his face and looked into the mirror. What was he going to say when he saw her? How would he react?

Okay, so she got cold feet at her wedding. So why was she here? Why didn't she just run home to mommy and daddy? To her expensive, posh life instead of just slumming with the boys who ran a bar?

The air locked in his chest as realization hit him. Because maybe that's exactly what she wanted. A break. To slum with the so-called bad boys who ran a bar.

The irritation slipped past that fine line and turned to anger. Was that truly her motive? God, talk about a serious mind fuck.

He slapped his hand against the mirror and swallowed the sharp bite of hurt.

You're an idiot, Marco. To ever think there was more there. She doesn't give a rat's ass about who you are. You're just a glimpse of what it's like to be wild. You're her ticket to have a little fun.

And he'd better get that through his head because Brandy would be back any minute.

It still stung. Even a half hour after getting her eyebrows waxed and plucked into society's idea of perfection.

Brandy walked into the bar, actually slightly waddled due to the dull ache of her now freakishly bare genital area. It had taken a good twenty minutes to talk her into getting the Brazilian wax.

She regretted ever confiding her botched Nair attempt to Val because the woman had wielded it over her head as the main reason to get her southern region waxed. To 'fix things' and start with a clean slate.

She kept a hand covering her forehead as she headed straight toward the bathroom. She wanted to check to see if the redness had diminished at all.

"Brandy," Sebastian called out before she could reach the bathroom.

She winced and slowed to a stop, not removing her hand from her forehead as he hurried over to her.

"What's up?" she asked.

He blinked and shook his head. "Do you have a headache?"

"No." She didn't remove her hand. "So what's going on?"

He hesitated and stared at her.

"Why are you looking at me like that, Sebastian?"

His face filled with color. "Like what? I promise I'm not imagining you naked."

"*What?*"

He cleared his throat, his face going redder. "You should go speak to Marco."

Her mind reeled with confusion and it took a second before she could answer. "I need to speak with Marco? Now?"

"Yeah." He shoved his hands into his jeans pockets and sighed. "You do, luv."

What was going on? She gave a slow nod. "All right."

She stepped past him, her heart thudding a bit faster. Something had happened. Something had changed. But what?

Her mind raced through the possibilities and then landed on one. One that made her stomach about drop to her feet.

Crap, please don't let that be it.

She headed towards the back and then pushed into Marco's office.

He glanced up the moment she appeared in the doorway. As usual, just the sight of him was enough to send her pulse into overdrive and awaken all her girly parts.

"Hi," she said, hating the hesitation in her voice.

He didn't smile, and there was little warmth in the look he gave her.

Ugh oh.

"What's wrong with your forehead?"

Her forehead?

Oh.

She jerked her hand away from her eyebrows.

"Good god. What did they do to you?"

"Oh jeez. Is it that bad?" She hurried over to the mirror above the filing cabinet and groaned.

The perimeter of her eyebrows was still as red as it had been when she'd left the beauty shop.

"I had my brows waxed," she muttered.

"And do they normally look like that afterward?"

"I don't know, Marco. I've never had them done before today. But, I have sensitive skin." She sighed and folded her arms across her chest. "Sebastian told me I should come to talk to you."

Marco's gaze once again became hooded. "Did he now?"

"Yes." She held her breath, hoping he wouldn't say what she thought he was going to say.

"Why didn't you tell me who you were?"

And there. He said it. The air hissed out from between her teeth and her heart skipped a beat.

The accusation in his eyes didn't surprise her, but the hurt in his voice did.

"I tried to," she said lamely.

"When? When did you try and tell me, Brandy?"

She sighed and looked away. "The other night."

"You did?"

"We were just starting to...you know...go at it on your desk."

He was silent for a moment and then gave a short laugh. "You tried to tell me who you were when we were about to have sex?"

"Yes."

"*Not* the best time to have a chat. I'm pretty sure my mind was on one track at that point."

"Okay, I'm sorry. It wasn't the best time to try and bring it up," she agreed and turned to look back at him. "How did you find out?"

"Your parents and Gordon held a news conference on TV."

She gripped the edge of his desk as her knees threatened to give out.

"You can't be serious."

"I am. Completely. Sebastian and I saw the whole thing about an hour ago." He gave a hard shrug. "They haven't filed a missing person report yet, but you can tell they're getting close."

"Shoot." She winced and bit her lip. "I meant to call my parents. I just thought...."

"You were just having too much fun playing me for a sucker?"

"What?" Brandy reared back, her eyes widening. "Of course not. Look, after all that's happened between us, should it even matter who I am?"

His jaw clenched. "You tell me."

The room spun and for a moment she thought he meant to end it. Not that there was a lot to end. She'd known him an entire five days. But those five days had already changed her significantly. He had changed her.

She stared at him, watching the uncertainty and anger flicker in his eyes.

"I'm still the same person I was when I left here an hour ago, Marco."

"No, you're not. When you left you were just a damned choir teacher." He scowled. "And now you're some rich heiress to bra-selling parents."

"Bra-selling parents?" She lifted an eyebrow and gave a soft laugh. "Oh, god. If they could hear you reducing them to bra-selling parents right now they'd have a conniption. *Sugar and Spice* is the fastest-growing lingerie chain in North America. We just opened our first store in Europe."

His fingers curled tighter around the pen in his hand. "Well. You must be worth a pretty penny then."

"Yes. I am. Is that a problem?" Brandy's anger fully ignited at his petty response.

The tic in his jaw was his only reply. And then it became all too clear.

"You're an idiot," she said softly and shook her head.

"What did you say?"

"You are..." She pushed the door shut and then walked behind the desk, sliding onto his lap. "An idiot."

Obviously, he didn't think he was worthy of her now that he knew who she really was.

She breathed in his spicy scent, watching the mix of heat and hesitation in his gaze.

"Look. I've known who you were since the moment we met," she said, cupping his cheek and stroking her thumb over the stubble. "And it doesn't have any effect on how I feel about you. I would hope you could say the same about me."

She felt the tension in his muscles ease, before he caught her wrist, placing a kiss on the inside.

"Brandy," his voice grew husky, but the hesitation still remained.

"You know what? Just stop thinking about it so hard and kiss me." She brushed her lips across his.

His arms tightened around her and she opened her mouth to his seeking tongue.

She parried the slick intrusion by stroking her tongue against his. Heat built with each passing second in her belly, before sliding low between her legs.

He pulled back and brushed a kiss against her neck.

"You know," he murmured. "They think I kidnapped you."

Her pulse increased steadily as his lips brushed an ultra-sensitive spot.

"Who does?"

"Your parents. Gordon. Everyone."

She blinked, his words finally sinking in and she jerked away. "But that's ridiculous! If anything I kidnapped you."

A smile played around his mouth. "That's what I said. And something's fishy. Not once did Gordon mention the wedding in the interview. It was like your parents didn't know anything about it. He said you were last seen in front of a restaurant."

Her lips pressed together. Why had Gordon lied? She looked away and shook her head. It shouldn't come as a complete shock.

"My parents wouldn't have approved of it," she admitted. "That's probably why he didn't tell them."

"You need to call them, Brandy. I know you're trying to keep a low profile from Gordon, but your parents are worried. Sebastian and I were surprised to hear no one's recognized you yet—but how long can that go on?"

"I'm not worried about it. People never paid all that much attention to me anyway. Well, not until I started dating Gordon. And now with the new look, I'm even more unrecognizable." She twisted her finger around one of the curls in her hair. "Which is part of the reason I agreed to the makeover."

"And the other?"

She glanced back at him. Her heart thudded a bit faster. "Well, for myself. And to convince you to go to bed with me."

His nostrils flared, even as his smile stayed casual. "You didn't need a makeover." He shook his head. "You've been driving me crazy since the moment you jumped my bike."

"Really? In a good or bad way?" she asked, ridiculously pleased by his words.

"A good way." He ran the pad of his thumb across her bottom lip. "Now why don't you go call your parents?"

"I suppose I'd better." She slid off his lap, regretting the loss of warmth and intimacy. "I'm sorry, Marco. You're right. I should have told you earlier. It's just," she hesitated and then shrugged. "I'm having a lot of fun with you. You don't treat me the way everyone else does."

"And that's what you want? To be treated...normally?"

"Pretty much. It's why I picked a normal career. That and I love music." She lifted her head and gave him a brief smile. "Let me go make that call and then maybe we could head back to your house."

The sympathy and understanding in his gaze put a lump in her throat.

"Of course we can," he said after a moment. "Go call them."

"Okay." She drew in an unsteady breath, her belly warming with pleasure. "I'll be back in a few."

Tucking a curl behind her ear, she gave him one last tentative smile and then left the office.

Reaching into her purse, she pulled out her cell phone and moved to the far corner of the kitchen.

She crouched down between the bread rack and the walk-in freezer, not wanting anyone to overhear this upcoming conversation.

Her parents' phone barely rang once before her mom picked up.

"Brandy! Where on earth are you?" The relief in her mom's voice rolled in waves through the connection. "For the love of all things holy, do you have any idea what your dad and I have been going through?"

She bit her lip. "I'm sorry. I meant to call."

"Where are you? When Gordon told us that you ran out on him at the restaurant—"

"We had a fight."

Should she mention the wedding? Hmm. Probably not a good idea. She really had no intention of marrying or even dating Gordon again at this point.

"So I gather," her mom said. "Which I think is great. You know how I feel about him. In fact, I hope you dumped that loser on his pasty ass. I just wish you would have called us sooner."

Pasty ass.

Not for the first time, she questioned whether she might have been adopted. Her parents were just so outspoken, so raw, so...hmm. Almost like Marco.

"Brandy? Are you there?"

Brandy grimaced and snapped her attention back to her mom. Evil, stupid, tangents.

"Yes. Sorry."

"Where are you? Do you want us to send the plane to pick you up?"

Send the plane.

While most people would consider sending a driver outlandish, she'd grown up with *send the plane* if she strayed more than a few hours from home.

"I'm still in Nevada," she admitted. "And no, I don't need the plane. I need a break. I met someone—"

"You met someone?" And just like that the dynamics of the conversation changed. "Have you gone to bed with him yet?" Her mom laughed. "Wait, ignore me, I almost forgot who I was talking to."

Brandy bristled, but resisted the urge to get offended. "Mom—"

"I bet he owns a casino."

Try a bar.

"Mom—"

"Have fun with him, Brandy. Or her. Whoever it is. You're young. You need to experience life! Go out and party for once."

Brandy closed her eyes and counted to three.

"Why I'll bet you've never stepped foot into a bar in your entire life," her mom went on.

"Actually I have."

In fact I just had sex in one the other night. Brandy stopped herself before she could say the rest.

"Good. It warms a mother's heart to hear that. Anyway, my point is I want you to enjoy your time with this person. Maybe even get in some kinky sex—"

"For fuck's sake, mom, stop already!"

Another pause. "Brandy Elizabeth Summers. Did you just swear?"

Brandy winced. God she had. What the heck was happening to her? The Marco influence. Or wait, no, she'd learned that one from Sebastian. You got around those guys and you couldn't help picking up their habits.

"Sorry, mom. I just—"

"No don't apologize, honey. That's wonderful." She could hear the smile in her mom's voice. "This person is good for you. I can tell you're loosening up a little already."

Only her mom would think drinking and swearing were good traits. In moderation of course. Everything in moderation was her mother's motto.

"Look, I'm going to go." She sighed. "But will you do me a favor?"

"Sure. You name it."

"Tell the media you heard from me, and that I went on some spontaneous trip to the Mediterranean or something. Don't tell them I'm in Nevada." She gripped the phone tighter. "And whatever you do, don't tell Gordon where I am. If he calls, you can tell him the same thing. Just please... *please* don't tell him where I am."

"All right, honey. I won't. You just be sure to check in with us."

A pair of denim-clad legs suddenly appeared in front of her, and Brandy raised her gaze upward until she found Sebastian grinning down at her.

"Thanks, mom. I love you."

"We love you, too. Have fun, honey. Oh and use a condom."

Brandy ended the call and her cheeks heated with color.

"Having fun, luv?"

Chapter Twelve

"How much did you hear?"

"Not as much as I'd have liked." He winked and put out his hand.

"Good. Eavesdropping is considered in poor taste." She took his hand and let him help her up. "Thank you."

"You're welcome."

"So," she folded her arms across her chest. "I take it you know who I am now?"

"Yes, I have to say I do."

"And you're not really imagining me naked, are you?" She tilted her head and narrowed her eyes with amusement.

"Only for the briefest of moments." His grin broadened. "But I don't have a death wish from you or Marco."

Brandy's lips twitched. "So can I trust you to keep it quiet?"

He placed his hand over his heart and winced. "You wound me, Brandy. Truly you do. To think I'd utter a word to anyone."

She wrinkled her nose at him. "I didn't say you'd out me. I just had to cover my bases."

"Another baseball term?"

"Of course. So if anyone asks, no I am not the same Brandy as that heiress chick who ran off to the Mediterranean."

"You went to the Mediterranean?"

"No." She gave him a pointed look. "But that's what the media will be saying within the next few hours."

"Got it. Well, my lips are sealed," he promised and shoved his hands into his pocket. "Look, I came back to talk to you because I wanted to make sure you and Marco are still cool."

"Ah, Sebastian. You were worried?" she teased and started back toward Marco's office.

"A little." He stopped her, placing a hand on her shoulder before she could pass him.

"That's sweet." She glanced toward the office door. "We're fine, I smoothed things over. Though I think he was a little hurt that I didn't confide in him."

"He was," Sebastian said quietly. "I don't think you have any idea how good you are for him."

Her heart did a little flip, but she shook her head and tried to sound casual. "It's only been a few days. We're just having fun."

"Right. You both just keep telling yourself that." Sebastian smiled and stepped back, letting her walk by.

Brandy moved past him, her stomach knotting now as she questioned the truth in Sebastian's words.

Just having fun? Was that really all it was?

Porcelain exploded into hundreds of pieces as Gordon threw the seventeenth-century Chinese vase against the wall.

"Fuck!"

He thrust his hands into his hair and paced in front of the living room windows of his Hollywood home.

Fuck. Fuck. Fuck.

The Summers were lying through their billion-dollar teeth. Brandy needed time alone and had fled to the Mediterranean?

Bullshit!

Brandy didn't want to be found, by him or anyone else. It was obvious she'd asked her parents to cover for her.

He was running out of time. If he didn't come up with the money, he might as well pack his bags for that *long walk in the desert* his bookie had threatened him with.

Sweat trickled down the back of his neck and he eyed the broken vase with regret and guilt. He could have easily got a million at least for that. Not that it would have even made a dent in the money he owed.

He had to find Brandy. She was his only option. But how the hell did he find her? It was like she'd disappeared off the damn planet.

"Shit." Grinding his teeth together, he picked up his phone again and dialed an old contact.

"I need a favor," he snapped when the man answered. "I need help locating a woman and want you to track a credit card for me. Yes, I know it will cost me... Well, they fucking lied, I have plenty of money... Look, just do it."

He gave him the details and disconnected the call. With unsteady hands, he went to pour himself a shot of Jack Daniels.

Marco dumped their dishes from dinner into the sink. He cast a glance back down the hallway and wondered what the hell was taking Brandy so long.

"What are you doing in there?" he called out.

"I need to brush my teeth."

He grunted at her response and went to sit down on the

couch. The remote was just inches away on the table, and he reached over to grab it, flicking on the news.

Across the screen flashed an image of Brandy's parents; again speaking to the media. He turned the volume up until he could hear what was being said.

"Brandy? When are you going to the Mediterranean?" he asked, his mouth curving in amusement.

"I'm not. I just want everyone else to believe I'm there." Her voice grew closer.

He turned his head, expecting to see her in another one of his baggy t-shirts. He couldn't stop the strangled groan that escaped when he saw her.

"Do you like it?" she asked hesitantly. Each step closer to him displayed more of her body under the short, flimsy red negligee.

His attention first caught on those perfectly shaped legs to her toenails, now painted a dark red to match the lingerie.

Dragging his gaze back up his body, he locked on the hard pink nipples of her full breasts pressing against the see-through fabric.

"I thought you were brushing your teeth," he choked.

She grinned and placed a hand on her hip. "Well, yeah, I was doing that, too. You never answered my question. Do you like it?"

"Hell yeah, I like it." He swallowed hard and resisted the urge to just undo his fly now and ease the discomfort.

The lingerie was sexy, tiny, and looked expensive as hell. It had to have come from her parents' shop. Had she had it the entire time? Jealousy pricked deep as he realized why she likely had it.

"Do you wear that for Gordon?" he asked before he could stop himself.

"What? Of course not. Gordon and I had sex maybe a

handful of times, and I can guarantee you neither of us put any effort into it. It was awful. Kind of like the few times, I tried yoga."

Surprise took the place of jealousy, but he didn't dwell on it as she crossed to the couch and straddled his thighs.

"I picked this up at *Sugar and Spice* the other day during the shopping trip with Val."

He barely managed to lift his gaze from her breasts which were now in his face. "Before we'd slept together?"

"I was optimistic." She took his hands and slid them up her belly until they covered the soft fullness of her breasts. "Oh, god. Marco, I've needed this all day."

He kneaded her flesh, feeling her nipples tighten against his palm.

"You can say that again," he muttered and lowered his mouth towards hers. Brushing his mouth across her parted lips. "You're my Lingerie *Goddess*."

"Goddess? Really?" Her body tensed against him, and she pulled back. "That's not funny."

"What's not funny? Hey, wait a second." He grabbed her wrist when she tried to step away. "What's wrong? What did I say?"

Her cheeks flushed and she shrugged. "Nothing. I mean...it's just you don't need to call me a goddess, okay? I know what I am."

Confusion drew his brows together. "Oh yeah? And what are you?"

"I'm plain. I've got a little extra meat on my bones—"

"Stop it." His grip around her wrist tightened and he drew her forward, pulling her onto his lap. "Brandy, you are a sexy woman. Don't you have any idea what you do to me?"

When she didn't respond, he traced his thumb over the fast-beating pulse in her wrist.

"Brandy."

"I do, it's just," she grimaced. "You know who I am now. And how I grew up in the shadow of the Goddesses—the models for our lingerie line. I admired them. And I compared myself to them."

The air whistled out from between his clenched teeth as realization dawned.

"Why would you compare yourself to them?"

"How could I not? I was immersed in that world. God, it seemed like forever that I compared myself to *Sugar and Spice* models. I mean I figured out from a very young age I would never match up—"

"Jesus, Brandy, no one matches up. They're fucking supermodels."

"I know that. Now." She swallowed. "When I was a teen I decided to not even try. I knew I had the smarts to be whatever I wanted, but I doubted my looks."

"You shouldn't have."

"Maybe." She lowered her gaze. "But I remember the first time it hit me. That I was the ugly duckling heiress to a business that was created for beautiful women."

She wasn't ugly. He stayed silent for a moment, letting her finish what she obviously needed to purge emotionally.

"So I focused on my love for music and didn't worry about my looks so much. Downplayed my appearance in a manner that wouldn't draw attention to me."

Fuck that must have been a shitty way to grow up.

He brushed a soft kiss across the inside of her wrist and was rewarded when some of the tension eased from her muscles.

"I'm not sure why I just told you all that." She looked away. "I thought I'd stopped comparing myself to them years ago. I just don't really ever get called sexy. Definitely not a Goddess.... Wow, I'm really sorry. I freaked out on you."

"Jesus, don't apologize, sweetheart. I'm glad you told me." He shook his head and cupped her cheek with a gentle hand, turning her back to look at him. "Now promise me you will never hold yourself to that asinine standard again. You're the kind of woman any man would be proud to have on his arm." He pressed a hard kiss against her mouth. "And you *are* a Goddess."

"Thank you." She blinked quickly, but he'd already spotted the sheen of tears. "You know, I'm really glad I chose your bike to hijack last Friday."

"Me too." He gave a husky laugh, sliding his hand up her ribcage to cup the underside of her breast. "I'm glad you had the guts to do it."

"I am too," she admitted and tilted her head. "And you might be pleased to see what else I have the guts to do."

She pulled back and slid off his lap.

"Wait a minute, where are you going?" He reached for her again, but she'd already crossed the room.

"I want to try something," she called out and picked up one of the wooden chairs at the kitchen table.

"You want to try something?" he repeated and shifted on the couch, tugging at his jeans. "Now? Couldn't you try something later?"

"You'll like it. I promise." She grunted and adjusted the chair in her arms as she stumbled across the floor. It would have been comical if she didn't look so damn sexy in that red thing.

She dropped the chair in front of the couch and rubbed her hands together.

"Sit on it," she instructed.

"What?" He lifted an eyebrow and glanced at the chair. "I'm pretty comfortable right here—"

"I'm going to give you a lap dance."

Marco blinked, going one hundred percent hard at her

casual statement. Realizing he was stupid to even question her reasoning, he lurched off the couch and planted his ass onto the chair.

"All right, here's my lap," he patted his legs. "Feel free to dance."

"Now I want you to work with me here," she warned, clearing her throat. "I've been thinking about doing this after...well after that day first when you thought I was a stripper."

He opened his mouth, ready to admit he'd never actually thought she was a stripper, but then decided against it.

Hell, why ruin all her fun?

"Is that right?" he asked instead.

"Yes." She licked her lips and he could see the hesitancy and excitement flickering in her eyes. "Are you ready?"

"I was ready about a second and a half after you said lap dance."

She laughed before her expression turned serious again. "Okay. Let me just turn on some music."

"Are you sure you want to do this, princess? I'd be happy just having you naked and on top of me."

"I bet you would. But I spent an hour with Val getting a lesson on how to do this."

"You practiced on Val?" He lifted an eyebrow, finding it hard to imagine Brandy doing a kinky lap dance for Val.

"No." She rolled her eyes. "I practiced on Slasher—Val's boyfriend."

"Like hell you did," he growled.

"No, you're right. I didn't." She wrinkled her nose at him. "But it's nice to know you care."

He grunted, not wanting to admit just how much he did care.

"I knew you were bluffing."

"Sure you did." She hurried across the room to his stereo. "Actually, while I was getting waxed Val told me that she and Slasher split last night. Which is a bummer since apparently, he had a tornado tongue. Or something like that she said."

He gave a soft laugh and before he could respond, she started the music. A second later some straight-out-of-a-bad-porno music started going. Nice. He'd have to thank Val later for this sudden inspiration.

"Here goes nothing." She drew a loud breath in, before moving to stand in front of him.

He watched as she started making slow circular movements with her hips. Even though her execution was a little stiff and jerky, watching her run her hands up and down her thighs made the whole thing sexy as hell.

She leaned forward abruptly and placed her hands on the back of the chair on each side of his head. Her breasts were once again in his face as her lower body brushed against his erection through his jeans.

"*Brandy*." He gripped the edge of the chair, his jaw clenching.

"Mmmhmm?" She pushed his legs apart and then fell to her knees between them.

She moved her hands up and down his thighs, tossing her head and making the curls stand up a little higher.

The blood pounded through his veins, his breathing grew heavier.

His reaction to her dance must have been obvious because her confidence blossomed visibly. Her smile widened as she lowered her head and kissed him through his jeans.

The air hissed out from between his teeth and his hips lifted involuntarily from the chair.

"Mmm." She gave a soft laugh and then moved back up his

body, kissing his chest and moving oh so slowly towards his mouth.

Then her head rammed into his chin.

"Ouch!" Pain radiated down his jaw.

"Oh my god, I'm so sorry!" She pulled back and covered her hands over her mouth, her eyes wide. "It wasn't supposed to happen like that."

"Yeah, so I gather." He gave her a lopsided smile.

"Do you want some ice?" She brought her hands to her mouth. "Oh god. I didn't knock out any of your teeth, did I?"

He rotated his jaw and shook his head. "No, the teeth are fine."

"Okay." She lowered her hands and bit her lip. "Let me start the music again and I'll start over."

He stood up and shook his head. "I have a better idea."

Her perfectly formed brows drew together into a frown. "This wasn't a good idea?"

"It was a great idea," he murmured and scooped her up into his arms, ignoring her squeal of surprise. "But I have one that's a hell of a lot more geared for the birthday girl."

"But you've done enough for my birthday." She wrapped her arms around his neck and pouted. "I wanted to do something for you."

"You can another day," he promised. "Right now I want you in my bed." He stared at her mouth. "Beneath me, making those sweet little sounds you make when you come. And then I want you screaming my name."

"Oh. Well, that's certainly specific." He heard the shift in her breathing and her tongue darted across her mouth. "But you know what? I kind of like the sound of that idea."

"I thought you might."

He kicked open the door to his room and moved swiftly to

the bed. He braced one knee on the mattress and lowered her down.

She stretched her arms above her head and stared up at him with an intoxicating combination of desire and trust.

He set his other knee down so that he straddled her waist. Using his hands to bracket her ribcage, he moved his thumbs over the slippery red negligee.

"I really like this on you," he murmured and stroked up the swell of her breast.

"Good." The haze of desire in her eyes increased and her chest rose as she drew in a deep breath. Her lips parted on a sigh.

Somehow she managed to embody the ultimate temptation of sex and seduction, while at the same moment exuding vulnerability and innocence.

The blood in his veins quickened, and his throat grew tight with the need to touch her. He slid his hands down to her waist, catching the fabric in his hand and pushing it up her body until it gathered below her breasts.

Nudging her thighs apart with his knee, he moved to kneel between them. He leaned down and brushed a kiss over the curve of her belly.

"And I really like this." He snapped the string on the side of her panties. "But I think I'll like them even better off."

He curled his fingers around the string on each side of her hip and pulled downward. She lifted her hips, making it easier for him to draw the scrap of lace off.

"Jesus." His breath caught and his erection increased to a painful level. "You got more than your eyebrows waxed, huh, princess?"

She gave a soft laugh and lifted her head to look down at herself.

"Mmm hmm, and you'd better appreciate it, because doing that hurt like the devil."

"Hell yeah, I appreciate it." His words sounded husky to his own ears.

He cupped her smooth pussy possessively, sinking a finger into her slick heat.

"Oh." Her eyes drifted shut with the soft moan.

He watched her reaction as he slipped his thumb up to rub her swollen clit.

Her brows drew together, her breathing heavy. He bit back a groan and used a second finger to penetrate her.

Monitoring her pleasure, he adjusted the pressure with this thumb and murmured a husky, "Come for me, sweetheart."

Her hips lifted against his hand and she cried out, gripping the sheets. He kissed her belly, loving the tremors that rocked through her body from the orgasm.

Moving his mouth lower, he kissed his way toward the sweet taste that was becoming his addiction. He dragged his tongue over her pussy, before seeking out her clit.

"Marco," she gasped and squirmed beneath him. "What are you doing?"

He circled the sensitive flesh with his tongue again, knowing it would make her lose control. He just kept sucking and flicking her clit until she was riding his mouth and pleading for him to make her come.

She gripped his head, holding him to her as he answered her plea.

When she was limp, with her thighs trembling on either side of his head, he murmured,

"I was giving you an orgasm," he finally answered.

"But I," she groaned and then began to pant. "I'd already had one."

"Good. That means we have twenty-eight to go before

morning." He lifted his head from between her legs and grinned. "Thirty birthdays, thirty orgasms."

"I thought that was spankings," she protested weakly, even as her hips rocked again toward his mouth.

"Would you rather I spank you?" He kissed her clit again and hid a smile. "Or lick you?"

It was her birthday, if that's what she wanted, hell he'd have no problem indulging her.

The silence that followed stretched on.

Well, well, well.

"I want both," she finally whispered.

He sat up and moved to deftly flip her onto her stomach. When she gasped, he smiled and dragged her backward and across his lap.

Her little negligee was over her hips still, and her pale round ass waved like an invitation in his face.

He took a moment to smooth his palm over the soft skin, before lifting it again and then bringing it back down in a firm slap.

She made a low groan in her throat, but other than that made no protest.

So he did it again—harder this time.

Her hips lurched as if she were trying to get away, but her groan was all pleasure.

He smacked her again, this time with enough force to leave his red handprint on her cheek. The sight of it made him pause.

Her whimper was a pretty good indication she'd found her limit.

He kissed his fingers, before placing them on the red mark. Then smoothed his palm over the warm flesh, before sliding his fingers lower, past her cheeks and into the slit of her pussy.

He pushed them deep and groaned at the wet silk of her gripping him.

"More?" His question was gruff, as he waited for her to answer if she wanted more spankings.

It took a moment before she shook her head.

"I just want you, Marco," her voice cracked. "Inside me."

That was all he needed to ease her off his lap and into a kneeling position. He eased the gorgeous red gown up and off her body, leaving her completely naked.

Then, he went to grab a condom from the bedside table, before removing his clothes too.

"I want to try being on top."

Her words surprised him. Excited him.

"I think that's a damn good plan." He slid on the condom and laid back, waiting for her to take charge and go at her own pace.

A moment later, when she was sliding down onto his rock-hard dick, he wasn't quite sure he had the willpower to let her handle it all.

But then she started moving, her eyes glazed with pleasure as she rocked up and down on him.

Unable to resist touching her, Marco slid his palms up to cover her breasts and flexed his hips, driving himself deeper.

Soon they were at a steady pace, and she figured out exactly what she seemed like.

He licked his finger and then moved to touch her clit while she rode him. Her cry of pleasure and pussy clenching around him was his reward.

His eyes nearly crossed at the pleasure of how tight she became around him. Wanting to make her come again, he stroked her harder as she started to move faster.

"Marco," she whispered. "Oh my god, do you even know what you do to me?"

"Same thing you do to me, princess." And then he pinched her clit and sent her flying. "That's three? Or is that four?"

"I've lost track," she mumbled, eyes glazed with pleasure. "It's going to be an amazing and long night."

"You complaining?"

"Not even a little bit." She closed her eyes and continued her ride.

Chapter Thirteen

"We've had fifteen bands sign up for tomorrow's event," Brandy called out.

She dropped two empty pint glasses and a burger basket into the sink and stepped into the doorway of the back office.

Marco glanced up from his paperwork. "That's good, right?"

Her heart fluttered at the intimate smile he gave her. She was still exhausted from all the hot and heavy nights and figured surely she'd stop thinking about sex all the time. And yet all he had to do was smile like this to prove her wrong.

"That's *great*." She nodded. "Because if you think about it, each band competing will be bringing their own little support group of family and friends—all wanting to buy drinks and food."

He leaned back in his chair, pursed his lips, and gave a thoughtful nod.

She hurried on. "Also, that's exposing *Dante's* to a bunch of people who may never have heard of you guys before."

Rolling a pen between his fingers, he continued to stare at her. "Brandy, you have been so good for this place."

Her face flushed with pleasure.

"Thanks."

How had it only been a week and a half since she'd first jumped his bike?

The time with Marco and everyone at *Dante's Place* had been life-altering. She looked in the mirror every morning and tried to reconcile the woman she once was and the woman she had become.

"Is everything all set up for tomorrow night? Is there anything else you can think of that we need?" he asked.

Brandy walked all the way into the office and sat down on the edge of his desk.

"Well, it'll be tight staff-wise that night, but we'll make sure everyone who can be here will be. So we should be able to handle it," she hesitated. "But, still, you should look into hiring a couple more waitresses. I'm telling you, your business is going to double if not triple after this event."

His foot, which he'd kicked up on the desk, nudged her hip and he grinned.

"I'm on top of it, princess. I placed an ad a few days ago." He cleared his throat. "Besides, I know you won't be hanging out here with us forever."

Her bubble of happiness slowly deflated from the puncture wound he'd just inflected.

Was he already gearing up for her to leave?

The idea hadn't even crossed her mind. Or maybe it had, but she'd fiercely shoved it back into the cobwebs in the back.

"I'd better get back up front." She glanced away. "I just thought I'd give you the latest number."

He didn't say anything, but his mouth grew taut. Without another second's hesitation, she slid off the desk and left his office again. Pushing through the swinging doors to the front of the bar, she tried to ignore the ache in her heart.

You knew it wouldn't last forever. So you shouldn't get in a tizzy the minute he brings up that fact.

Besides, she had a life back home. Her thoughts turned to her classes that would start in the fall.

Who was she kidding? This wasn't who she was.

She could never give it all up to be a waitress. Sure it had its fun moments, but her heart was still in teaching. Taking a group of half-talented, half tone deaf students and getting a decent sound out of them as a whole.

Still. Would that mean the end of her and Marco? Would she leave here and have things just go back to...life as normal? Did she want that?

No. Not entirely.

She sighed and looked around. The bar was still empty with their last customer having left an hour ago. Sebastian and Val wouldn't be in for another couple of hours.

Light poured into the bar as the front door swung open and the silhouette of a woman was illuminated before the door closed again.

Brandy narrowed her eyes and crossed the floor to approach the woman who didn't look much older than some of her students. She wore baggy cargo pants, a tight tank top, and the aura of someone with a serious chip on their shoulder.

"Hi there," Brandy called out. "Do you mind if I check your ID?"

The woman, almost a girl really, gave her an appraising glance with dark eyes. She was a slip of a thing, barely five feet, but obviously confident with herself.

"I'm here to sign up for the Battle of the Bands," the girl said after a moment and lifted a flier that had been clutched in her other hand.

Nice how she skirted the issue of identification. Brandy drew herself up to her full height and cleared her throat.

Pulling out her teacher's tone, she asked again. "I'll need to see your ID first.

The girl's eyes narrowed before she began to dig in her purse.

Brandy blinked, the hairs lifting on the back of her neck. There was something familiar about the girl—those eyes.

"Here." The girl thrust her license at Brandy and then turned to look around the bar again.

Brandy took the plastic card from her and glanced down at it, looking over the license to shed some light on whether or not she might know her.

Her mouth parted in surprise, her heart pounding as she jerked her gaze back up to the girl's face.

"Elena?"

Marco's voice split through the silence at the other end of the bar. Elena grinned and strode past her to her brother.

"What's up, mi hermano?"

Brandy turned around to watch the young woman run full speed into Marco's embrace.

He wrapped his arms around her slight form, squeezing her tight. His eyes closed and a visible tremble racked his body.

"I told you not to come," he reprimanded her, but there was no anger in his voice.

"As if that would stop me." She pulled back and scowled, all affection vanishing. "How dare you, Marco."

Marco gave a weary sigh. "How dare I what, Elena?"

"Avoid us for so long. You haven't seen dad in almost two years. He's—"

"Dad doesn't give a shit about me anymore, Elena, and we both know it."

Brandy bit her lip and glanced toward the kitchen. This was obviously a conversation she shouldn't be sitting in on.

"He cares about you, Marco. You're both just being stubborn and proud, and it's ridiculous."

Right. Time to make an escape.

Brandy drew a quick breath in and moved toward the kitchen, hoping they wouldn't notice her leaving.

"Where are you going?"

No such luck.

She turned back and faced Marco and his question. "I thought I'd give you two a moment."

"Don't bother. Elena was just leaving."

"I'm not leaving, so deal with it. This is a public bar and I'm a paying customer." His sister folded her arms across her chest and lifted her chin.

"We have the right to refuse service to anyone."

"Oh stop it. Plus, I'm here to sign up for the Battle of the Bands."

Marco's jaw hardened. "You're in a band?"

"Umm, yeah, and have been for at least two years. I told you that last year when you called. Maybe if you came by once in a while it would stick."

"Elena, it's not a good idea."

"What isn't?" she challenged.

"Everything. You being here. Signing up for the Battle of the Bands."

"So, what? You going to throw me out? Your own *hermana?* Are you going to forbid me from signing up for the Battle?"

Marco sighed and jerked his glance up to meet Brandy's. The frustration in his gaze made her heart ache for him a bit.

She shrugged and shook her head. What could she say? She had no idea of the history between the two, but obviously, there was some kind of dispute between Marco and his dad.

"Where are you and the other girls staying?" he asked tersely.

"Girls?"

"The other band members."

"Oh." Elena tossed her hair and gave a broad smile. "They're guys. I'm the only girl in the band. And Phil and I have a room at the Excalibur."

"Phil?" he asked with deceptive calm.

"He's the drummer. We've been dating for five months."

Brandy watched Marco's brows draw together, then the flash of disbelief and outrage. Knowing he was about to go into big brother protective mode, she stepped forward and grabbed Elena's arm, and moved her toward one of the booths.

"We haven't actually been introduced. I'm Brandy, one of the waitresses here." She decided to not go into full disclosure on her identity as she sat down across the table from Elena and asked, "Are you hungry? Can I get you something to eat?"

"A little bit." Elena gave a half smile and then glanced at her nails which were painted a metallic purple. "I could eat. We ate these awful breakfast burritos a couple of hours ago and it totally didn't fill me up."

Marco stepped forward. "Brandy—"

"How about a burger? They're fabulous here."

"Sounds good to me."

"Brandy—"

"Marco," Brandy turned her head and gave him a furtive warning glance. "Why don't you ask Dave to grill up one of *Dante's* famous burgers and I'll go ahead and get Elena signed up for the Battle of the Bands."

He met her stare, his eyes flashing. He wasn't pleased, that much was obvious. Finally, he gave a terse nod and spun on his heel, walking back to the kitchen.

"Thanks."

Brandy turned her attention back to Elena. "For what?"

"For not letting him kick me out of the bar. He probably would've if you weren't here." Elena glanced up at her. "I called the house a couple of days ago and he told me not to come and see him. Then I found that flier for the Battle of the Bands and knew it was the perfect way to get him to see me."

Why didn't Marco want to see his sister? Brandy bit her tongue to avoid asking the question. It was evident that part of him was pleased to see her—the way he'd hugged her had been proof enough.

When she'd overheard the phone call that morning the same question had run through her head. And like that morning, she realized if she was meant to know then either brother or sister would talk to her about it.

"I'm sure Marco is glad you're here. Whether he wants to admit it or not is another thing," she finally said with a gentle smile.

"I know he loves me. And he loves dad, too. They're just too proud to apologize to each other." She shrugged and rolled her eyes. "But then they're guys. What can you do?"

Brandy's lip twitched. "Not a lot. So...what's the name of your band?"

"Bitches Brew."

Brandy's lips parted and she made a little whimper. "Oh. That's...nice. And what kind of music do you play?"

"Alternative metal type stuff."

"I see. And what role do you have in the band?"

"I'm the lead singer," Elena said with a smug grin. "The bitch. They chose me over thirty-eight other people who auditioned."

"Hey, that's great. Congratulations." Brandy paused. "You know, during the school year I actually teach choir at a private school in California."

"No kidding?" Elena leaned back in the booth and gave her a considering look that she was used to seeing on Marco. "Well, I did choir back in middle school. No offense, but it kind of sucked, so I quit and took woodshop instead."

Brandy laughed and shook her head. "You know, you probably just had a bad teacher. When you have a good one, I promise it doesn't suck."

"Maybe. I bet you're a good teacher. But you look kind of young to be one."

Oh lord, she could've kissed the other girl.

"Hope you're still hungry." Marco crossed the bar and set down a basket with a burger and fries in front of his sister.

Elena snagged a fry and ate it in two bites. "Mmm. The fries are delish."

"Wait until you try the burger. *Dante's* is famous for them." She smiled at Marco. "Your brother talked them up until I finally gave in and tried one."

"You know, if I recall," he raised an eyebrow. "It really didn't take that much convincing."

"Actually he's right. Thanks for the reminder."

"Sebastian and Val will be in any minute," Marco murmured. "I'll go count down the till."

"Oh, you know, I can do it." Brandy started to stand but he waved her back down.

"Stay, hang out with Elena since it's dead in here."

Her brows drew together and she gave him a hesitant look. "Are you sure?"

"I'm sure."

When he didn't immediately look away from her, she felt her cheeks warm.

Finally, she murmured a husky, "Okay. Thanks, Marco."

"No problem." He glanced back at his sister. "I'll see you ladies in a bit."

Brandy watched him go, her heart fluttering. When she looked back at Elena, the girl was watching her with open curiosity.

"So what's up with you two?"

Brandy stole a fry and shrugged, trying to appear nonchalant "What do you mean?"

"Are you guys screwing each other?"

The fry stuck in her throat. "What?"

"Are you sleeping together?"

Brandy nearly choked.

"Umm." Her cheeks burned and she stared at the table. How the heck did she answer that? Would Marco want his sister to know—

"Never mind. It's written all over your face." Elena laughed. "You absolutely are."

Brandy lifted her head, unsure whether the news would be upsetting to Marco's sister or not.

Elena picked up the burger and took a hefty bite. "Damn this is good," she muttered between chews. "You don't lie."

"Why did you ask about Marco and me?"

Elena shrugged and swallowed the food in her mouth. "I was just curious. I'm glad he's out getting out there again. Marco pretty much stopped dating after Anna. Though who knows what he's been up to the past couple of years."

Anna? Who's Anna?

Tension slipped through Brandy's muscles.

"You look kind of surprised, but seriously, I know he probably never mentions her anymore. But they dated for like three years while they were in school."

"Did they?" Brandy murmured, trying for a casualness she nowhere near felt.

"Yeah. But then she trashed his heart and ditched him for some guy with deeper pocketbooks." Elena leaned forward and lowered her voice. "She said Marco would never be able to financially support the kind of lifestyle she was used to. Can you believe that?" She shook her head and picked up another fry. "What a materialistic bitch."

"I'll say." Brandy nearly massacred the french fry in her hand.

No wonder Marco had been so weary of the fact she had money. Had been so slow to trust her. The poor guy.

She closed her eyes, not wanting him to come back out and find her all pissed off looking.

Never before had she experienced the need to kick someone's ass, and it was a little odd to be experiencing the sensation for the first time at thirty years of age.

"So," Brandy cleared her throat and opened her eyes again, eager to change the subject. "You really like this Phil guy you're dating?"

Elena nodded, but not before a slight hesitation. "He's pretty cool."

It was on the tip of Brandy's tongue to ask if they were 'getting it on' because surely Marco would love confirmation on that tidbit.

Then again, maybe that knowledge wouldn't be so welcome. He certainly hadn't handled the fact that she was even dating a guy very well.

"Sometimes I think he's a little immature though."

Brandy held her breath and waited for her to continue, surprised Elena was being so forthcoming.

"Sometimes he parties too much and gets a big head over the band thing."

Elena pushed her half-eaten basket of food to the side.

"You know how it goes. Women come up and flirt with him after a concert and he flirts back pretty hard." She folded her arms across her chest and scowled. "He says it's all part of the promoting aspect and getting our name out there."

"Hmm."

Brandy drummed her nails on the table and gave the other girl a closer look. Elena's words had been casual, but the flash of annoyance and vulnerability had lingered beneath the pretense.

"Well," she said carefully. "I guess you need to decide how much you're willing to put up with."

"Yeah." Elena's mouth curled downward and she looked away.

Brandy was willing to bet the girl had been told the same thing before, maybe by other friends. Because she didn't look surprised or even too upset.

"You ladies ready to head out?"

They both turned as Marco crossed the floor to them again.

"Did Sebastian show up?" Brandy asked, sliding out of the booth.

Marco winced and nodded. "Yeah. He's in the back."

Something about his tone made Brandy make a mental note to ask Marco later what was going on with Sebastian.

"So do you have your car here, Elena? I just have my bike, and Brandy and I rode in on that."

"Yeah, I have my car." Elena stood up from the booth and placed her hands on her hips, lifting an eyebrow in challenge at her brother. "Are you both game to ride with me?"

Brandy exchanged a quick glance with Marco. He gave a slight smile and nodded.

"Let's do it," he curled his hand over Elena's shoulder. "That way it'll give us time to talk."

"So are you mad?"

Marco, still drowsy from just getting the world's best blow job from Brandy, tensed at her unexpected question.

They lay in bed after a long day and an evening of traveling all over Vegas with Elena.

"No, I'm not mad," he said quietly after a moment. "I know I told her not to come, but of course she didn't listen. Elena's a stubborn young woman."

"Kind of like her brother."

"Hmm." His lips twitched. "Maybe."

"You're glad to see her." It was a statement rather than a question.

"Yes."

Seeing his sister again had knocked the wind from him, and thrown his balance off kilter.

It had hurt seeing her, but it had also been so incredibly wonderful.

Two years had gone by since he'd seen her in person, but in that time she'd grown up so much. Too much. The pain that swept through him settled in his gut.

"Would it be too personal for me to ask why you haven't seen her in so long?"

The tension in his body increased.

Yes.

"I had a falling out with my dad a couple of years ago," he replied, which covered about only a quarter of the story.

But what could he say without spilling all the sordid details of the past few years? Truth be told, he just tried to ignore it.

Never think about it. Because when he did it just ripped the band-aid off a wound that would never heal.

"What happened between you and your dad?" She caught his chin gently and turned his head so he had to look at her. "Will you share with me?"

She asked too much. He didn't share it with anyone. Only

Sebastian knew.

"Brandy..."

"Please, Marco."

His chest rose from the deep breath he drew in. How much could he tell her without baring his soul?

"We had a falling out...over my career choice. He pretty much told me to get lost and stay away from Elena." He gave a grim smile. "Thought I was a bad influence."

"Oh my gosh." Sympathy flickered in her eyes. "That's terrible. Why would he do that? Just because he didn't like the idea of you opening a bar?"

"For the most part." His mouth twisted.

But then he couldn't really blame his dad for reacting the way he did. His son had given up a job as one of the best damn defense attorneys in the state of Nevada to open a bar instead.

How would Brandy react if he'd said those words aloud to her? If he'd filled in the blanks.

She'd probably keel over in shock. He knew when they'd met she'd written him off as a kind of a bad boy who lived to have fun—little did she know he was the man who used to defend those guys.

The thought of his former career sent a wave of nausea through him. He rarely thought about it. Preferred to stuff that part of his life back in the emotional closet where it belonged.

She didn't need to know about his past. It had nothing to do with where he was today.

Besides, right now when she looked at him there always seemed to be a bit of respect there and maybe even some hero worship. He'd hate for that to be replaced with disgust, with accusation when she found out what had happened.

"Marco, I'm so sorry." She dropped a kiss on his chest. "I'm glad Elena ignored you when you told her not to come."

"Me too." He closed his eyes and tightened his arms around

her. She snuggled deeper into the curve on his body.

He stroked her back, pushing all thoughts of who he used to be out of his mind and focusing on the woman in his arms.

"Elena really likes you, you know."

"Does she?"

"Yes. It's kind of shocking. She's generally pretty bitchy and wary of other women." He hesitated. "Has been since mom took off with a neighbor when Elena was only twelve."

"Ouch." Brandy lifted her head to look at him. "That must have been horrible for you both."

He shrugged, the years of anger and pain had long since faded to a dull ache. One he rarely bothered to acknowledge.

"She would never have won any mother of the year awards anyway. Spent more time drunk than sober." He closed his eyes to hide the possible bitterness reflected there. "We were probably better off without her. And dad did a great job raising Elena and me."

Brandy didn't respond, but showed her compassion by dropping another kiss on his chest as her arm tightened around him.

"I'm sorry," she finally said. Then, "So what was going on with Sebastian tonight?"

Marco drew in a deep breath, grateful for the change of subject.

"Bitter divorce stuff. It's really fucking with his head," he hesitated. "And then last night he took home another ditzy blonde from the bar. I think he regretted it."

"Does he do that a lot? Take women home?"

"Not a crazy ass amount, but I'd say there's been at least a handful since his wife filed for divorce."

She sighed. "Poor Sebastian. He's always so funny, but sometimes... I just sense this sadness in him."

"Yeah, I have too." He grunted. "But the Battle of the

Bands tomorrow will be a good distraction for him."

"Yes, it sure will. Speaking of, your sister is really excited about the competition."

"So I gathered from our conversation at dinner." He paused. "You don't think it's a conflict of interests? Letting her band compete when she's my sister?"

"It would be if you were judging, but the audience judges. And no one actually knows you're her brother."

"True. Do you think they'll suck?"

"Marco!" She swatted his stomach and giggled. "I have no idea. Let's hope not. Because I'll be honest with you, I'm a tough critic."

"I'll bet you are Ms. Choir Teacher." He chuckled, then yawned. "We'd better get some sleep. We're pretty much pulling a double tomorrow."

"It'll be worth it," she murmured. "*Dante's Place* is going to be the most popular bar in town after tomorrow night."

"Yeah, well hopefully we get some responses to the ad."

Earlier today he'd brought up the fact that she would eventually stop waitressing for them. It was a foregone conclusion.

He'd tossed it out as a feeler, almost hoping she'd declare that she had no intention of quitting.

Instead, she'd muttered something about having to go up front and had completely evaded the topic.

He sighed and stroked his hand down her back. That had sucked a little. More than a little. The last thing he wanted to think about was Brandy leaving him.

His brows drew together. She'd gone awfully quiet now. Had she fallen asleep?

"Good night," he said quietly on the off chance she still lay awake.

There was no response for a moment, then she whispered, "Good night."

Chapter Fourteen

The flare from the match briefly lit the motel room. Gordon held the flame to the tip of his cigarette and then waved it out.

He scowled and sat down on the edge of the bed with a shudder, biting back a groan.

Who knew what kind of germs and body fluids had been left behind on the bedspread from the previous guests?

He took a long drag and closed his eyes.

For the last year, he'd tried to hide his vices while dating Brandy. Never having more than an occasional smoke or drink at a party.

He'd tried to keep his image squeaky clean to convince her he was husband material. But none of it mattered now.

Brandy was keeping a low profile—didn't want to be found. And he was hiding out in some cheap hotel he was forced to pay for in cash—because he was a dead man if that fucking bookie found him.

His mouth twisted downward with a bitter sneer.

God, that bitch Brandy deserved to be smacked into the

next zip code when he got his hands on her. But that could wait until after he got her down that aisle.

He took another drag and closed his eyes.

And it appeared he was getting closer. The source he'd sent out to track her had provided some fairly interesting information.

Just as he'd known all along, she wasn't in the god damn Mediterranean. She was still in the Vegas area. And she'd been shopping—a lot.

But the kicker was she didn't appear to be staying in a hotel. Unless she was paying cash like he was.

No. Otherwise, she would've been careful not to use her card in other places. The possibility that Brandy had found a friend to stay with just didn't add up.

"Hmm." His brows drew together and he shook his head.

Brandy didn't have many friends that he knew of, and she'd never mentioned any in the Vegas area.

Which left one odd and puzzling possibility. The man whose bike she'd jumped on when she'd fled the chapel. The one he'd seen running from their hotel room.

But why? His mouth curled in dismay. Brandy had about as much energy as a sack of flour during sex. Surely she hadn't made her way into another man's bed.

He stood up and crushed the cigarette out on the chipped wooden side table. Striding into the bathroom, he hit the light switch. The lighting cracked and whined before the light reluctantly flickered on.

He leaned in toward the mirror and stared briefly at his once-perfect smile. Already the smoking habit had stained his veneers.

With a snarl, he flicked off the light again and went back to sit on the bed. It didn't matter. Any of it. He'd find out where she was. Even if he had to go from door to fucking door to find her.

Chewing on a fingernail, he paced through the room and took a moment to admit the seed of doubt that had begun to take root.

He needed to consider the possibility that she may not be easily persuaded to marry him. That the chances of getting her to say 'I do' were growing slimmer each day.

His soft laugh held no humor and was swallowed up in the tiny room.

He reached for another cigarette with unsteady hands and shook his head. No matter what, she'd give him the money one way or another.

The wall of sound inside the bar had reached its peak about a half hour ago. Marco glanced around the room and let out a whistle that got sucked up into the mass of noise.

He spotted Brandy walking by and grabbed her arm. "Can you believe this? This place is packed."

"I told you it would be." She grinned and pushed a strand of hair out of her face. "You see that one guy with that totally awesome teal-spiked hair?"

"I do. Wondered if he was one of Val's friends." His gaze drifted around. "It's crazy in here."

"It is. It's wonderful." She tugged away. "I've got a ton of drink orders to fill. I'll talk with you later when the insanity dies down."

Yes, she had warned him. But there was a part of him that could have never predicted this. This was...amazing.

He glanced around the bar again. Over a hundred people crowded the building. The sound of instruments, chatter, and laughter filled the air. People of every variety had shown up to support their family and friends.

Val and Brandy had been going non-stop all night. Sebastian was a mad fool behind the bar, mixing up drinks at an insane pace. Fortunately, they'd called in another friend who bartended at the last minute to help out as well.

Marco lingered at the door, checking IDs as people came into the bar. He glanced around again and shook his head. They were nearing capacity, but fortunately, the performances would start soon.

He sensed movement at the doorway and turned to see two men entering the bar with camera bags and other photo gear.

"Hey there," one of the men stuck out his hand. "I'm Fred with the *Vegas Times* and am here to do a piece on this event."

Reporters?

Unease stirred in his gut and he glanced back to where Brandy still waited tables. She'd freak out if she realized there were reporters in the bar.

Why hadn't he realized media coverage was a possibility?

What could he do, though? It'd only arouse suspicion if he refused them entry. And hell, it would be great to get *Dante's Place* a write-up in the local paper.

He forced an easy smile and shook the man's hand. "Thanks for coming by. I'm Marco Vargas, one of the owners of *Dante's*. Grab a seat if you can find one and enjoy yourselves."

"Thanks, Marco. Nice little joint you got here." The photographer glanced around and nodded, before following the reporter into the crowd of people.

Shit.

Marco let the air hiss out from between clenched teeth and left the doorway for a minute to go warn Brandy.

He found her dropping off an order at one of the booths in the back.

"I need to talk with you for a second," he yelled above the noise.

"What, now?" Her brows rose. "We're slammed—"

"Brandy." He tried to silently convey that it couldn't wait.

She held his gaze for a moment longer, before she gave a quick nod. She set down the last drink and then walked past him, straight into the back of the bar.

She turned around once they'd reached the office, uncertainty in her eyes. "All right. What's going on?"

He caught her hand and gave it a small squeeze. "I just wanted to warn you that there's a reporter here with a photographer."

Brandy's eyes widened and her mouth parted. She grabbed onto the desk and looked away.

"They're here for the bands, princess." He cupped the back of her head, stroking his thumbs over the nape of her neck.

"Of course." She gave a jerky nod but avoided looking at him. Her tongue ran across her lips. "It's just...what if they recognize me—"

"They won't. You look nothing like you did a couple of weeks ago." He hesitated. "Just don't make eye contact with them, and try and stay under the radar."

"I'm one of two waitresses working. It's going to be kind of hard to stay under the radar —tonight, especially."

"I know." He lowered his head and touched his nose against hers, trying to ease some of her tension. "Just don't think about it."

"Easier said than done. Hey, point them out to me when we go back out there and I'll have Val wait on them."

He angled his head to brush his mouth across hers and she trembled against him. "Sexy girl."

She rolled her eyes and murmured a husky, "Oh please."

"Beg me later, sweetheart. Right now you need to get back

to work." He looked her over from head to toes. "By the way, I like that black leather dress thingy you've got going on."

"Do you?" She pulled away and did a little wiggle, making all her female curves bounce in the most provocative way.

Christ, she was a freaking bombshell.

He bit back a groan, his body responding in all kinds of ways it had no right to at this point in the evening.

"You know I do. Now go."

She stuck her tongue out and stepped past him. He couldn't resist giving a light swat on her leather-clad bottom when he followed after her.

Brandy yelped and turned around to glare. "Nice. We'll see who's begging later."

"Touché." He winked and moved after her out into the main bar area. "Remember, no eye contact."

"Got it."

He looked around the floor. "Okay, they're the two guys standing on the left side of the stage area. One is wearing a Raiders T-shirt."

She remained quiet for a moment and then gave a slight nod. "I see them. Thanks, Marco."

"You're welcome." He noticed more people entering the bar. "And now I'm back to door duty. Good luck. We start in about five minutes."

"Good deal." She didn't hesitate, just charged off into the mass of people.

Marco headed toward the entrance to let in the customers lingering there. A quick glance at the clock a few minutes later confirmed it was time to get the performances rolling.

He shut the door to the bar and headed up to the makeshift stage. Picking up the microphone, he glanced over the crowd. A sea of faces stared back at him and he bit back a sigh.

Shit.

He should've convinced Sebastian to MC the Battle of the Bands. He would've been so much better at this kind of thing.

After clearing his throat, he called out, "How's everyone doing tonight?"

The bar roared in response and clapped wildly.

"I know everyone's excited, so we'll go ahead and get this contest started. Each band will perform one song." He fumbled in his pocket for the slip of paper that had the line up of bands on it. "All right first up performing will be...ugh...Spanking Monkeys."

Seriously?

Marco shook his head and stepped off the stage as fans of the band erupted into screams.

The band moved into position on the stage and counted off before a wall of heavy metal music erupted in the building.

Marco glanced back at the sound tech they'd hired, making sure he would be able to handle everything okay. The man gave a thumb's up and went back to twisting all kinds of knobs and levers.

Marco breathed a sigh of relief. Things started off without a hitch. He went to stand behind the bar, by Sebastian.

"So what do you think?" he yelled.

Sebastian turned to him. His eyes were almost glassy, fatigue drawing lines around his mouth.

"I think, mate, we're going to have to speed up the hiring process." He shook his head and grinned. "I'm absolutely beat —but I love it."

"Me too." Marco gave a slight nod. "Can you handle it for a minute? I'm going to run into the back and run some numbers on how much we've made so far tonight."

"I got it."

Marco slapped Sebastian on the shoulder and then headed into the back.

. . .

Brandy dropped off three bottles of beer at a table of rowdy men who kept a running tab, and then hurried away before they could waylay her with more flirting.

She grimaced as off-key singing and bad lyrics filled the room.

Who the heck was performing now? She stole a quick glance at the stage and immediately regretted it.

The two girls in the band danced provocatively in bikini tops and tiny shorts.

Their singing sounded comparable to a wounded animal, while the guy behind them who was strumming guitar had probably never had a lesson in his life.

"Oomph." She slammed into someone and stumbled backward.

"Sorry about that, ma'am."

Brandy turned to look at the man who'd spoken and then quickly looked back down.

"No problem." She moved past him, her pulse quickening.

Nice job trying to stay inconspicuous. She'd run right into the reporter Marco had warned her about.

"Brandy?"

She froze. Oh no, he'd recognized her.

Wait, no. That had definitely been a woman's voice calling her name. She turned around to find Elena weaving through the crowd toward her.

"Elena?"

"Hey," Elena came to a stop in front of her and folded her arms across her chest.

"You guys did great tonight," Brandy raved.

Elena's band had blown her socks off, and the younger woman had some seriously talented pipes.

"Thanks." Elena tucked a strand of hair behind her ear and cleared her throat. "Do you have a second?"

Brandy glanced back at the crowded floor, hesitant to leave Val by herself again.

"If not, don't sweat it," Elena went on in a rush. "It's nothing really. I just..."

The crack in the younger woman's voice clearly indicated that it was indeed something.

Brandy gave a quick nod and softened her expression. "Sure. Come into the back with me."

She tucked the drink tray against her side and turned back toward the kitchen. Pushing through the doors, she set the tray down on the counter and waited for Elena to follow her inside.

The moment the door swung shut behind Elena, the girl's face crumpled and she let out a ragged sob.

Holy crap.

For a moment Brandy was too stunned to move, seeing the strong and tough young woman she'd just met turn into a vulnerable sobbing mess right before her eyes.

"Come here, honey." She opened her arms to Elena and pulled the girl into a hug. "What's wrong?"

Thankfully they were alone. The kitchen had closed down at ten, two hours ago, so Dave had already left

"Everything. You know how I..." she sniffled between sobs. "How I said Phil was a big flirt?"

"Yes?" Please don't let this be going where she thought it was going.

"Well..." Elena gasped in a breath and her eyes squeezed tighter closed.

"Go on." Brandy saw movement out of the corner of her eye and lifted her head.

Or maybe they weren't alone.

Marco stood in the doorway to the office, watching them with narrowed eyes and a warning stillness in his body.

He lifted an eyebrow in question.

Brandy shook her head, hoping he'd go back into the office and give them a moment. He didn't, just continued to watch from across the room.

Elena drew in a ragged breath. "Like I said, Phil is a big flirt. And today I went shopping, and when I came back to the room...."

"When you came back to the room?" she prodded, though she knew pretty much without a doubt what the other girl would say.

Elena groaned and then said on a rush, "Phil was in bed with another woman."

Bingo.

"Oh, Elena...." Brandy rubbed her hand up and down Elena's back and tried to comfort her. "I'm so sorry."

And she could completely understand what it felt like. She'd just gone through the same thing with Gordon. Only she hadn't been nearly as devastated as Elena appeared to be.

Elena began to sob twice as hard. "I'm sorry. I shouldn't be t-this upset."

"Of course you should." *Why wasn't I this upset with the man I was supposed to marry?* "You have every right to be—"

"It's just that I really thought he loved me." She choked in a gasp. "I waited twenty-one years to give up my virginity, and for what? A bad kisser with a little dick?"

A door slammed.

Brandy jerked her gaze across the room and her eyes widened when she saw Marco storming towards the bar.

Oh dear god!

She'd forgotten he was even there.

"Marco, don't do it!"

"Holy shit." Elena lifted her head, her eyes rounding with horror. "Tell me my brother wasn't just here."

"*Was* being the keyword," Brandy said grimly and set the girl aside to head out after Marco. "Stay here."

"Stay here?" Elena bounded after her. "Are you loco? I don't think so."

Brandy pushed through the double doors and sent them slamming into the wall.

Sebastian glanced up at her in surprise and yelled, "What's going on?"

"Where did Marco go?" she hurried over to him. "You need to stop him."

"Stop him from what?"

Brandy turned away, scouring the crowd in search of Marco. "From beating up Elena's punk ass boyfriend."

"Oh for fuck's sake." Sebastian threw down the bar towel and moved out from behind the bar. "What did the boyfriend do to Elena? Did he hurt her?"

"Hey, wait up." Brandy hurried after him, weaving through the throng of people. She spotted Marco moving towards the far wall.

"There he is! Grab him, Sebastian."

Sebastian lunged forward but was too late. Marco grabbed onto the shoulder of a guy at least half a foot taller than him, spun him around, and sent his fist flying into the man's face.

The crowd scattered, startled cries and cheers mixing.

"What are you doing?" Elena shrieked, pushing past them all to grab her brother's arm.

"Stay out of this, Elena." Marco shook his fist and winced.

Brandy folded her arms across her chest and groaned. Five seconds earlier and she could have stopped this.

And now Marco would be lucky if he hadn't broken his hand on the other man's jaw.

Customers crowded around them, talking excitedly.

"Why did you hit him?" Elena placed herself between the man and her brother and glared.

"Because of what he did to you—"

"You hit Tony. The bass player."

"So?"

She placed her hands on her hips and glared. "So I was dating the drummer, you idiot. *Que pendejo.*"

"What? I thought—" Marco's head snapped to the left as a massive fist connected with it.

The room lit up from the flash of a camera as Marco stumbled backward.

Someone yelled, "Look out, he's going down!"

Brandy lurched forward as Marco staggered toward the side, and pulled him out of reach of the bass player.

Marco's unfocused gaze landed on her, the left side of his face already starting to swell.

The bass player shook his head and walked away with a scowl.

"You," Sebastian snapped at a man standing back a bit looking on in dismay. "You're the drummer, right? Did you hurt Elena? You'd better get your sorry arse out of here while you still can."

He paled, and his skinny body shook. "But they haven't announced—"

Marco lunged forward again and Brandy yelped, holding onto his arm for all she was worth to keep him from getting in another punch.

"Yeah, hit him, too!" Someone else in the crowd yelled. "He looks like an asshole."

"Okay, okay. I'm outta here." Phil stepped away and glared down at Elena. "Nice little drama you started, bitch."

Oh no.

Brandy winced and held onto Marco for all she was worth, trying to stop him from nailing the other guy.

But from the corner of her eyes, she saw someone else's fist go flying. She turned just in time to see Sebastian knock the drummer on his ass.

Elena stumbled back with a gasp, lifting a fist to her mouth. Sebastian turned to face her, his hand gently closing over her shoulder as his eyes narrowed with concern.

"Are you all right, kid?"

She nodded, clearly in shock, but her eyes were locked on his.

Brandy was distracted from the exchange when Marco jerked away from her grasp.

"Asshole got what he deserved." He cast one last glance at Phil, before turning to walk through the crowd and toward the back office again.

"What? What the hell just happened?" Valerie rushed over, her eyebrows raised.

Elena sighed and looked back at the chaotic scene before her. "Fight between my brother and a few members of my band."

"No *way*. I run to the bathroom for two minutes and miss all the fun? I have the worst damn luck."

Brandy rolled her eyes and approached Sebastian. "Can you please escort Phil out of the bar?"

He blinked, seeming to come out of his concern for Elena, and then gave a brisk nod.

"Will do." Sebastian stepped forward and grabbed the younger man by the arm pulling him up. "Let's go, you little punk ass."

Brandy turned away from the drama of watching him escort the drummer out the door. She nodded and switched into teacher mode.

Time to get things back to normal. Or as close to normal as it could after a bar fight.

"The show's over, people. We'll announce the winner of the Battle of the Bands shortly."

The crowd, half-drunk and all riled up from the fight, slowly dissipated.

"Good lord, what a mess," Brandy muttered and shook her head.

There'd been a fight once during a choir class, but it hadn't been nearly as chaotic and ridiculous as this one. And at least there she'd been able to send the boys to the principal's office.

She glanced toward the back of the bar where Marco had disappeared.

Should she be mad at him for going after Phil, or proud of him? Maybe just a little of both.

Rubbing the back of her neck, she sighed and set off to make the rounds through the bar.

Chapter Fifteen

arco rotated his jaw and winced. His face was throbbing.

Christ, he was an idiot. He leaned back in his chair and kicked his feet up on the desk, trying not to think about the colossal fuck up he made an hour ago.

He glanced towards the door to the office, cocking his head to listen for the sound of customers. The noise level inside the bar had gradually begun to die down and now seemed to be gone completely.

The monitor on his computer showed it was just after two. The silence just confirmed that everyone had been kicked out.

Had Brandy left as well? Disappointment pricked and he bit back a sigh.

He wouldn't blame her if she had. She was probably pissed as all hell at him. And she had every right to be. They all did.

He kicked his feet off the desk and his chair rolled back on the wheels.

Standing up, Marco shut down his computer and was about

to hit the light switch when he heard the door into the kitchen swing open and hit the counter.

"How's the face?" Brandy walked slowly toward him, stopping a few inches away.

She hadn't left? A bit of the tension in his muscles eased, but he kept his tone neutral.

"It's fine."

"Liar." Her lips pursed. "You know you deserved it."

"Do you hear me saying that I didn't?" He finally scowled and the movement made his face throb more. "Shit."

Her expression softened. She drew the pad of her thumb in toward his mouth and across his lips.

"You look like you went a few rounds with a gorilla."

"I feel like it. That guy was a giant. But I'll live."

"Let me get you some ice." She stepped back from him and went to the ice bin.

"I don't need ice."

"You do. Now stop being such a guy and listen to me."

Propping open the lid, she scooped a handful into a paper towel and then returned to him.

"Here." She laid the makeshift ice pack against his cheek. "Hold this."

The abrupt cold stung for a second, but then slowly began to numb the inflamed skin.

"Thanks." His voice came out gruffer than he intended. "Did everyone leave?"

"Mmm hmm." She turned and lifted herself onto the metal counter. "Val left a few minutes ago."

"And Elena?"

Brandy sighed. "Sebastian got her out of here."

Good. Sebastian would make sure she didn't get into any more trouble. Specifically make sure she stayed the hell away from that bastard drummer, in case she got any ideas in her head to make up with him.

"They won you know."

"Who did?"

"Your sister's band."

His chest expanded with pride as he drew in a slow breath. His mouth curved upward. "Really?"

"Really. When we tallied the audience votes, they chose Bitches Brew hands down." Brandy crossed one leg over the other and the leather skirt hiked up another inch on her thigh.

Oh damn, had she done that on purpose? The blood rushed south in his body and he flexed his jaw.

"I think she was pretty disappointed that you weren't out there to see her win."

"Elena probably would have hit me herself if I'd come back out there." He shook his head and averted his gaze from Brandy's legs.

"That's not true. In fact...I think it pleased her. Having her big brother stick up for her that way." Brandy smiled and cleared her throat. "Even if you, err, hit the wrong guy."

"Yeah. Minor mistake. Sebastian fixed it for me though."

"Yeah, he did. But I know you were itching to get in a punch too."

The light feminine giggle she made broke any control he had left.

He tossed the ice pack in the garbage can and closed the distance between them. Stepping between her legs as she sat on the counter.

Her eyes widened even as she slid her hands onto his shoulders.

"You're not mad at me?" His voice turned husky as he kissed the spot just below her ear.

"I...ah, no, I'm not mad." Her words were breathy. "I understand how much you care about your sister. I actually think it's sweet you went to her defense."

"Mmm." He caught her earlobe between his teeth and drew his tongue across the soft flesh. "You know what?"

"What?" she gasped out the word and squirmed against him.

"I don't want to talk about my sister anymore."

"Good thing, because I don't either." She gave a ragged sigh and tilted her head, giving him access to the side of her throat.

He nuzzled her neck and breathed in the familiar scent of apples—her perfume which had once seemed so strange, now drove him wild anytime he got near her.

"Marco..."

"Yes, princess?" He slid his hands up her legs, pushing the leather dress further up her thighs.

"You know that scene in *Pretty Woman* where Richard Gere does Julia Roberts on the piano in the bar?"

He lifted his head, her random question making him pause. "No. I've never watched *Pretty Woman*."

"God, you should be arrested."

He shook his head, his thumbs moving over the inside of her thigh. "So what are you saying? You want to have sex on a piano?"

"It could be fun." She met his heated look head-on through lowered lashes. "What do you think?"

His dick jerked in response, his mind already imagining the possibilities. He'd made the suggestion as a joke, in no way thinking she could be serious.

Hell, why wouldn't she be though? The woman *was* a choir teacher.

"It's a fantasy of mine," she went on in a rush. "And since we brought in that piano for the Battle of the Bands..."

"Yeah."

"So, umm," she ran her hands down his chest and he drew in a swift breath. "You think you can accommodate me on that Mr. Vargas?"

"I think, Ms. Summers," He slid his hands under her bottom and lifted her up. "You'll find me incredibly accommodating."

He closed his mouth over hers and slid his tongue past the seam of her lips. She sighed and wound her arms around his neck as her legs wrapped around his waist.

Catching her fleshy bottom lip between his teeth, he gave it a light nip before running his tongue over it. Her soft cry sent his pulse into overdrive.

"God, I want you," he rasped. He adjusted his grip on her, his fingers digging into her bottom as he carried her into the bar.

"I want you, too." She buried her face against his neck, her breath warm against his skin. "I haven't stopped wanting you since the minute I hijacked your bike."

Her words sent a thrill of possessiveness through him. *Mine.* The need to possess her, claim her, came on fierce. He set her down on the edge of the shiny black surface of the piano.

"We should probably be careful," she warned hesitantly. "Actually, this may not be the best idea seeing as we borrowed it from one of your customers. And if anything happens—"

"You're right. We should just fuck on the counter of the bar."

Her eyes widened and then she gave a soft laugh. "You're so naughty, Marco."

His mouth curved. "And you love it."

She rolled her eyes. "Maybe we should save the piano fantasy for the one at my house sometime."

Her house? Was that an invitation into her world? The idea didn't seem so intimidating; in fact, it kind of pleased him.

He dropped a hard kiss on her mouth and then lifted her up again, carrying her to the bar counter and then setting her on top.

She sat a few inches above him now, so that she looked down at him, her lips swollen from his kisses and her eyes shiny with desire.

His blood pounded a little faster and he couldn't tear his gaze from her. Damn, she was so beautiful. Such an amazing woman in every aspect. He didn't deserve her.

"So are you going to just stand there looking?" she asked with an arch of her eyebrow. "Or were you going to, err, fu—fu...make love to me on the bar."

He gave a husky laugh and pushed her legs apart to step between them. Hmm. This position might be a little bit of a challenge as well. But hell, nobody said he didn't like a challenge.

He cupped the side of her face and smiled. "Can't quite bring yourself to say fuck, can you, princess?"

She didn't answer right away and something in her expression shifted. There was hesitancy in her eyes. A vulnerability.

"I can say it," she said quietly and her tongue swept across her bottom lip. "I'm just not sure I can reduce what we do together as fucking anymore."

His pulse slowed and then sped right back up again. The meaning of her words resounded in his head. It was more than sex to her.

More than sex.

"Oh jeez, I'm so sorry," she whispered. "I shouldn't have said that. I just made things weird, didn't I? I tend to do that sometimes."

His mouth dried out. Did this mean she cared for him? It

couldn't be love. Hell, they hadn't even known each other for two weeks.

"I'll take that as a yes," she whispered and tried to slide off the counter.

"No," he said fiercely and caught her around the waist, holding her still. "No. Nothing's weird."

Uncertainty flickered in her eyes. "Are you sure?"

It wasn't weird at all. What was weird was the fact he wanted to admit he felt the same. That whatever they had together had bypassed the just sex part a few days ago.

Fear and doubt roared up inside him. Along with the knowledge of how exposed, he'd be if he admitted his feelings aloud. The words locked in his throat.

Seeing the raw vulnerability on her face, Marco answered her in the only way he could.

Her lips parted with a sigh of relief when his mouth closed over hers. His tongue moved inside in search of hers. They met in a collision of hot, wet friction as they teased each other.

Sliding his hands up her waist and behind her, he found the zipper on the leather dress. He tugged it down over her breasts, never moving his mouth from hers.

She tugged his shirt from his jeans and lifted it upward. He ripped his mouth from hers just long enough for her to pull it over his head and off his body. Then his mouth covered hers again as her fingernails raked down his naked chest.

He fumbled with the hooks on the back of her strapless bra, attempting patience until each hook had been undone and he was able to tug the smooth bra from her body. Her breasts fell heavily into his hands and his breath caught, his thumbs already stroking the hardened nipples.

She angled her head with a sigh, giving him deeper access to her mouth. Her tongue rubbed against his in a quick sensual stroke and then retreated.

She repeated the process until his blood pounded thick in his veins and his erection became painful.

Marco pulled his mouth from hers and drew in an unsteady breath. "I want you."

"Yes," she whispered and reached for the fly of his jeans.

He curled his fingers around her wrist, halting her progress. "But not here. Not on the counter in a bar."

Her brows drew together. "I don't understand."

"You were right earlier." His jaw hardened. "You deserve more than getting fucked on the counter of a bar."

Brandy could almost feel her heart expanding to let Marco inside a little more.

Her breasts ached for his mouth, already she could envision the sensation he'd create when he touched her that way. And a heavy pressure lingered between her legs that only he could ease.

She pulled his hand up to her face and laid it against her cheek.

"Thank you. For wanting to take me back to your place and make it more romantic." She tilted her head against his palm and kissed the tip of his thumb. "But right now I just need *you*. I don't care if it's in a bed, on your desk again, or half on the counter of a bar."

His nostrils flared and she heard his swift indrawn breath.

"You kind of like that last visual, don't you?" she asked, her voice husky.

"Hell yeah." He pressed his thumb against the seam of her lips, his gaze never leaving hers.

She opened her mouth and drew the padded tip of his thumb into her mouth. Her tongue played with the tip, her lips curving into a smile.

A shudder visibly racked his body. "Are you sure, princess? I can wait until we get back to my place."

"Noble of you." She released his thumb and dragged his hand down her body, not stopping until she reached the final destination between her legs. "But I can't."

"Well then." He rubbed her clit through her panties. "I guess we'd better do something about that."

She barely bit back a groan. "I guess so."

"Damn, Brandy." He groaned and glanced down at where he touched her. "Undressing you is like opening a different present each time. I never know what I'm going to find underneath your clothes."

Brandy gave a soft laugh and lifted her hips so he could dispose of the silky black thong. Then he tugged her dress down over her hips and off her body.

"Well, I'm glad my underwear gives you such a thrill. Especially since I'll be in control of the company that makes it someday."

His gaze jerked up, his eyes narrowing. "Really?"

"Well, they don't call me the Lingerie Heiress for nothing." She gave a light shrug.

Why had she brought this topic up now? It'd never been one of the more comfortable discussions.

"But who knows, I may step down."

Marco's brows drew together. "Why would you—?"

"Can we not," she cut him off quickly, running her hands over his naked chest. "Talk about this now. It was a mistake to bring it up. Especially at this moment."

He stared at her for a second longer before giving a slow nod.

"Of course. We don't have to talk about it. Besides, we were just about to...."

"About to?" She raised an eyebrow and swung her legs

which dangled over the counter. She arched her back and her breasts moved closer to his face.

"We were about to." He smiled and cupped her breasts again. His head lowered and then his tongue swept across one of her nipples.

Fire jolted through her body at the first touch. He drew the tip into his mouth, sucking, and her muscles turned to mush. He slipped an arm around her waist, encouraging her body to arch into his touch.

"I love the way you taste," he murmured, moving to pay attention to the other nipple.

She gave a strangled groan, and then teased, "Like Brandy?"

"Better than any Brandy I've ever tasted." He buried his face between both her breasts and sighed.

"You've obviously never had Hennessy Ellipse." She laughed and drew in a ragged breath.

He lifted his head, a smile on his mouth but his eyes serious. "I don't want Hennessy when I can have you."

His comment should have sounded a bit cheesy, yet it made her want to sigh like a schoolgirl with a crush.

She lowered her eyes. Her body still hummed from his touch, wanting more of it. The need to have that complete physical connection hit sudden and powerful.

Trying to keep things light, she murmured, "You know. If you take your jeans off, we can get to the fun part."

"You mean this isn't the fun part?" He grinned and stepped back from between her legs.

Her gaze dropped to where his long fingers unbuttoned his jeans. Then the slow, drive-you-crazy way he pulled the tab down through the teeth of the zipper.

"Marco," her voice cracked. "Please."

He paused and grabbed a condom out of his pocket.

"Come here," he whispered a moment later and pulled her hips off the bar.

She slid half off the counter, wrapping her legs around his waist but kept her elbows braced on the bar.

He kneaded the cheeks of her bottom and kissed her neck, but didn't enter her yet.

She groaned in frustration and tried to lower herself onto his cock.

"*Marco.*"

He gave a soft laugh and adjusted his hold on her, before slowly lowering her down onto him. She released the bar and wrapped her arms around his neck, letting him support her weight.

The breath locked in her throat as he slid inch by inch inside her. Only when he fully joined their bodies and was buried to the hilt, did she release the air stranded in her lungs.

They stayed locked together, not moving right away. He fit so perfectly inside her.

She listened to his ragged breaths and felt the pounding of his heart against her chest.

"What are you doing to me?" he asked in a hoarse whisper.

She closed her eyes. "I have no idea. But you do the same to me."

He moved his hips, sliding out of her a bit, and then thrust back inside.

"It's damn crazy."

"Complete madness," she agreed and gasped when he hit an ultra-sensitive spot inside her.

The conversation died as they found their rhythm together. He moved inside her with slow, deliberate thrusts.

Each time he sank back inside her her heart seemed to swell with emotion. The closer to tears of happiness she came.

Her mind turned to mush and it became impossible to

think. Except for one terrifying little thought. A phrase that looped in her head as the pleasure inside spiraled her higher toward a climax.

I love this man.

"Brandy." He groaned her name and then his mouth covered hers again.

She kissed him back as if her life depended on it. Her eyes burned with sudden tears as she stroked her tongue against his, slanting her mouth to bring him deeper.

His movements inside her quickened. Became more urgent. Not quite as steady. She met each one, pressing herself down onto him and gripping him with her inner muscles.

He gasped against her mouth, his fingers biting into the flesh of her ass. He angled their bodies so there was just enough pressure in the right area to send her over the edge.

Pleasure spread to every inch of her body, all thoughts scattered with a wave of lightheadedness and color behind her closed eyes.

He thrust deep into her and stayed. His groan ripped through the bar as he found his own release.

"Brandy, oh god, I think I'm in—" He went still.

Her heart pounded faster and she stared with wide eyes at the wall.

I think I'm in... what had he been about to say?

Marco sighed, his grip tightening on her as he buried his head into the curve of her neck.

"It's late," he finally said.

She closed her eyes, disappointment blooming in place of the fading pleasure. What had she expected? That he'd confess his love for her?

Her lips twisted into a scornful smile.

Silly fool, you always were too romantic.

"We should head back to my place."

She gave a jerky nod, drawing in an unsteady breath. "I am a little tired."

"Just a little?"

He set her down on her feet and her legs wobbled. She gripped his shoulders to keep her knees from buckling.

"Okay, a lot." She gave a wan smile and glanced around the bar. "I'm glad we cleaned this place up before I came back to get you."

"Ditto. I don't have the energy to do more than pass the hell out." He stepped away and disposed of the condom into the garbage.

Brandy picked her clothes up off the floor and slipped back into them, stifling another yawn. She glanced at the clock and noted it was after three.

"Good lord, do we really have to be here at ten tomorrow?"

"No." He pulled on his jeans and gave her a slight smile. "Sebastian is going to pull a double and Valerie's coming in early."

"Really?" Brandy slipped her shoes on and gave him a sideways glance. "What's going on?"

He shrugged, obviously trying to look casual, but she wasn't convinced.

"Elena convinced me to go have dinner with my dad."

Brandy's lips parted and she took a slow breath in. "Marco, really? That's wonderful."

He gave a tight smile and thrust a hand through his hair. "Yeah. I...it's overdue. Would you come with me?"

Her surprise doubled. "You want me to come with you?"

"If you don't want to that's all right. I can—"

"I want to," she said quickly and then softened her voice. "Of course I want to. I'd love to."

"Thank you." He gave a tight smile and grabbed her hand, giving it a squeeze. "It means a lot."

"I'm glad I'll be there." She held his gaze. That magnetic pull she always experienced between them increased until her heart fluttered wild in her chest.

He traced the inside of her palm and then cleared his throat. "Why don't you grab your stuff and we'll head out? I'll lock up."

"All right. Give me just a second." She tugged her hand away with reluctance and went into the back to grab her purse.

When she came back out front Marco stood waiting by the door, fully dressed.

"Ready?"

She nodded and pushed open the door, stepping into the warm night. Marco followed after her and they made their way toward his bike.

"Tonight went pretty well, I think," she said once they were standing under a street lamp beside his motorcycle.

"Except for that whole fight part." His lips twisted.

"Oh, I don't know." She batted her eyelashes and climbed onto the back of the bike. "I have to say seeing you in angry, protective brother mode was a bit hot."

"Was it?" He leaned down and brushed his mouth across hers.

"Mmm hmm." Her eyes fluttered closed and she sighed.

"Thank you for tonight, Brandy. For everything."

Her pulse skipped. "You're welcome."

He pressed his forehead against hers and then pulled away, climbing onto the bike in front of her. He handed her a helmet that she promptly put on.

Her smile widened as she wrapped her arms around his waist. She'd really gotten this whole motorcycle thing down in her time with him.

Marco started the bike and gunned them out of the parking lot and onto the highway.

She sighed and snuggled her body close to his, wondering if she'd ever been this happy.

Gordon tugged the baseball cap down over his eyes and pocketed the cigarettes he'd just purchased.

"Hey," the clerk said suddenly. "Aren't you on that one show?" She snapped a bubble with the gum she chewed and narrowed her eyes. "*New You* or something? I don't watch it much, since it pretty much sucked, but you look familiar."

"No." He shook his head and scowled, heading toward the exit.

The bottled blonde's IQ was probably smaller than her bra size. What the hell did she know anyway? *New You* had been a great show.

Ugly chicks, like the bitch behind the register, had been made into something a little less repulsive. It was utterly ridiculous the show had been canceled.

In fact, this entire situation was ridiculous. Having to sneak around the city like some damn criminal.

Hell, three weeks ago he'd been fucking worshiped when he'd visited this town. He'd been that 'hot dentist from the reality show'. He'd had a different woman every night—sometimes two.

He'd get that back. He would damn it. He refused to accept anything else.

Once this money thing was settled, he'd find another job—maybe even on another reality show. Hell, those shows still popped up left and right like invincible fruit flies.

He pushed open the door to the store, put one foot outside, and then froze. He stepped back inside, letting the door close behind him, and then glanced down.

Eyes wide, he reached with unsteady hands to pick up a local paper.

It couldn't be. How in the hell...? Was it really her?

He took the paper up to the register and dug some quarters out of his pocket.

Well, well. It looked like today might be the day when his luck changed. His heart rate doubled and a tight smile crossed his face.

"I gotcha now, love muffin."

Chapter Sixteen

R olling over in bed, Brandy stretched her arms above her and gripped the headboard. Every inch of her body still tingled and warmed with awareness, doubling so when she glanced over at Marco.

He lay on his side, his fist next to his head on the pillow and his mouth parted; his expression soft and relaxed with sleep.

Her gaze flickered over the left side of his face and she winced. The fight last night had certainly left a mark. She leaned over him, running a finger lightly over the swollen black and blue flesh.

Marco's eyes snapped open. His hand shot out and his fingers curled around her wrist.

"Good morning," she drawled with amusement, a shiver running through her at his touch.

"Mmm." He gave a drowsy sigh and released her wrist. "Good morning, princess."

With her hand free once more, she trailed her fingers across the ridges of his chest. "What time are we heading over to your dad's house?"

The muscles tensed under her fingers and she glanced up at him again. His jaw had hardened and there was a brief flash of panic in his eyes before it disappeared.

"Are you nervous?" she asked softly.

He didn't answer, just looked away and gave a slight shrug.

"Okay, answer me this." She leaned on her elbow and propped her head on her hand. "Before your falling out, was he a good father to you? Or was he a bad father?"

"No." Marco shook his head, a slight smile on his lips. "He was an outstanding father. Raised two kids on his own...put me through college."

"Yes, see? He sounds like a great dad. He's probably just as eager to put this behind him as you are." Her brows drew together. "Where did you go to college?"

Marco tensed and then jumped out of bed as if she'd jammed a needle into his leg.

"We should probably get ready."

She sat up. "Oh. So soon?"

"It's what," he glanced at the clock. "Ten? It's an hour drive and I told them we'd be there by noon."

Brandy watched him stride over to the dresser and search through it.

Okay.

So obviously he wasn't going to reply to the *where did you go to college* part. But why?

She sighed and gave a slight nod. Maybe he'd attended a junior college and was embarrassed, which was ridiculous. Or maybe he hadn't completed school—had never received his degree.

"I'm going to grab a shower." He turned, clothes dangling over his arm. "Did you want to join me? Or would you prefer your own?"

"Silly question." She winked and climbed out of bed after him, not at all self-conscious about her nudity.

"Yes," he replied, his voice suddenly hoarse as he looked her over from head to foot. "It was a silly question."

She strode toward the bathroom but paused next to him.

Reaching up, she cupped the back of his head and pulled his mouth down to hers.

"You forgot to say good morning properly," she chided, her lips just a breath away from his.

"My bad."

"Oh my god. You just sounded like one of my students."

"My bad." His smile widened.

"Stop it!" She giggled and tugged his head down further until his mouth covered hers.

All her muscles grew pliant the moment their lips touched, a sensation she'd quickly become used to.

Marco gave a growl of approval and deepened the kiss, his arm sliding around her waist to hold her up. He lifted his head a bit later and the naked desire in his eyes locked all the air in her lungs.

"Good morning," he said thickly.

"I'll say." She ran her tongue over her lips. "Now how about that shower?"

Marco's cell phone started to ring and they both glanced at it.

"Or did you want to get that?" she asked.

"It can wait." He scooped her up into his arms. "I'm feeling the need to get dirty—mmm, I mean clean."

The drive out of the city gave Marco some much-needed time to think. With the hot Nevada air against his face and Brandy's arms around his waist, he relaxed enough to enjoy the ride.

This morning's conversation had started down a road he wasn't quite prepared to go down. He should have never even said the word college to her.

What college had he gone to? Hell. She'd probably been shocked to hear he went to college at all.

The moment he admitted that he'd graduated from Duke with a degree in law, he'd better be ready to revive her. Or at least be willing to lay it all out on the table. And he couldn't do that. Not yet...but soon.

Last night he'd come to the realization that he wanted to share it with her. The entire experience—his sordid, not-so-pretty past. And he could only hope it wouldn't affect her feelings toward him.

Marco turned the bike onto his father's lot a few minutes later. The land wasn't extensive, but his dad had always kept it up nice and neat. And the house appeared to have undergone some minor renovations.

Two years. Had it really been so long since he'd last been here? Since he'd seen his father?

Parking the bike on the side of the house, he killed the engine.

The front door slammed open and Elena came charging down the stairs.

"You guys made it!"

Marco swung off the bike, removed his helmet, and then assisted Brandy down.

"We made it," he agreed with a grin. Unease pricked his gut again as he glanced up toward the front door. His father hadn't come out yet. "And it looks like you got back all right, too."

"I did. Actually, Sebastian brought me home."

"Sebastian did?" Brandy asked, stepping up between them.

There'd been some weird shift in the other girl's tone. "All the way back out here? That was nice of him."

"Yeah, it really was." Elena's lashes fell and she glanced away.

Was it Brandy's imagination, or did Elena's cheeks just get a little pink?

"Well, I'm glad you got home safely." Marco gave a sardonic wince and touched his jaw.

Elena leaned forward and narrowed her eyes. "Jeez, Marco. That looks terrible. I'm surprised you let Tony kick your ass so badly."

"The man is almost over six and a half feet tall! And he hit me when I wasn't looking."

"Excuses, excuses. Did you put some ice on it?"

Marco glanced over at Brandy, and this time it was her turn to blush.

"I did last night," he murmured.

The door slapped against the side of the house again, and he glanced back up to see his father standing in the doorway.

His muscles tensed and he couldn't breathe. They stared at one another and everyone went silent. The anguish and regret on his father's face finally gave him the motivation to close the distance between them.

"Papa," he said roughly and drew his father into a tight embrace.

"*Lo siento*, Marco," his father said raggedly and his arms wrapped tighter around Marco. "*Lo siento.*"

Tears he hadn't thought possible burned behind his closed eyes.

So much time had passed. Been wasted without his family. Marco drew in an unsteady breath, regret eating a hole in his gut.

"Papa, you must let me introduce you to Brandy," Elena

said finally and tugged the other woman up the steps. "Brandy, this is my father, Alfredo."

His father turned to look at Brandy.

"Ah, Brandy, *tu eres bella.*" He stepped forward and took her hand, brushing a kiss across her knuckles. "Beautiful, you are so beautiful."

"Oh wow. Thank you, sir." Her cheeks flushed and she glanced at Marco.

He gave her an intimate smile. She had helmet hair—flat on top, while the bottom half of her hair fluffed out in every direction. And still, she was the sexiest woman on the planet—

"More beautiful than your picture."

Marco and Brandy jerked their head to look at his father and blurted at the same time,

"My picture?"

"Her picture?"

His pulse began to thud a bit faster. How in the hell was it possible that his dad had recognized Brandy? He never watched television and could care less about Hollywood circles.

"Yes, your picture." Alfredo stepped back into the house. "Come, come. I'll show you."

Brandy and Marco exchanged another look before following them inside. Elena followed close on Brandy's heels.

"I can't believe you didn't tell me, girl," Elena chided and tugged on Brandy's sleeve.

"Tell you what?" Brandy turned around.

Elena rolled her eyes. "Umm, who you are."

"Ah, here it is. The beautiful picture."

Marco blinked at the newspaper his dad threw down in front of him. Brandy leaned forward to peer over his shoulder.

"Oh my god," she whispered.

Brandy lifted a hand to her suddenly warm cheeks.

This wasn't happening. This couldn't be happening. But apparently, it was.

In big, bold letters on the front page of the paper it read:

Brandy, The Bar Brawling Heiress

She stepped back and spun away from the paper, her heart pounding.

The bar-brawling heiress? That's what she'd been labeled? Oh god.

Pacing the room she went to stand by the window.

"Brandy? Are you okay?" Elena rushed to her side. "Really, it's a great picture of you. I mean, yeah, you have kind of a crazed look in your eyes. But your boobs look fantastic in that dress."

A great picture? The image on the paper flashed before her eyes again.

She'd been gripping Marco's arm, with indeed a crazed look in her eyes, right after he'd slugged Tony. A good picture? She'd looked exactly like what they'd called her. A bar-brawling heiress.

Dear lord. Nausea swirled in her stomach. Could she lose her teaching job over this? No, that wasn't likely. Or was it?

"Brandy, it's okay, princess."

She shrugged off Marco's arm and shook her head.

"It's not okay. Now everyone knows exactly where I am—and it sure as heck isn't in the Mediterranean. I'm...in the midst of a bar fight in that picture. I look like I'm ready to roll up my sleeves and start throwing punches myself."

"So?" Elena snorted. "Lots of people get in bar fights. Oh my god, this one time? This one chick called me short and I totally knocked her on her—"

"You don't understand. I don't get in the middle of fights. Before last week I'd never even been in a bar!" Brandy spun around and gave a shaky sigh. "I mean I've avoided this kind of publicity my entire life."

"Brandy, it's all just crap." Marco threw the paper into the garbage and stepped toward her. "It'll blow over—"

"No. You guys just don't understand." She shook her head and choked back a watery laugh. "I'm not this person. I'm *not*. This puts me in the same class as *other* heiresses who are tabloid fodder."

"Shit, and that's a bad thing? Tell me who I have to sleep with to get my ass on the front page."

"*Elena*." Alfredo gave his daughter a sharp look, before turning back to Brandy. "It is not that bad, is it?"

"It's just a place I promised myself I'd never end up."

"Well, it's not like you do it all the time." Elena grinned and grabbed her arm. "And you have to admit being a little bad can be fun."

"Oh, jeez. I need—"

"A drink," Elena said quickly and urged her into another room. "That's just what I was thinking. Come with me."

"I don't need a drink." Despite her half-hearted protest, she followed the other girl out of the room.

"Tequila?" Elena offered.

"Oh god no."

"What about a hard seltzer?"

Brandy sighed and gave a weak shrug. "Okay, why not."

"Okay. You make yourself comfortable and I'll grab you one." Elena turned and winked. "Papa doesn't like to keep alcohol in the house, so I keep a stash in my room."

"Of course." Brandy closed her eyes.

When she opened them again Elena strode toward her with a tall thin can in her hand.

"Here you are."

"Thanks." Brandy cracked it open and took a sip of the seltzer.

Elena folded her arms across her chest and gave her a pensive look. "So you're really the Lingerie Heiress?"

"Yes."

"I always thought it was kind of cool that you never got in trouble like those other chicks..." Elena shuffled her feet. "Well, before the bar fight. But I take complete responsibility for that."

"It's not your fault."

"You're right, it's Marco's. We'll kick *his* butt."

Brandy laughed and some of the tension eased from her body.

"I am getting pretty worried over nothing, aren't I?" she asked after a soft sigh.

"Yeah. Maybe just a little." Elena shrugged. "Here's my theory. People know you. People know what to expect from you. One picture and a bullshit article in a newspaper doesn't mean squat. They'll know it was a one-time deal."

"You're probably right."

"I know I am. Now come on," Elena stepped forward and looped her arm through Brandy's. "Let's go back and get you back to my brother."

They arrived back into the living room and found Marco and his father deep in conversation. The offensive article lay nearby half hanging out of a garbage can.

"Gonna make a quick phone call, back in a few." Elena gave her a pat on the shoulder and disappeared.

Marco glanced up and his gaze connected with Brandy's. She gave a slight smile and conveyed a silent apology.

He returned her smile with a small one and then turned back to his father who was saying something.

Little flutters gathered in her tummy and her pulse

skipped. Last night, while they'd made love, she'd thought herself in love with him.

And now? She knew. Without a doubt. She was one hundred percent in love with this man.

"Well, kids." Alfredo clapped his hands, his eyes extra bright and his smile wide. "I'll go fire up the barbeque and we can grill some steaks. Is that okay with everyone? Do you eat meat, Brandy?"

"I love meat." She grinned at Marco. "In fact, your son recently turned me on to bratwurst."

"Bratwurst is good."

"I think that's pretty much what I said."

His father laughed and his grin expanded. "I know I'm going to like you, Brandy. Anyway, you guys just hang out while I get the food going."

"That sounds great, thank you," Brandy murmured and watched as the older man headed out the back door.

Marco stepped toward her and picked up her hand, giving it a slight squeeze.

"How are you doing?"

"Better." She bit her lip and winced. "I'm sorry, I totally freaked out."

"It's understandable." He pushed a curl back off her forehead.

She leaned into him and sighed. "Was the article terrible?"

"I didn't read it—tossed it in the garbage where it belongs."

"Thank you."

"You're welcome." He kissed her forehead. "And really, thank *you*."

"For?"

"Coming with me today." He placed a finger under her chin and tilted her head so she looked up at him. "I've got too much damn pride, and I don't think I'd have come here alone. You're too good to me, Brandy."

Her cheeks warmed with pleasure. "I could say the same. You basically let me take over your life for the past couple of weeks."

"You know damn well I didn't mind." His eyes darkened. "Let's go sit outside."

She curled her fingers around his and followed him into the front yard again. He led her to a porch swing and sat down, patting the spot next to him.

She settled down on the padded swing and snuggled her head against his shoulder. He slipped an arm around her waist and leaned his head on top of hers.

"Tell me about *Sugar and Spice*."

The random question drew her brows into a frown. "What do you want to know?"

"How did your parents get into the lingerie business?"

"Hmm." She smiled. She stared out over the brown mountains and vast land. Stark and beautiful in its own way. "They fell in love young. Both were always the real artistic type. My dad made his own pottery and my mom loved to design and make her own clothing. Specifically lingerie. They'd travel to festivals and shows and sell their stuff."

"That's how they started? For real?"

"Well mostly." She shrugged. "My mom's stuff sold like hotcakes. People devoured it, and couldn't buy enough. When it became clear they had something good going, they sold half their possessions, applied for a loan, and opened their first shop in a little strip mall in Santa Barbara."

"Obviously it did well."

"It did great. Within two years they had opened three more shops and from there it just snowballed." Her chest swelled with pride. Her parents had started out so small, with just a dream and a couple of bucks. "Now it's the largest lingerie chain in the United States."

Marco shook his head. Talk about living the American dream. The question of the hour was why didn't Brandy want anything to do with it?

"That's great. And now they've expanded to Europe you said?"

"Yes. Just recently they opened their first store in Paris. I went along for the opening, of course." She laughed softly. "I mean, come on, it's a trip to Paris."

"Not to mention you'll own the majority of the stock someday," he said in a quiet voice, testing the waters.

Her body tensed against his. "Yeah, there is that whole part."

"But you want nothing to do with it?" He decided to push her, hoping she wouldn't resent him for it.

"It's not that," she sighed. "I love *Sugar and Spice*. I love the quality and beauty of the items we sell. I have no problem standing behind the company itself."

"Then what is it?"

"I just don't think I'm necessarily the best face to put behind the company."

His grip tightened around her waist and disbelief rushed through him. "I hope to god you don't mean that literally."

"Marco...I'm a choir teacher. I don't fit the bill of someone who'd run a massive lingerie chain."

"Bullshit. Just find someone you trust. Someone who can give you good advice when you need it."

"Like who?"

He drew in a deep breath in and looked away.

Like me.

He may have graduated with a law degree, but he'd minored in business.

He couldn't very well admit that. Not yet. He fully intended to open up and confess everything, but right now, at his father's house while they were here for dinner wasn't the best time or place.

Besides, reuniting with his dad seemed like more than enough emotional drama for one day. And the bomb about his past that he planned on dropping on Brandy wasn't exactly light discussion material.

"There are people who can help."

"I just don't know," she murmured after a long pause. "Have you seen my mother? I mean, she's the type of woman you want behind *Sugar and Spice*. I'm..."

"Her spitting image." Marco turned in the seat and cupped the side of her face. "Princess, I *have* seen your mother. And you have her beautiful smile—and sexy long legs."

Her eyes widened. "Okay, I'm going to try not to think about the fact that you just called my mother's legs sexy. But thank you."

He grinned and dropped a kiss over her parted lips. "All I'm saying is think about it. They're giving you their legacy. Your parents worked their asses off to build *Sugar and Spice* into what it is today. Do you really want to just hand over the reins to someone else?"

"No, I don't," she admitted and her lashes lowered to brush against her cheeks. "I just never thought I had much of a choice. Thank you, Marco. I'll think about it. I didn't consider myself worthy...until I met you."

How could she have ever thought that way? He gently drew his fingers across her cheek, ready to say the words aloud, but she wasn't through.

"You've just been so good to me. For my self-esteem, for helping me to relax and have a good time. You even helped me be a little bad." She gave him a crooked smile. "You've never been anything but honest with me. And I want you to know it means a lot."

Shit.

His gut twisted and his throat went tight as her words hit his guilt button hard.

Maybe he should open the doors to his past, just give her a hint there were some things she didn't know.

"Brandy—"

"Steaks are ready." Elena stepped out onto the porch and gave them a curious glance. "Hope you guys weren't about to make out or anything."

Marco rolled his eyes and pulled his arm free from Brandy.

"Yes, we were. You've got crappy timing, twerp."

"So sue me, hermano," his sister teased with a grin. "I'll see you both inside."

Marco blinked, winded for a moment, and then glanced over at Brandy, almost expecting to see her shocked. She appeared perfectly normal, with just an amused smile on her face.

Elena had meant the comment to be a pun on his former career, but Brandy wouldn't know that. To her, it'd be just another bad joke between siblings.

"I'm hungry," she said and slipped her hand into his. "I can smell those steaks. Does your dad put teriyaki sauce on them? Is that what I'm smelling?"

He tightened his fingers around hers and gave her a slight smile. "He sure does. I hope you don't mind."

"Mind? I love the stuff. Lead the way, handsome."

Chapter Seventeen

ordon's lips curled into a sneer. From his spot parked behind a tree down the road, he had the perfect view of Brandy following that punk-ass bartender into the house.

The bitch had been all over the guy. And, hell, Gordon barely recognized her with all the makeup, new hairdo, and skimpy clothes.

She looked good, he could admit reluctantly. A helluva lot more fuckable, for sure.

He laughed, the sound high and almost manic in the car. Fuckable. Had he really just called Brandy, the unfuckable, fuckable?

Well, obviously the bartender thought so. He hadn't been able to keep his hands off her. That man was nothing but trouble.

He flicked the ashes of his cigarette out the window of the car and narrowed his eyes. What did she even see in him? When he finally got her into the car he'd ask. Maybe.

How long would he have to wait to get Brandy alone? Hell, she'd already been there for close to an hour.

He shook his head and reached for another piece of pizza. He shoved half the slice in his mouth and chewed slowly. He'd picked up a large pizza earlier in the day and had been living off the thing since.

Methodically he tapped the barrel of a revolver against his thigh. One way or another he'd get Brandy alone. Even if it meant shooting her new boyfriend.

Hell, the world would be better off rid of another lawyer anyway.

Not that he even practiced anymore. What kind of person gave up a prominent law career to open a bar? The man obviously had no sense.

He'd read that little tidbit in the paper this morning, and his rage toward the bastard had doubled.

That article in the paper had covered anyone who'd gotten within five feet of Brandy in the past few months. Not only had they dug up all the garbage on Brandy and this Marco fuck up, but they'd also written a nasty little paragraph about Gordon.

His lips curled into a sneer. All lies of course. What the hell did some pimply-face reporter know? Calling him a gambling addict? He was no addict. He'd just had shitty ass luck lately. And damn it, the tide would change.

It'd all change. Once he paid off the little debt he owed he'd be back on television, making money, and maybe even finding a way to dispose of his bitch of an heiress wife.

He grabbed another slice of pizza and wiped the grease off the corner of his mouth with his shirt.

Shoving the slice into his mouth, he tapped the gun against his thigh again.

They'd be married by the end of the day. All he had to do

was wait. Unfortunately, patience had never been one of his virtues.

"That food was wonderful. Thank you, Alfredo." Brandy tossed her napkin onto her empty plate and leaned back in her chair, hand on her belly.

Good lord, when was the last time she'd eaten so much?

"Although I think you're going to need a wheelbarrow to get me out of here."

Marco laughed and took another sip of beer. "I'll join you."

"No way." Elena shook her head. "That leaves me to push you guys, and I'm too lazy."

Alfredo beamed from across the table, still slicing into his steak.

"You should come and check out Marco's bar, papa," Elena said. "He's got a great place there."

Alfredo's grin slipped a little and he lowered his head.

Brandy sensed the sudden tension in Marco and laid a hand on his thigh, giving him a reassuring squeeze.

His father looked up again and gave a slight nod, his smile back in place.

"Yes. I would like to."

Marco's thigh relaxed under her hand and she heard his slow exhalation. He'd obviously still been worried about his father's feelings about his career choice.

Opening a bar wasn't a bad thing. She glanced over at him, pride swelling in her chest. He was a great man who loved what he did.

And that's why she loved him. What you saw was what you got with Marco.

His hand covered hers and squeezed. She looked over at him and smiled.

"Did Elena tell you her band won the Battle of the Bands?" she asked Alfredo.

He looked at his daughter and his eyebrows rose. "*Si?* Was this before or after the fight?"

Elena laughed even as her cheeks turned red. "We performed before. We were awarded after."

Their dad beamed. "That is wonderful. Congratulations, *mi hija.*"

"Thank you, papa."

Alfredo looked around the table. "How about we celebrate with a cake? Marco and I will go pick one up down at the market."

"Cake sounds great," Brandy replied and then frowned. "But are you sure you want to go all the way to the store?"

Marco glanced at his father for a moment and then turned to her.

"No, you go ahead and hang out with Elena for a few. I don't mind going for a little drive."

Brandy gave a slow nod. Of course. The men wanted time to speak alone. Understandable.

"Great," Elena grinned. "I can show her where the band practices. Maybe even get her to sing. I haven't heard her yet. Have you, Marco?"

Marco's gaze slipped to hers and the weirdest expression crossed his face before it turned into a look of amusement.

"Just once," he replied. "When she was in the shower."

Brandy's cheeks flamed and her eyes widened. Oh god. She'd forgotten all about that morning.

"All right," Brandy stood up quickly. "Show me where you rehearse with your band."

Marco's soft laughter followed her when she left the room with Elena.

His sister led her down the hall and looked back over her shoulder with a knowing look.

"I take it that was a private joke?"

Brandy cleared her throat and looked away. "Something like that."

Elena giggled and pushed open the door that led into a garage.

"Wow," Brandy stepped inside. "You've turned this into a nice little rehearsal room."

"Yeah, we did. We all went in on having it soundproofed." Elena rolled her eyes. "God knows we don't want the neighbor calling the cops on our noisy asses."

"Good call."

"Okay," Elena turned around to face her and folded her hands across her chest. "I didn't bring you in here to just show you where we rehearse."

"You didn't?"

"No. I just wanted a second alone to thank you."

Brandy cocked her head, her brows drawing together. "For?"

"For being so supportive. For convincing Marco to see me again and for being so nice about the asshole boyfriend slash drummer situation." Elena sighed. "For everything. You're just really cool and I'm glad Marco found you."

Brandy's heart melted a little and emotion thickened in her throat.

"Ah, sweetie." She stepped forward and hugged the younger woman. "How are you doing with the Phil situation?"

"Ah, he's a scumbag. I knew it all along but was in total denial. It's all good." Elena sniffled and shrugged. "On the drive home, Sebastian talked to me a lot and made me realize I can do better. And that maybe I should reconsider dating members of the band in the future."

"Yeah, that might be something to think about." Brandy pulled away and gave her a gentle smile. "And you know, I'm glad Marco found me, too."

Elena's smile widened and her expression turned pensive.

Brandy looked away, not sure how she felt about that gleam in the younger woman's eyes.

"Hey, so why don't you show me around the rest of your house?"

"All right. Not much to see though." Elena stepped past her and then shut the garage door behind them. "And you still have yet to sing for me."

"Some day, I promise." Brandy gave a soft laugh and followed her down the hall. She glanced over at the pictures hanging on the wall and frowned, leaning forward.

"So, I have a question for you."

"Okay. I just may have an answer. What's up?"

"Do you get free stuff from *Sugar and Spice?* And if so, do you think you could hook me up?" Elena nudged her arm and grinned. "Especially since you'll probably be my sister-in-law by the end of the year."

Brandy's laughter died at Elena's last comment.

"Sister-in-law?" she repeated weakly, her head spinning. "Oh. I don't think..."

"Don't even tell me Marco isn't serious about you."

"Marco doesn't...." She trailed off and looked away. Her attention landed on a group of photos on the wall again.

"Brandy, come on! I see the way my brother looks at you. The way he always finds a reason to touch you." She snorted. "I know my brother and let me tell you, I'll stick a fork in my hand if that man doesn't propose by Christmas."

A lump formed in Brandy's throat and she closed her eyes. Warmth rushed through her body and left her knees weak.

Marry Marco. She hadn't even allowed the idea to cross her

mind. Not until Elena mentioned it. But now that it had...the imagery it created sent her mind spinning, made her legs go a bit weak.

She swallowed hard and gripped the edge of the table next to her. Opening her eyes again, she focused on the pictures on the wall and frowned.

She shook her head and glanced away.

"Listen, I can hook you up with some lingerie, but as to Marco and me...we only just met," she argued, telling herself as much as Elena. "I can't even begin to—okay, it's driving me nuts. Is that your cousin?"

Elena followed her gaze to the pictures on the wall and her brows drew together.

"Which one?"

"That one." Brandy jammed her finger into the picture of a man who looked to be in his early twenties.

Elena laughed and shook her head. "No, that's not my cousin. That's Marco. Or was back in the day."

Everything shifted inside her. Brandy leaned forward to look at the picture again, convinced she must be seeing things. Her mouth opened, but no words came out. The picture remained the same.

The man staring back at her wore glasses, had a closely cropped haircut, and sported a suit and tie. Only the face—specifically the eyes, had convinced her that the man must be a relation to Marco.

But this was no relation—this was Marco.

"I don't understand," she said finally. "When was this taken?"

"Ah, a few years ago. Back when he was in school." Elena shrugged. "He used to be so damn clean cut and I swear to god he even wore a pocket protector."

"Pocket protector?" Brandy squeaked. "Marco?"

"Oh yeah." Elena rolled her eyes. "He was the epitome of a dork all through high school and college. And then one day he shows up with tattoos and a freaking Harley. Tells us he's quitting the firm and opening a bar."

Her stomach dropped. "Firm? Like Law Firm?"

"Yeah." Elena frowned. "Wait a minute, why do you look so surprised? Didn't he tell you?"

A sharp knock came on the front door.

"Hang on. Let me grab that real quick." Elena stepped past her and walked toward the other room.

Brandy stared at the picture. Her phone began to ring, and she fumbled in her pocket for it.

"Hello?

"Hey, it's me," Marco said softly. "Do you have a preference for white or chocolate cake?"

"Cake?"

"Yeah. We—"

"What firm did you quit?"

Dead silence met her question.

"Marco," her voice cracked. "Answer me."

"Brandy...I was going to tell you."

"Are you a..." This couldn't be right. There was no way. "Lawyer?"

"Was. I was a lawyer," he said quietly. "Listen, princess, we can talk more—"

"Don't...call me princess. Please. Not now." She gripped the table in the hallway again and looked at the picture. "I'm staring at this funny-looking picture of you...I didn't even know it was you. And then—god, you're really a lawyer? I just don't understand. Marco, who *are* you?"

"Look, it's in my past," his voice took on a harsh edge. "It doesn't matter."

"Of course it does! I told you everything about me. *Every-*

thing. You never thought to mention you're a lawyer? And you...you never mentioned Anna, your ex-girlfriend. Elena said she'd hurt you—"

"*Anna?*" He cursed. "God, Brandy, I haven't thought about her in years."

"Look, it just hurts that you didn't trust me enough to tell me the truth." She closed her eyes, emotion choking thick in her throat. "The stuff I told you...I haven't told any—"

"Hey, back the hell off, buddy." Elena's sharp voice came from the other room.

Brandy spun around and her focus changed in an instant as she encountered the man gripping Elena's arm.

"Gordon?"

"Gordon?" Marco's voice sharpened. "Is he—?"

Brandy ended the call and stormed across the room.

"Are you *insane?*" she demanded and stepped forward to jerk Elena from his grasp. "What are you doing here?"

"I'm picking you up. Let's go."

"Go? I'm not going—" Her words died when he stepped forward and pointed the barrel of a gun at her chest.

Her stomach dropped to the floor as she hurriedly thrust Elena behind her.

Her ex had officially gone off the deep end.

"Okay, take it easy, Gordon." She drew in a ragged breath, not taking her gaze off the barrel of the gun. "Maybe I shouldn't have left you at the altar like that, but don't you think pointing a gun in my face is a little—aah!"

He grabbed her arm and jerked her forward. "Don't you dare bring up that god-awful day." He snarled and swung her around, back toward the front door. "It's time to quit playing school teacher makeover. It's time to go."

"She's not going with you," Elena screamed and started to dial into her phone.

Gordon grabbed her phone and threw it at the wall. Then he trained the gun on the younger woman.

"Hey, little senorita girl, sit your ass down before you find yourself shot in the leg."

Racist jerk. What had she ever seen in him?

Elena's lips curled downward and she looked ready to blow a gasket, but there was a flicker of fear in her eyes that Brandy recognized.

"It's okay, Elena," Brandy said quickly. Cold sweat beaded on the back of her neck. "I'll go with him."

"Damn right you will." Gordon strode forward and pulled some rope out of the bag he'd been carrying.

Rope? He'd brought *rope?*

And you're surprised why? The man also brought a gun!

"What are you doing, Gordon?" she asked warily.

"I'm tying her up. You can't honestly expect me to leave her free to call for help the minute we leave."

"Oh god." Brandy's stomach took a nosedive as she shot Elena a look of regret. "I'm so sorry."

Gordon sat the younger woman down in a chair, tying her hands behind her and her ankles to the chair legs.

"Let's go." He grabbed Brandy's arm again and jerked her toward the front door.

"My brother's going to kick your ass for this," Elena screamed after them. "And by the way, your show sucks major dick."

Brandy choked, almost convinced Gordon was about to turn around and shoot the girl for that last comment.

"I'm glad it got canceled!" she screamed again, right before Gordon dragged Brandy out the front door.

Canceled? His show had been canceled? The thought flitted through her head but was gone just as quickly as he forced her into an unfamiliar car.

She pushed aside the pizza box and sat down. Her pulse pounded and her hands shook.

Why the hell did Gordon have a gun? Or better yet, why was he kidnapping her while using one?

He slid behind the wheel and she kept her attention trained on the gun still gripped in his hand.

She took a deep breath in.

Calm. Stay calm.

Closing her eyes for a moment, she tried to put herself back into teacher mode.

"Gordon," she said as calmly as she could manage. "Perhaps you could fill me in on what's going on?"

"What's going on?" he snapped and started the car, slamming his foot onto the accelerator. "You want to know what the hell's going on?"

The car jerked forward and swerved onto the road.

"Yes. I really would."

"Don't talk to me like I'm one of your damn students." He turned to look at her and gave a broad smile, his eyes glittering.

She swallowed hard, staring at his teeth. Her eyes widened with shock.

His teeth had an abnormal yellowish tint. And was that...was that *cheese* stuck between his bottom teeth?

This man prided himself on a million-dollar smile—as any dentist should. But these teeth—not to mention god-awful breath—would never again sell a toothpaste ad.

Her unease increased. If Gordon's mouth was this much of a mess, then she didn't even want to know what was going on upstairs in his head.

"I'll tell you, Brandy." Gordon turned back to face the road and gave an unsteady laugh. "We're going back to *The Hunk-A-Hunk-A Burning Love* Chapel and we're getting married."

"Getting married?" she squeaked.

The man had kidnapped her at gunpoint and now wanted to force her to marry him? Gordon had *completely* lost his marbles.

She reached for the handle of the door, fully prepared to jump before they got on the main road and started going faster than 35 mph. She curled her fingers around the handle, took a deep breath, and then pulled. Nothing happened.

"Locked."

She glanced over at him and tugged on the handle again.

"Gordon, what's gotten into you?" Panic assailed her. "You're acting completely insane. You can't make someone marry you."

"More like *who's* gotten into *you*." He swerved to the side of the road and leaned over, gripping her chin. "Did you have to slut yourself up to get him to screw you, Brandy?"

Shock ripped through her and her eyes rounded. Her stomach revolted at the look of vehemence and lust in his eyes. Who was this man? They may have dated for a year, but the man before her was a stranger.

"Get your hands off me."

"Actually, I think I'm going to have fun breaking you in again, Brandy." His smile turned nastier and his grip tightened. "I bet you learned some great tricks in bed from the bartender."

"You piece of sh—"

He lurched forward and slammed his mouth across hers.

Brandy choked at the taste of grease and cigarettes. Planting her palms against his chest, she shoved him away and gagged.

She turned her head to the side, dry heaving, and her gaze landed on the road—and the car just passing them.

Marco and his dad. She turned in her seat, trying to wave him down, but Gordon slammed her back against the seat and hit the gas again.

"That's right, love muffin. We're getting married." His words were almost spoken in a singsong tone. "And then we're going to stop at the bank."

"The bank? You want to stop at the bank?"

"I owe someone a little bit of money."

"So pay them! For goodness sake, Gordon, you make plenty of money on your show."

"Show got canceled." He lifted his hand and bit the nail on his thumb, spitting the piece onto the floor. "And I'm flat broke."

Scooting to the edge of the seat, as far away from him as possible, she stared in complete disbelief at the man in front of her.

What was with these habits he'd picked up? Nail biting? Smoking? Deciding brushing his teeth was optional?

"How can you be broke? You've been on that show for a couple of years. You should have plenty of—"

"I had some bad luck a couple of nights while gambling," he snapped and then moved on to bite the nail on his next finger.

Brandy blinked and drew a slow breath in. The parts of the puzzle all fell into place.

Gordon had lost his job. He had a gambling problem. And the most obvious why-the-hell-hadn't-she-seen-it-before part...Gordon also happened to be dating her. A plain Jane worth billions.

"I can't believe you," her voice dropped an octave. "All this time we dated, were you ever interested in anything but my money?"

Gordon looked over at her again and scowled. "Of course I was."

"Really?"

"Really." He bit into another nail. "I wanted access to the same social circles your parents are part of. No matter how famous I became, it didn't matter, nobody let me in. Just slammed the elitist door in my face."

No wonder she hadn't loved him. She must have sensed somewhere deep down his intentions were crap.

Between gritted teeth, she muttered, "Yes, well you see if our friends let every person who landed themselves a spot on a reality show into their lives, they'd be renting out the state of California just to have a party."

Gordon's face turned an unhealthy shade of red. "You dumb bitch. You think you're so much better than me. Always have. Well, you're not. And neither is that punk bartender."

"Marco is three times the man you are," she fired back. "And you know nothing about him."

"I know enough." He snorted and pulled the car onto the highway. "He's an idiot. The man had a huge career on the rise. The most impressive defense attorney in Nevada, they said. The ruthless rookie they called him."

Marco had been a defense attorney? Ruthless Rookie? Her stomach roiled.

"And just how do you know all this?"

"How do you *not?*" He laughed suddenly. "Oh that's great. He didn't tell you any of this, did he? Apparently, you were good enough to sleep with, but not good enough to confide in." He glanced over and clucked his tongue. "Poor Brandy. I hope you didn't really care for this guy."

"Go to hell." Tears burned behind her eyes and she turned to look out the window.

Why *hadn't* Marco told her any of this?

"So you probably have no clue about his glorious downfall."

"I don't want to hear it." She gritted her teeth and looked out the window. This was not a conversation she should be having with Gordon.

"So his last case? Yeah, he's defending some hugely famous boy band singer accused of rape."

"I'm not listening."

"The case was cut and dry, should have nailed the bastard." He leaned over into her face and laughed. "Marco got the guy off on some obscure technicality."

Her gut ached, but she refused to give Gordon any reaction.

"Anyway, that's not the best part. The best part?" Gordon laughed harder. "The woman who was raped? She offed herself. Jumped off an overpass during rush hour. Isn't that amazing?"

Chapter Eighteen

randy's eyes squinted shut, her heart pounding furiously in her chest.

Oh god. Oh god.

This couldn't be true. It just couldn't.

"Apparently he didn't handle it very well," Gordon went on, ignoring her. "Quit the field of law and went underground. No one could figure out what the hell happened to him. To The Ruthless Rookie."

He leaned over again, she could feel his breath hot on her face. She swatted at his head and arched away into the door.

"But that all changed yesterday. When they stumbled upon you at that bar, all they had to do was dig a little to discover just who owned the joint." He gave a musical laugh. "It was kind of a coming out party for you both, huh?"

"Fuck you." She seethed, tears burning the back of her eyes.

Gordon's laughter increased. "Wow. I never thought I'd live to see the day when I hear you say *fuck*."

She drew in a deep breath and crawled deeper into herself

emotionally. Her thoughts circled back to what he'd said about Marco and that case.

The guilt and pain Marco must have felt. No wonder he hadn't shared this part of himself with her. He'd probably buried that piece of his life long ago.

"You know it's amazing. You really have changed, love muffin. You've got this spunk in you—though, I can't say I like it all that much." He sighed. "Two weeks holed up with some defense attorney-turned-bartender and you've suddenly grown a spine."

She bit down on her lip, refusing to be goaded by him anymore.

"Hmmph." He went quiet for a moment. "Are you hungry? There's some pizza left in that box. It'll only take another half hour or so before we get to the chapel."

Her gaze jerked back to him again, the shocking conversation about Marco subsiding a bit. "You can't be serious about this, Gordon."

"Serious about what?"

"This marrying me thing. I wouldn't marry you if you—"

"Put a gun to your head?" He glanced sharply at her, his mouth tight. "Because if that's what it takes I'll do it."

"Why?" Her voice rose. "I'll just tell the Elvis minister I'm not willing. I'll say no."

"Then I'll shoot him, too."

"You're crazy!"

"Maybe."

"Gordon," she drew in a deep breath, hoping to reason with him. "You do realize that by kidnapping me you've committed a felony. If you take me back now, I promise I'll just forget this little incident happened."

"Okay, you know what? This conversation is over." He slammed his hand on the steering wheel and shook his head.

"We're getting married. What part of that don't you understand? We'll be good together, Brandy. We were before. And now that you've fixed yourself up a bit, I think we'll do just fine in the bedroom."

The thought of sleeping with Gordon again was enough to make her throw up a little in her mouth. She folded her hands in her lap and chewed on her lip.

Marco had seen them driving by, right? Surely he'd find Elena and she'd explain what had happened.

He'll come after me.

She closed her eyes, her heart thudding extra hard in her chest.

He will.

Fists clenched and nausea rolling through him, Marco stared out the windshield in stoic silence.

His dad cleared his throat. "That almost looked like your sweetheart in that car that passed."

Marco drew in a deep breath and said flatly, "I didn't notice."

The hell he hadn't. He'd spotted those brown curls from halfway down the road. Suspecting it was her, his confirmation had come when they'd pulled alongside the Toyota—just in time to see Gordon lean in to kiss her.

Marco closed his eyes, his stomach twisting and bile rising in his throat. Why had she done it? Gone back to him? From the entire time they'd been together, she'd insisted she was done with him.

That's before she found out you'd been lying to her.

His mouth tightened into a grim slash. Well, maybe not outright lied, but failing to mention his past could be perceived as lying.

When he'd called her and she'd asked about the firm, his heart had nearly stopped. All the anxiety and guilt had rushed to the surface. Guilt for where his former career had led him, and guilt for not sharing that time of his life with Brandy.

She had every right to be angry. After all, she'd shared about her past and her own fears.

And he'd heard the betrayal in her voice. The shock. And then that one word.

Gordon.

She had sounded surprised, but not necessarily displeased about his arrival.

Yes, definitely not displeased you dumb ass. Seeing as you just witnessed her kissing him.

Kissing him after she'd so obviously just left him.

"That lady in the car," his dad went on. "That couldn't have been your Brandy. Because she was, er... embracing that other guy."

Marco's teeth snapped together, his stomach twisting even more painfully.

His dad wanted reassurance that they hadn't just seen Brandy. That the woman who'd so obviously claimed Marco's heart, and had already charmed his sister and father, hadn't just left Marco for another man.

He couldn't give his dad that assurance. Hell, the evidence had been right in front of them.

"Maybe you'd better let me out here," he said thickly. Not altogether certain he wasn't going to get sick. "I can walk the rest of the way."

"Marco." His dad's voice gentled. "Ah, damn it all to hell. That was her, wasn't it?"

"Dad, could you just pull over? I need some air."

His dad slowed the car with a sigh, but before Marco could open the door he hit the gas again.

"No," Alfredo said with a firm shake of his head. "Elena is still at the house, maybe Brandy left a message."

"And I know exactly what the message would be," his words came out harsh. "You lied to me, so go to hell."

"No. Brandy? She's not like that."

Marco shook his head. "I never told her, dad. About any of it." He gave a bittersweet smile. "She thought I was just some random bartender who could give her a good time. She never signed up for this."

"Signed up for what?" His dad glanced over at him. "The woman fell in love with you."

"She doesn't love me—"

"The hell she doesn't!"

Marco reared back at the vehemence in his father's tone.

"I know what a woman in love looks like, and Brandy was head over feet for you, boy."

Marco's lips twitched. "Head over heels."

"That's what I said."

He glanced out the window, his brows drawing together. How could he have forgotten?

One of the last comments she'd made had been about the man she loved being an illusion.

His blood pounded harder and his hands curled into fists. Was it possible? Had Brandy fallen in love with him?

The past couple of weeks had certainly seemed to send them both spiraling down that road of love—like it or not.

But that was before Brandy had discovered he'd been keeping a major part of his life from her. What kind of relationship could be built on that? How would she ever trust him again?

"Stop it, Marco," his dad said harshly. "I know where you're going with those thoughts, so just stop it."

"I can't. I want to, but I can't. Knowing about my own past

makes me sick to my stomach. How can I expect her to look at me any differently?" He asked, emotion thickening his voice. "For god's sake, someone killed herself because of me."

"*Not* because of you," his dad shot back sharply. "And don't you ever imply that again. You were not the reason that woman killed herself."

Marco bit his tongue, not wanting to go down that familiar road. Hell, this was the first time since he'd changed careers that he'd seriously dug into the topic of his former life at all.

"I hope you never thought I believed that about you." His dad glanced back over at him, pain written all over his face. "That you were the reason that woman died."

"No. Of course not." Though Marco spoke the words, he wasn't so sure how much he believed them.

"I think part of you does," his dad said thickly. "I'm damn sorry for the way I treated you when you came to tell me of your decision to quit. Sure, it was a shock, but that didn't give me the right to say the things I did."

"It's all right, dad."

On the drive over to the store, they'd already hashed all this out. Got their apologies in order and put aside their falling out. Marco's throat tightened and he exhaled slowly. But now, the raw emotion in his father's voice really sank in.

Alfredo pulled the car into the driveway of the house and turned off the engine.

"Let's go find out what Elena can tell us."

Grabbing the handle, Marco pushed open the door to the car and bit back a sigh. Whatever Elena had to say, it couldn't be much.

Before they even reached the front porch, the sound of angry screams and cursing reached them.

Marco stepped past his father, his brows drawing together as he pushed open the door to the house.

"Is that you guys?" Elena screamed from the other room. "Marco? Get in here and untie me!"

Untie her?

Marco's pulse went into double time, his mouth drying out. He broke into a run and rounded the corner into the living room.

Elena sat tied to one of the kitchen chairs, her eyes flashing with rage and fear.

"That crazy fucking dentist took her, Marco. He came in here with a gun!"

A near-debilitating panic swept through him, and his gut twisted with guilt.

Damn.

He hadn't even given her the benefit of the doubt. How could he have been so stupid to assume she'd have gone willingly?

"I swear to god, Hollywood breeds the craziest assholes. He's got a big gambling problem, you know. I bet he took her for her money."

"How do you know he has a gambling problem?" Marco made quick time undoing the knots and freed Elena from the chair.

She rubbed her wrists and shook her head. "It was in that article about Brandy this morning. His show got canceled, too." She paused, her look incredulous. "Did you even read the article, Marco? I left a message on your phone this morning about it."

"No. I didn't check my message or see the article until we got here. And then I saw the headline and tossed it in the garbage."

"Ah, well, um. I should warn you," she cleared her throat. "There's also a big article on you, too."

"Fanfuckingtastic. Look, I need you to call the police," he

instructed, sounding a hell of a lot more composed than he felt. "Tell them to be on the lookout for a grey Toyota with male and female occupants, likely heading toward I15."

"That's it? Did you get the license plate?" she asked, pulling her cell from her pocket.

"No." His jaw tightened and he grabbed his keys, heading for the door. "I'm going after them."

"I can come with you." His dad stood in the doorway, his eyes wide.

"Thanks, dad, but I'm taking my bike. I can make up time and maybe catch up with them." He grabbed the door handle and pulled open the door.

"Careful, son."

"Yeah be careful!" Elena shouted. "He's a real—oh, hey. Yeah, I need to report a kidnapping. Some dentist from a shitty reality show just kidnapped my future sister-in-law."

Marco ran down the steps, jumped onto his bike, and gunned the engine. Rolling back the throttle, he shot out of the driveway and onto the small road. Dust rose around him as he pushed the bike to the limits.

Once he reached the main road he looked left and right. The real question was where would Gordon take her?

Back to Los Angeles or back to Vegas? He ground his teeth together and tried to put himself in the mindset of the other man. He wanted Brandy back. Bad. Had made it all too clear he still wanted to marry her.

A possibility took root in his gut.

The idea was ludicrous. Completely insane.

And yet so was Gordon right now.

Rolling back the throttle again, he turned left onto the highway toward Vegas.

· · ·

Why hadn't she thought to bring her cell phone? Grab her purse? Brandy cursed herself for not being more prepared.

Yeah right, like you can really be prepared to get kidnapped by your nutty ex who you already ditched once at that altar.

Biting back a groan, she stared out the window and watched the approach of the lights and buildings of Vegas.

How could Gordon be so off his rocker to actually think he'd convince someone to marry them when she so obviously wasn't willing?

She turned to glance at him again, just in time to see him grab a cigarette and light up. Fumbling at the window, she pushed the button that slid it down.

"What are you doing?" he asked sharply.

"Putting the window down so I don't have to smoke with you."

She turned her face toward the small breeze, grateful for the fresh air. Not only was the smell of smoke overwhelming, but it was clear Gordon hadn't showered in a while.

"We'll be there in a minute," he muttered. "I'm sorry we don't have a dress for you this time, love muffin. But I'm sure you can understand the urgency of the situation."

Umm, I can understand you're batshit crazy.

She bit back the response, having decided a while ago that trying to talk sense into him was a complete waste of time.

"Ah, there it is now." Gordon swerved across the boulevard, the car bouncing as it plowed over the cracked pavement in the parking lot.

Brandy shook her head. Good Lord, please let Marco and his family have called the police by now. Not that they'd know where she was heading.

"Okay, out you go."

The lock on her door clicked open and she reached for the handle. Maybe she should just make a run for it.

"And I'm keeping the gun on you, so don't do anything stupid."

Brandy sighed and jerked open the door, glaring at Gordon across the roof of the car when he climbed out.

"You won't shoot me. You need my money, remember?"

Gordon scowled and he jerked his head toward the dumpy chapel.

"Come on. You first."

"What is it with you and this place?" She folded her arms across her chest and walked ahead of him into the dark chapel.

Her nose wrinkled as the familiar smell of stale beer and B.O. assaulted her.

"It's sentimental to me," he sneered. "And it's the cheapest chapel I could find."

Here she was, almost two weeks since she'd run from her wedding and she was right back where she started. She'd come full circle.

Only this time she had absolutely no chance of running, and even if she did Marco wouldn't be outside waiting on his bike.

"We're closed early for the day, ma'am." A voice came from the shadows below the stained-glass window.

"God, I'd love it if you were," she muttered under her breath as Gordon pushed past her.

"Can you marry us?"

The man stepped out of the shadows. Obviously, they'd caught him in the process of getting dressed.

His white jumpsuit was half undone and gathered at his waist; a black T-shirt that said *She looked legal* sprawled over his beer belly.

"Now, folks, I done told you we're closed. There're plenty of chapels on the Strip, I'm sure—"

"I don't want any chapel." Gordon pulled the gun and waved it at the Elvis/minister. "I want this one."

"Welcome to the party," Brandy muttered.

"Well, hey now. Settle down, buddy." The man took a quick step backward, his brows drawing together. "Say, aren't you that same couple who came in here a couple of weeks ago?"

"Yes," Gordon snapped.

It *was* the same guy who'd tried to marry them before. Brandy groaned and shook her head. Of all the luck.

"Well, didn't this little lady run out on you once?" The Elvis glanced her way. "Did you change your mind?"

"No."

"Yes."

They both answered at the same time.

"It's irrelevant. She's going to marry me and you're going to perform the damn ceremony," Gordon yelled, spittle flying from his mouth.

"Come on now, son," the Elvis glanced at Gordon's gun. "Even if I did marry you this marriage will never stand up in court—"

"Uh yeah—tried telling him that already." Brandy shook her head. "The man's not playing with a full deck right now."

"Damn it," Gordon screamed. "Don't *make* me ask again!"

The click of the safety being removed had all of Brandy's frustration draining into fear. She hadn't really thought he'd shoot someone, but now she wasn't so sure.

She glanced over at him and went still. That hadn't been his gun making that noise.

Gordon's gun now rested at his side. His face was pale and his eyes were wide, as the man behind him pressed a gun to the back of his head.

"Who are you?" Brandy hadn't realized she'd spoken the words aloud until the gigantic man turned his attention to her.

Her pulse jumped and she took a quick step backward. This was not a guy you messed with. And, unlike Gordon, he looked completely calm and in control of his emotions.

"I'm a friend of Gordon's." He gave a hard smile that held no amusement. "Aren't I, buddy? I just stopped by to pick up that money you owe me. Now drop your gun."

Gordon leaned down to set the gun on the floor.

A friend? Brandy shook her head.

"You're not a friend, you're his bookie. I've seen enough movies."

The man didn't respond to her statement, though she thought she heard him make the tiniest grunt of amusement.

The Elvis/minister cleared his throat. "Bookies aren't actually illegal in Nevada. Though...I'm not sure I've ever seen them carrying around guns."

"I'm not a Vegas bookie."

"Oh I see. Look, can I leave and just pretend this never happened? You know, what happens in The Hunk-A-Hunk-A Burning Love Chapel stays in the The Hunk-A-Hunk-A Burning Love Chapel?"

The bookie stared at him for a moment. "You remember that slogan, and you'll be just fine. You call the cops and I'm coming for you next. Now get the hell out of here."

The Elvis/minister turned to flee from the building, his jumpsuit still half off his body.

"After repeated attempts to collect the money from you, I'm giving you one last chance to hand it over now, Mr. Perry."

Brandy swallowed hard. God. Is this how it would all end? Getting shot by a freaking bookie because her ex-boyfriend had a stupid gambling problem?

"I don't have your money," Gordon said tightly. His gaze rose to meet hers. "But my fiancée does."

· · ·

Still no news from Elena. Which meant the police hadn't found them yet. Marco shook his head and hoped his only idea would pay off. It was a long shot, though.

Gordon couldn't possibly be stupid enough to take Brandy back to the chapel he'd first tried to marry her in. That'd be ridiculous.

Even knowing the chances were slim, Marco turned onto the Strip and headed back to the chapel where Brandy had first jumped on his bike.

Ten minutes later he spotted the run-down chapel. Hell, the place ought to have been torn down years ago. What a shit hole.

He slowed his bike and turned into the chapel, driving to the back where the parking lot was almost empty. His pulse slowed and then snapped right back up to pound through his veins.

Holy hell, the man *was* stupid enough.

Marco pulled alongside the building and killed his engine.

Reaching into his pocket he grabbed his cell phone and dialed 9-1-1. After relaying the situation and location to an operator, he promised not to go into the building himself.

Fat chance of that happening. He turned off his phone and climbed off the bike, heading for the front door of the chapel.

Before he could reach it the door swung open and Brandy came walking out.

Her eyes widened, relief sweeping across her face. "Marco—"

She stumbled forward as the giant of a man behind her nudged her forward with the barrel of a gun.

A wall of rage slammed into him as Marco lifted his gaze to connect with the other man's.

"Do you want to tell me what's going on here?" Marco asked, his voice ice and his jaw hard.

"Look, you don't want to get involved." The man sighed and gave him a once-over, eyeing his black eye. "Especially since it doesn't seem to have gone so well for you in the last round you fought. Now move."

Marco straightened—matching the other man, in height at least, and refused to back down or acknowledge the comment about his bruised face.

"Let her go. Whatever your issue is, it's with Gordon, she has nothing to do with it."

"Well, now, I'm going to have to disagree with that. Seeing as she's the one holding the purse strings."

Marco narrowed his eyes. So the giant before him was related to Gordon's gambling problem.

Speaking of, Gordon stepped outside of the chapel, pale-faced as he followed the bookie. His lips shriveled when he spotted Marco.

"Oh god. Not you again."

"My car is over there," the giant nudged Brandy with the barrel of the gun. "Let's go, princess."

Oh, *hell no*. That was his nickname for Brandy, and no one, not even a gun-toting bookie was going to walk in and take it— or his woman away.

Marco stepped forward and blocked their path.

"I asked you to move." The giant turned the gun on Marco. "Don't *make* me ask again."

Marco caught Brandy's gaze and noticed the flare of anger in her eyes. Her lips pursed and he knew she was about to do something. Sure enough, she let out a war cry worthy of a samurai and drove her elbow back into the giant's gut, diving away from him.

"Oomph!" The man doubled over and Marco delivered a swift kick to the wrist that held the man's gun.

There was a satisfying crunch before the gun skated across the parking lot.

"Ouch. Jesus, *ouch*." The man gripped his hand, his eyes watering.

Taking the window of opportunity, Marco grabbed Brandy's hand and jerked her away, putting as much distance between her and the bookie as possible.

"I knew you'd show up." Her fingers tightened around his hand as they sprinted across the parking lot.

The sound of a gunshot had them both ducking behind a car and hitting the deck.

"He's shooting at us," she screamed in disbelief. "I can't believe he's freaking shooting at us!"

Marco pressed her head back toward the cement and peeked around the tire.

"It's Gordon. Gordon just shot that other guy."

Their confirmation came in the tirade of curses that echoed in the parking lot.

"Oh, you've got to be kidding me." She scooted forward and peered around the tire.

"Brandy? Come out, love muffin. I won't hurt—god damn it!" Gordon screamed as another gunshot rang out. He fell to the ground, clutching his calf. "You shot me! Oh, god it hurts."

Marco shook his head. "It is way too easy to get a gun in this country."

The sound of sirens resonated in the distance and she reached over to clutch his arm.

"Please tell me those are for us."

"They should be." Relief spread through him.

He turned to look at her. She stared straight ahead in obvious fascination, watching the two men crawling toward each other screaming threats.

Cheeks flushed and hair all a frizz, Brandy was beautiful.

More beautiful than any woman he'd known. And he could admit now that he'd never experienced a deeper connection with someone.

The real question was would she still want him? Knowing he'd withheld the truth about his past. And even still she didn't quite know everything.

He reached for her hand. "Brandy—"

The police cars bounced into the parking lot, sirens blaring. Doors slammed.

"Drop your weapons! Stay where you are!"

The sound of people running toward them came, and then two officers appeared at the end of the car they were hiding behind.

"Move away from Miss Summers. Now!"

Move away, what the hell? Marco's brows drew together.

"Wait," Brandy protested. "He's not—"

"I said now!"

Before they got trigger-happy, he rolled away from her. Rocks bit into his bare arms before he was jerked to his feet and dragged away from Brandy.

They shoved him against the back of the car and out of her reach. He had the perfect view of Gordon and the bookie, still cursing each other out, being read their rights.

From the corner of his eye, he watched as three officers helped Brandy up and rushed her toward one of the squad cars. The car started again and pulled out of the parking lot.

His world shrunk as he watched her press her face against the window, pounding on the glass and yelling as she stared at him.

Marco closed his eyes, willing the tightness in his chest to fade.

It was possible that just as quickly as she'd entered his life, she was gone from it.

Chapter Nineteen

arco shoved a hand through his hair and kicked his feet up on the desk of the office. The myriad of emotions that had been plaguing him for the last couple of days had left him an utter mess.

He grabbed a pencil off the desk and spun it through his fingers, shaking his head.

Three days. Three days and there'd been no contact from Brandy. It had been bad enough when some bitchy assistant from her parents had shown up on his doorstep to collect her stuff.

And that's all she'd done. Took the stuff and left. No message from Brandy, no thank you for your help, nothing.

His brows drew together and gave a choked groan. At the two-day mark was when he'd finally given up on hearing from her. Had realized she had no intention of coming back for him.

The pencil between his fingers snapped in two as he tightened his grasp.

He shook his head and leaned back in the chair. Maybe it had been because he'd hidden his not-so-pretty past from her. It was altogether possible. She certainly had seemed upset enough on their last phone call.

Or maybe it was something else entirely. He gave a self-deprecating smile. Maybe it's what he'd feared all along.

That she'd just been biding her time with him. Slumming with the boys from the bar and now she'd move on back to her normal life.

A hoarse laugh escaped from his throat. He pulled his legs from the desk and leaned forward, resting his elbows instead and laying his head in his hands.

"How you doing, mate?"

Marco tensed, heat rushing through his body as he realized Sebastian had just seen him in a complete moment of weakness. Christ, he'd held it together pretty well in front of them for the most part.

He lifted his head and forced an easygoing smile. "I'm doing fine. Just a little tired."

"Don't bullshit with me," Sebastian gave him a knowing look and then sat down on the edge of the desk. "Why don't you just call her?"

"Because she doesn't want to hear from me."

"And you know that how?"

"Look," he sighed. Why the hell put up a pretense with Sebastian? They knew each other too well. "I gave the lady who came to my house a letter to give to Brandy. A letter that pretty much laid out how I felt about her. And I explained why I hadn't told her about my past."

"And?"

"What do you think?" he offered a stiff shrug. "I never heard back."

"Hmm." His friend frowned and pursed his lips. "That doesn't sound like Brandy."

"Yes, but how well did we really know her?"

"Pretty damn well I'd say."

Marco shook his head, half convinced his friend was just blowing smoke up his ass. The deadpan expression on Sebastian's face convinced him otherwise.

"Look, I don't know what happened," he finally admitted. "I wish to god I knew what was going on in her head. But I don't."

"So call her."

"I don't have her number."

"She didn't fill it out on the application?"

Marco paused. "She put a number that's no longer in service."

"So you tried."

"Of course I did," he said wearily. "And it's not like she just advertises her address. All she put was a P.O. box on the application."

"Send her another letter—"

"Come on, Sebastian," his words cracked and his gut twisted with disappointment. "Let's be real here. She doesn't respond to my letter, does not attempt to contact me, and disconnects the only number I have for her?"

Sebastian's jaw hardened and he looked away.

Marco gave a sad excuse for a laugh. "Exactly."

"It just doesn't make sense." Sebastian turned to look at him again and sighed.

"So how about you?" Marco asked, turning the tables. Wanting to shift the conversation from the source of his current depression. "You gonna see that blonde again that you took home the other night?"

"Not at all." A look of revulsion swept across Sebastian's face. "The woman kept screaming '*Screw me harder, you dirty Brit.*' I tell you it freaked me out after about the tenth time. Shite, I don't know why I took her home in the first place."

"To get laid?"

"There is that aspect, yes."

"You'll find the right girl, buddy. She's out there."

Something close to unease flickered in Sebastian's eyes before he shook his head and looked away.

"I'm not exactly looking right now." He cleared his throat. "Look, I didn't come back here to just bring up Brandy, though."

"No?"

"No. You have some big reporter out front who wants to interview you."

"Again?" Marco cursed and straightened a stack of papers on his desk.

"Yeah. I don't think they're going to leave you be until you give one of the blokes an interview."

"Well, hell."

"Just make it clear you're only giving one and be done with it."

Marco's mouth tightened. Damn, this was not going to be pleasant. But Sebastian was right, it needed to be done.

"Okay. Tell them I'll be out in five minutes."

Sebastian nodded and left the office again.

Marco turned to glance out the window, attempting to gear up for the god-awful questions that were sure to come his way.

Questions about why he'd quit his career as a prominent defense attorney on the rise. Questions about why he'd chosen to open a bar.

But those weren't the questions he dreaded. Not by any means. The worst would be the question about Brandy.

He drew in an unsteady breath and stood up. Now he just had to figure out how the hell he'd answer them.

· · ·

Brandy snuggled deeper into the couch, curling her legs up under her bottom and cradled the small glass in her hand.

Her mother walked by and covered the mouthpiece on her cell phone, admonishing a quick, "Drink your Jack and Coke, honey."

Wincing, Brandy took another sip. The fiery drink warmed her belly but did little to ease the numbness in her heart.

She set the glass down on her side table and fiddled with the edge of her T-shirt. Well, not really her shirt, but Marco's.

She pulled the hem of the shirt outward and glanced down at the words *Dante's Place* scrawled across. She lifted the shirt to her nose and inhaled, hoping to find the scent of him still there.

Nothing but her perfume by now.

Tears pricked the back of her eyes, but she blinked rapidly to dispel them.

"You need to get out of the house, honey." Her mother came back into the room and sat down next to her. "You're so depressed."

"I'm not depressed."

"Oh, but you are." Her mom shook her head. "Ever since you watched that *Entertainment Hollywood* show and saw that bartender you stayed with on there."

Brandy closed her eyes. It had already been four days since the show had run, but the interview had been looping in her head repeatedly since it aired.

When Marco had spoken about his new life running a bar, and why he'd left his past career, she'd bawled buckets of tears for him. She'd been struck by the anguish and pain in him that had never healed.

But her tears for him had turned into tears for herself when they'd asked about her.

A pity party? Maybe. But being described as some random

woman who'd just happened to turn to him for help kind of hurt a bit.

And then when the reporter had probed to find out if there was a romantic connection between them, he'd paused and looked at the camera before saying quietly *she's not really my type.*

Which is what she'd known all along. She wasn't Marco's type. Right? She bit back another sniffle.

Good thing she'd seen that show in time. She'd actually had plans to fly back to Vegas the next morning to see him again.

To see if he still wanted her. Her chest tightened and she blinked rapidly. The interview had answered that question well enough. Marco had only been amusing himself with her.

"You really liked that man, didn't you?"

The sudden question from her mom threw her for a curve.

"I'm sorry?"

"That bartender."

"He used to be a lawyer, and he actually owns half that bar, you know."

"I realize that," her mother crossed her legs and gave her a considering glance. "And your father used to make pottery."

"What does that have to do with anything?"

"Nothing, I'm just saying you like the man. Maybe you even loved him?" She cleared her throat. "Or was it all about the sex?"

"*Mom.*" God, if her mom had any idea how on the spot she was about the love stuff she'd never stop probing. Like a dog with a bone....

"Sorry, honey. Just checking."

"Yeah, well, check something else please."

"All right, since you insist." Her mom stood up and crossed the room to pick up her Versace purse. "I have something for you."

"I don't need any money," Brandy protested wearily.

"I'm not offering you money. I'm offering you this."

Brandy finally noticed the envelope her mother held out. Her brows drew together.

"What is it?"

"A letter."

"From who?"

"From the bartender."

Brandy snatched the letter from her mother's hands, her mouth suddenly dry. "Where did you get this?"

"I found it this morning while I was sorting through the bag of clothes you left at the bartender's house. It was at the bottom of the bag." She sat back down on the couch. "I fired her, you know. My assistant. The very same day I sent her to pick up your stuff. That girl was terribly moody and I caught her stealing some of my silver."

"That bartender has a name, mom," Brandy replied in exasperation and opened the letter—which already appeared to have been opened.

"Yes, it's Marco."

"Did Svetlana read this? It's open."

"No, I found it unopened. She must have forgotten to give it to you—or maybe she was just annoyed I canned her butt and decided to let you find it months down the road." Her mom waved her hand. "In any case, I read it."

"*You* read it?"

"Yes, and it's really a rather good letter. You should read it, honey."

"Oh my god. I can't believe you read my letter. And I *would* read it if you'd let me."

She shook her head in disbelief and turned her attention to the letter in her hand. Her hands started to shake after the first line, and by the time she'd finished her vision was blurred with tears.

"How could that bitch of an assistant forget to give me this?" she growled.

"Yes, well, like I said, it may have been deliberate." Her mom patted her blonde coif and cleared her throat. "I can't say she was too happy about being let go."

"This letter…" The words died as a flood of tears choked off her ability to speak.

"It's quite good, right? I mean, he loves you."

Brandy set the letter down and whispered. "Yes. He does."

"So that's why I was asking if you loved him."

Brandy closed her eyes, her heart pounding as warmth spread to every inch of her body.

That interview he'd done with *Entertainment Hollywood*, when he'd said she wasn't his type had probably been a lie.

Hell, he'd sent this letter a week ago and in his eyes, she'd just never replied. What else could he be thinking?

She opened her eyes and leaned back against the couch, relief making her dizzy. "Yes, mom, I love him."

"Wonderful! I can't wait to meet him! You'll have to bring him by the—"

"Mom, could you let me work some stuff out with him first?" She stood and stretched.

"Of course! It's just after your dad read the letter he was a bit anxious to meet him—"

"*Dad* read the letter, too? Oh for fuck's sake." She shook her head.

"Brandy! I just adore this new side to you." Her mom stood and gripped her hands. "You're really letting loose and having fun."

"Yes, well that fun needs to curb itself when I start the school year." She winced and touched her forehead. "The kids will keel over if I come back in mini skirts and cussing like a sailor."

"Ah, yes, so true."

Brandy headed toward the bathroom, already debating what to wear.

"And, Mom?" She turned around before she reached the door.

"Yes, honey?"

"Thank you for being so supportive." She hesitated. "I've always been so proud of you and Dad, and how you built *Sugar and Spice* up from the ground."

Her mom's brows raised and she saw the flicker of surprise and pleasure in her eyes. It made Brandy realize she'd been stingy with the compliments and admitting how proud she was of them.

"And I just want to say," she drew in another deep breath and then purged on with the other thing that had been weighing heavily in her heart. "That I would very much love to be a part of the company in the future. Not give up my career completely, mind you. I love to teach. But *Sugar and Spice* started as a family business...and it should stay in the family."

Her mother's head bobbed up and down with obvious shock, and Brandy spotted the sheen of tears in her eyes.

"Okay, now I'm off to shower. Because tonight I *will* get my man back." She clenched her fists and moved out of the room, turning at the door. "Oh, one more thing."

"Yes, honey?" Her mom's voice trembled with emotion.

"I think tonight I'll take you up on that offer to use the plane."

"I'm locking up," Sebastian called from the front. "Do you want me to stick around until you finish up, mate?"

"I've got it. See you tomorrow. Don't forget we're interviewing for a few new waitresses."

"I'll be there. You know I love this part of my job."

"Pervert," Marco called and plugged some numbers into the calculator.

"That I am. Good night."

Marco listened to the door slam shut and then set down the receipts. Christ, he needed a vacation. He needed to get the hell out of Vegas for a while and hunker down on a tropical beach. Somewhere he could try and repair his shredded heart.

He picked up the receipts again and started tallying them, but the process stalled as he heard the door to the bar open.

"Sebastian, did you forget something?"

There was no reply, only the soft click of footsteps. He saw her shoes first—heels that made her legs look endless. Then a short denim skirt that ended mid-thigh.

He lifted his gaze higher and the immediate lust that had hit him faded into slight amusement. Covering her big breasts was an all too familiar purple shirt with a puffy cat on the front.

"Hey," she said softly.

Finally, he lifted his gaze fully to meet hers. Brandy was here. She'd actually come back.

"Brandy?"

"Mmm hmm." She sat down on the edge of the desk and her skirt rose higher. The familiar smell of apples teased his nostrils. "Did you miss me?"

"What are you doing here?" He set the receipts down.

He wouldn't allow himself to be hopeful. Wouldn't jump to any conclusions until she explained why she'd returned. Especially after she'd blown off his letter.

"What do you think I'm doing here?" She gave a slight shrug and pushed her hair behind her shoulder.

His jaw hardened and several possible reasons hit him at once. Some darker and not as pleasant as the others.

"Stop it," she chided and leaned forward. "I know exactly where your thoughts are going, and you're wrong."

"And where should my thoughts go?" he challenged, his voice harsher than he intended. "You blew off my letter and then show up a week later—"

"I never received your letter." She traced a painted nail over his mouth. "My mom's crap assistant neglected to give it to me. We found it today. I read it, oh, three hours ago to be exact."

Relief weakened the muscles in his body. The hardness in his jaw dissolved and he grabbed her finger and pressed his cheek into the palm of her hand.

"Is that so?" he asked, his voice husky now.

"Yes."

"So you read it?"

She nodded, never looking away from him.

"And you're not appalled by me? Or disgusted in my decision to leave the firm?"

"Of course not," she said softly. "You're doing what makes you happy. And I Googled you like a mad fool for hours, Marco. You weren't responsible for that woman's death. You were a defense attorney—for Pete's sake. Of course, you're going to take some cases you'd rather not."

"I didn't want to take any. Law wasn't for me. I pursued it because of my dad. He always wanted to be a lawyer. When he realized I'd argue for hours with a fence post, he encouraged me to pursue the field."

"And it wasn't for you." Her fingers stroked feather-light along his hairline. "Shit happens."

"You just swore."

"Yes, a bad habit I picked up from a couple of crazy bartenders I met."

"They sound interesting."

"Well, one interests me a bit more than the other." She pushed her fingers into his hair. "Seriously, though, Marco. Why spend your life doing something that doesn't make you happy?"

He pressed a kiss into her palm and closed his eyes. God, he didn't deserve her. She was too understanding. Knew him too well, as if they'd been together years instead of just a couple of turbulent, amazing weeks.

"Besides, you have a fantastic little bar here. Getting busier every day."

"Damn, you have no idea." He shook his head. "We're interviewing for three more waitress positions tomorrow."

"Make it two."

He froze and pulled away. "I'm sorry?"

"Make it two," she repeated and leaned forward, brushing her lips across his. "I want to work here on the weekends."

His pulse slowed and then sped up again. "You want to commute from California?"

"No." She brushed another kiss across his mouth and lingered in a way that had the blood rushing to his cock. "I want to commute from your house."

He caught her wrist when she moved to pull away. His gaze searched hers, looking for any sign that she was joking.

"You want to live with me?"

"If you'll let me." Her gaze flickered with the first bit of uncertainty. She reached into her purse and pulled out a wad of folded papers. "I printed out a list of schools that are hiring music teachers in the area, and if I can't get a job at one of them I'll just teach private lessons."

His mouth opened and then closed. She wanted to move to Henderson?

"Why?" He touched her cheek, sliding his hand around to cup the nape of her neck. "Why would you do that?"

Her stare grew both heated and vulnerable. "Because I refuse to have a long-distance relationship with the man I love."

"You love me?" Swept by an unfamiliar possessiveness, his fingers tightened around the nape of her neck.

"Yes. Of course," she whispered, searching his face. "I'm surprised you couldn't tell."

"I wondered...and on the phone—"

"I love you, Marco. I love you more than I love my piano, and that says a heck of a lot."

"More than your shirt with the cat playing the piano?"

She arched a brow and tsked. "Now you wouldn't be mocking me, would you, Mr. Vargas from Vegas?"

"Hell no, princess. There are many other things I'd rather be doing that end in *ing* to you," he muttered thickly, before tugging her onto his lap and crushing his mouth down on hers.

His tongue delved past her lips, desperate and hungry to find hers. To have that connection that he'd missed all week. That had nearly driven him mad without.

"I love you so much, Brandy," he whispered and reached for the button on her skirt.

She drew in a shuddering breath and her eyes filled with tears. "I read the words in the letter, but to hear you say them..."

This woman would be his wife. He knew without a doubt. Already his mind flicked with the possibility of what kind of engagement ring she'd like.

"I know that look in your eyes," she teased and stood up. "Let me get out of these clothes."

Obviously, she had no idea where his thoughts lay. Good.

That meant he'd get the pleasure of surprising her with the ring.

"Hey, princess?" he said softly as she started to undress.

"Yes?" She lifted her beautiful blue eyes to look at him.

"Leave the cat shirt on."

Brandy laughed and a devious smile crossed her face. "I always knew you liked it."

"Yeah, I do. I love everything about you."

Once she was naked, he proceeded to show her just how much so.

Afterword

Thank you for reading Negligee Behavior! I hope you enjoyed it, and be sure to keep on the lookout for Sebastian's book which hopefully will be out this fall! Please help other readers find this book by:

1. Recommending it to a friend.

2. Writing a review.

4. Find and follow me on social media under Shelli Stevens at:

- TikTok
- Newsletter
- BookBub
- Amazon
- Facebook
- Goodreads
- Instagram
- Pinterest
- Twitter

About the Author

Shelli is a New York Times and USA Today bestselling author of romance novels. She's a wife and mom of two girls. As a born and bred Pacific Northwest native, she loves rocky beaches, sunsets and baking on rainy (and dry) days. Shelli is also known to frequently break into song.

Shellistevens.com

Also by Shelli Stevens

A is for Alpha Series (mild spice stand-alone stories with one spicy one)

- The Billionaire's Baby Bargain
- Beauty and the Sheik
- Taught by the Tycoon
- Corrupted by the Prince
- Taken by the Pirate Billionaire (spicy)

Bro Code Series (medium spicy)

- Losing It
- Her Fake Boyfriend
- Won't Back Down
- Nursing the Flame

The McLaughlins series (medium spicy)

- One More Round
- Straight No Chaser
- Top Shelf
- Last Call

Seattle Steam series (medium spicy)

- Dangerous Grounds
- Tempting Adam
- Seducing Allie

Chances Are novella series (medium spicy)

- Anybody but Justin
- Luck Be Delanie
- Protecting Phoebe

Holding out for a Hero novella series (medium spicy)

- Going Down
- Command and Control
- Flash Point
- Love Me Knot

Marshall Ranch Series (mild spice)

- Protect Me, Cowboy
- Falling for the Hometown Girl
- Christmas Lights and Cowboy Nights

Savage series (Medium Spicy Paranormal) The

- Savage Hunger
- Savage Betrayal
- Savage Revenge
- Savage Rescue (novella)

Stand Alone books (medium spicy)

- Foreign Affair
- Hot Zone
- Island Fever

www.ingramcontent.com/pod-product-compliance
Lightning Source LLC
Chambersburg PA
CBHW031119160726
47991CB00004B/1463